"Years ago, my parents, High Chief Peter & Lia Maivia, while promoting wrestling in Hawaii, worked closely for years with Diana's father, the one & only Stu Hart. I cherish the bond that I have with Diana Hart Smith. She's smart, funny, witty & classy woman who, herein within these pages, writes a powerful story about professional wrestling and how it can affect the family."

—Ata Maivia Johnson
Mother of Dwayne "The Rock" Johnson

"Diana Hart is the 'Daughter of pro-wrestling,' listen to what she has to say about pro-wrestling from joy to struggles. You will hear amazing stories in her fictional trilogy which you've never heard before, trust me. Your understanding of pro-wrestling will change."

—Ken Yasuda
Pro Bodybuilding Champ, Mr. Japan
and International Fight League (IFL) coach.

"Diana has done it again. But what would you expect coming from one of the most respected families in professional wrestling? Diana's secret knowledge of this world is now shared with the reader giving them insight very few attain. You will enjoy this novel as I have."

—Don Frye
"The Predator," UFC Hall of Famer, Actor, Pro-wrestler

CAULIFLOWER HEART
BOOK III

She Who Laughs Last

Diana Hart

Publisher Page
an imprint of Headline Books, Inc.
Terra Alta, WV

Cauliflower Heart: She Who Laughs Last Book 3

by Diana Hart

To order additional copies of this book or for book publishing information, or to contact the author:

Publisher Page
P.O. Box 52, Terra Alta, WV 26764

Tel/Fax: 304-789-3001
Email: mybook@headlinebooks.com
www.HeadlineBooks.com

www.OfficialDianaHart.com

Publisher Page is an imprint of Headline Books

ISBN 13: 9781882658909

Library of Congress Control Number: 2017931001

PRINTED IN THE UNITED STATES OF AMERICA

Dedicated to Stampede Wrestling
and many thanks to my family.

1

The Absolute Best

"Welcome, wrestling universe fans! We have a fantastic show for you tonight! We have sixteen of the very best submission fighters in the universe here to compete in the first ever CrazyyyyyBesttt!"

The crowd roared so loud that the announcer, Maxwell Potter had to wait for the noise to die down before continuing. In his black and white tuxedo, he looked like a penguin to most of the fans.

"The winners of the next eight matches will determine who goes on to the next round of fights. All matches are one fall apiece, with a fifteen-minute time limit. Tonight's main event, our final match of the night, has a 30-minute time limit.

"We have our panel of five judges sitting at ringside and two referees, all sanctioned by the Greater Manchester Boxing and Wrestling Commission. The luck of the draw determines who fights whom in the matches that follow our first round of combat. I promise you fans out there that this is sure to be an amazing night! Now that the formalities are out of the way, let me ask you: Are You Ready? I said, ARE YOU READY?" he shouted into his microphone again.

The cheers were deafening. Bullhorns went off and the fans screamed.

"Very well then! I love it!" exclaimed the announcer to the pumped-up, mostly male audience. "Let's get this show on the road then, shall we?"

Japanese electro-pop music suddenly blared through the speakers. Behind the curtains, Dempsey dimly registered that the music playing was his. He did not feel nervous, but his heart was beating faster nevertheless. His adrenaline was pumping and he felt very ready for his first fight in Manchester in five years.

Aaron nudged Dempsey in the back and he pushed his way through the heavy black velvet curtains. The crowd went wild! Aaron held the ropes open for Dempsey as he stepped into the ring.

"Our first fighter of tonight's CrazyBest WrestleFest Elimination Tournament, representing the Tokyo Dojo in Japan, at 6'4½," weighing in at 17 stone 8 pounds, wearing the white and red shorts and red boots, I introduce to you to Dempseeeeeeey Bellllllllllamy!"

The thunderous applause smothered the next round of ring entrance music - steady Native American drumbeats. Maurice Starlight, his trainer Keith Williams, and his two corner men walked down the aisle to the ring. A lean and lanky Native American Indian from the Stoney Indian tribe in Western Canada, Maurice specialised in kickboxing. As a teenager he had worn his hair in two shiny black plaits, Dempsey remembered from watching matches on TV. Now his hair was cut in a short, thick Mohawk, and his eyes were confident and calm. He danced around the ring, rolling his head from side to side and shrugging his shoulders.

"Our second fighter of tonight's CrazyBest WrestleFest Elimination Tournament," shouted the ring announcer "hails out of Gleichen, Alberta, Canada! He is Canada's reigning heavyweight kickboxing champion! At 6'3," weighing in at 16 stone, I introduce to you in the green and blue shorts, and bare feet, Mauriceeeeeeee Starrrrlightttttt!"

The crowd cheered as Maurice raised his left hand in the air.

Referee Hathaway checked Dempsey and Maurice's mouths, made sure they were wearing their mouth guards, and looked each fighters' hands over. He felt around their waists and underneath the bottoms of their feet. Finally, the referee pointed at the timekeeper.

Ding! Ding! Ding! Timekeeper Johnny Swingler rang the bell and the tournament began. The fighters shook hands and walked around each other. Fists in the air, both fighters got into standing guard positions, ready to lock up, swing, or block. Maurice raised his knee in the air, preparing to kick if he saw an opening.

Breaking the suspense, Maurice jabbed with his left hand then swung his right hand up towards Dempsey's face. Then he swung down, aiming for Dempsey's liver. Dempsey lowered his right arm to block it, feeling the impact on his thick, meaty bicep. Had this powerful punch connected with the liver area on Dempsey, it would surely have brought him to his knees.

Unperturbed, Maurice tried again, this time with a swift uppercut aimed right up into the ribs, but instead collided straight into Dempsey's elbow. His hand hit the point and Dempsey felt the crunch of bone and saw a flash of pain in Maurice's eyes. Something was wrong.

Maurice tried to punch again with his other hand, but Dempsey knew the match was already over. Referee Hathaway stopped the match and checked Maurice's right hand carefully and then checked Dempsey's elbow. Some fans booed the referee for interrupting; others applauded out of respect for the fighters.

Hathaway called Maurice's trainer, Keith Williams, into the ring. "I can't let this fight continue. Maurice has a broken hand, look," he said in a concerned voice to Keith. "It's been shattered, by the looks of it. The fight can't go on. Sorry mate, but them's the rules, fer yer own good."

Those fans who applauded knew it was a huge disappointment to both fighters to have the match stopped. Dempsey looked over at Aaron as if to say, "What happened?" before walking over to Maurice and shaking his good hand, raising it in the air. More fans cheered and fewer booed this time. He felt lucky that his elbow hadn't shattered the way Maurice's hand did upon the impact of his swift uppercut.

By the end of the first round of matches, only four fighters were left. The other twelve were either eliminated or too injured to advance onto the next round. Switzerland's Petter Pfister was the winner of his match, but he sustained a bad cut on his forehead that left him unable to advance; Matheus Andre of Brazil won too, but suffered a broken jaw; Bobby Canyon from the United States won his round via submission, but his eye was swollen too much for him to have enough depth perception to continue. CrazyBest was now down to Dempsey Bellamy representing

Japan, South Africa's Steven Peacock, Russia's Sasha Borshov, and England's Toasty Bonham.

Dempsey sat on a long grey bench in his dressing room with Aaron, watching the ring action on the TV and waiting for the announcement of the next fight. The locker room was intended for a whole sports team, with a row of showers and toilets and a series of standing metal lockers, painted a pale yellow color. It seemed so vast and empty with just Aaron and Dempsey sitting quietly in it. The only thing that made it look like a dressing room instead of an industrial-feeling locker room was the impressive and colorful flower arrangement from Dino, which was sitting on the counter next to the clinically white porcelain sinks.

Commissioner Sam Oakland climbed in the ring, about to make the suspenseful announcement for the next bout. He faced the live cameras filming CrazyBest for the pay-per-view audience as he addressed the crowd.

He joined Referee Hathaway who was holding a glass jar containing four white balls. Commissioner Oakland reached in and grabbed a ball, holding it up before grabbing a second one. Then, as the crowd watched, he pulled the balls apart right down the centre and unfolded two small pieces of paper. Now he held in his hand the names of the next two fighters. The two names inside other balls would fight after this next match. The audience went quiet as the commission began to speak into the microphone.

"The next two fights of the evening will be followed by a thirty-minute intermission. During that thirty-minute intermission, the fighters will rest and prepare mentally for their final match of the evening." The crowd was growing restless and noisy, not interested in all the rules and steps required to get to the next matches. Commissioner Oakland looked into the capacity crowd and motioned with his hand that he needed quiet. A few bullhorns still went off, but otherwise the audience went quiet and waited for Oakland to announce the next matches.

"Will the following wrestlers come down to the ring?" said the commissioner in a loud and clear voice, full of energy and inflection. "South Africa's Steven Peacock and Japan's Dempsey Bellamy." The fans went wild again, impatient for the next match to begin, knowing it could be extraordinary.

"Well, looks like you're up next," said Aaron to his young protégé. Dempsey's ring music began to play. "This Peacock guy is mainly an offense guy. He's not so great on the defense and you've got him in height and reach by about four inches. If you get on top of 'im, you'll tire 'im out and if he can't reach ya when yer standin', you'll tire 'im out that way. But he's got power in 'is legs and he's like explosive like dynamite, so just keep that in mind. But ah think you'll be fine. "

Dempsey stood and shook out his immense shoulders, as if to shake off any tension. "C'mon, let's do it," he said. Aaron held open Dempsey's dressing room door for him and they started down the hallway towards the curtain for the second time that night.

Steve Peacock was a stalky blond South African gold medalist in amateur wrestling. He was known as the Giant Killer because he was a master at overpowering bigger opponents with his own power that came the hard way from years of amateur wrestling at the lighter end of the heavy-weight class he usually fought in. With his big, bumpy cauliflower ears, tree-trunk neck, broken nose and hardened face, he looked like he'd been fighting his whole life. He was only thirty, but he looked like he was fifty. When he acknowledged Dempsey in the ring, he gave him a quick, respectful nod. Steve came in close to him and spoke sagely under his breath.

"I knew yer dad. He was a great fighter, he was," Steve said in a rough South Africana voice. "Do '-im proud, son."

"Thanks," Dempsey said decorously. His mind whirred as he stared down this pit bull of an opponent. He appreciated Steve's sentiments, but he quickly had to put them out of his mind for the time being. He had to take the emotion out of his heart and focus on what he needed to do to win this fight. Dempsey remembered his Grandfather Billy and Uncle Toasty telling him that no matter how big someone was, a smaller, less powerful guy to beat him if the smaller guy had knowledge and heart. Steve had both and he was a mat wrestler. He would probably try to get Dempsey down to the mat first thing or try to tire him out by making Dempsey chase him for hits if they stayed standing. Dempsey didn't take for granted that he outweighed and outreached his opponent. He knew Steve was tough as nails and a smart, strategic fighter. Dempsey knew he was young and not as seasoned as the Giant Killer, but he never let his youth get in the way of being experience. He had years of experience too, even if he was only 21.

The bell rang.

Dempsey threw jabs and caught Steve with a stiff punch to his spleen. Steve faked a right hook, then caught Dempsey with a beautiful uppercut. They danced around the ring for about a minute, exchanging crosses and hooks, knees and uppercuts. Steve backed up a couple of steps and Dempsey moved in for the kill. But it was at this moment when Steve managed to side-suplex the huge body and the pair went down to the mat. Rolling furiously, the two sweating wrestlers weaved and slipped in and out of each other's holds. The fans knew they were witnessing some marvelous chain wrestling and applauded many times in appreciation.

Steve, in an attempt to end the match, set Dempsey up for a wrist lock. Dempsey was on his back with his knees bent in a guard position when Steve quickly moved on top of him from a side mount, grabbing Dempsey's left arm and pulling him in. Moving in, he threaded his arm behind Dempsey's shoulder. He grabbed his own wrist, locking Dempsey's forearm into place. Believing he had the match won, he leaned down hard on Dempsey. The crowd was going crazy! They leaned forward towards the ring, still sitting in their seats, barely, stretching their necks to get a better look at how Steve Peacock, the Giant Killer was going to tap out Dempsey Bellamy.

Steve's decision now was the deal breaker. He kept his arms locked through Dempsey's and began to roll backward towards Dempsey's right hip. Dempsey, sensing the change, used his leverage and rolled Steve over. The hold was broken and Dempsey was on top now. The capacity crowd, now on their feet, sat back down, shaking their heads in disbelief at how Dempsey managed to break this bear-trap of a hold.

Thinking fast, Dempsey gave Steve a taste of his own medicine. He grabbed Steve's wrist, securely putting his opponent in a double-wrist lock.

Instead of trying to roll, Dempsey pushed his chest into Steve's stomach and lifted Steve's torso from underneath. Like a wrench tightening a bolt, he intensified the triangle lock he had on Steve's arm. Dempsey dug his elbow into the mat for leverage and Steve's elbow was sticking way out like a boomerang. Dempsey hadn't even begun to apply the pressure when Steve tapped out.

The fans, back on their feet again, cheered wildly! The two fighters stood on their feet and gave each other a respectful hug.

"You got me on that one, son. I think you made your dad proud. Good job," said Steve as the referee raised Dempsey's hand.

"Thank you, mate," said Dempsey, clapping the stocky wrestler on the back. He headed for the walkway, where Aaron was waiting for him, arms crossed and head nodding in approval. As they walked back to the dressing room, Aaron said, in a tone that combined speculation and confirmation, "Well, there's a fifty per cent chance now that you'll be fightin' your uncle."

Dempsey didn't say anything. Secretly, he hoped he would face his uncle in the main event. He didn't know if fighting Toasty was the best way to resolve their cold five-year war, but he was hard-pressed to think of any other solution to get past it all. All the loss and finality of the tragedies needed to be put behind them all. Perhaps it had to get a little bit worse before it really could begin to get better. If they didn't fight tonight, Dempsey had no Plan B for how he would get back into the British wrestling scene again and that is what he wanted now; he needed to give his face a rest in Japan. If Dempsey wanted to make a name for himself in British wrestling and once again call England his home, something drastic and severe needed to be done. Trying to appeal to Toasty's better nature wouldn't amount to any kind successful reunion, as the past proved. Ignoring his uncle wouldn't work either, as his uncle had ignored him and his family reaching out for him over the past five years; he just never reached back In the end, Dempsey reassured himself that the best way to get his uncle's attention, and hopefully his respect, was the daunting task of going toe-to-toe with him, even if Toasty was one of the smarted and gutsiest grapplers there ever was Sitting in his dressing room, with the television off so Dempsey could release some of his stress, he stared straight ahead while Aaron thoroughly iced his sweating body.

Grant knocked and let himself in. "Well, looks like it's going to be you against Toasty!" he said. "He just beat Sasha Borshov with a shin lock. You should 'ave seen it! Toasty dug his elbow into the Borshov's leg and 'e tapped in like two seconds!"

Dempsey nodded his head. "Chances were good that I was goin' to face him sometime in this tournament. Shouldn't be worse seein' it's the main event. I didn't come all this way to lose, though. Right then, thanks for the news, Grant." He was now about to go down that treacherous road that he had been preparing for since he signed up for CrazyBest.

"Well, I think after tonight, you and your uncle, maybe your mum too, you should all try to talk things out," said Grant amicably. He, along with everyone else, knew all about the notorious family feud.

"Well, I've bloody well tried to reach out to him and he's been a bastard to us for years," said Dempsey. "I'm thinkin,' as bad as this sounds, that the only hope in hell we have to move forward is to fight each other tonight. I know me uncle is not the losin' kind, but neither am I, as he'll soon find out."

Aaron stood up. "Thanks fer the news, Grant," he said. "Ah need to have a few words with Dempsey here, now."

"Sure thing," said Grant, turning to go. "Good luck out there, Dempsey."

Aaron squatted next to the bench Dempsey was sitting on, looking him square on in the eyes. "Jumbo, we've talked about this moment for months," he said. "Keep your focus on the prize. Right now, ah don't know if the prize is the £50,000 or getting your hands on your uncle, but either way, keep focused, like I just said to ya. Toasty's gonna try to psych you out. Don't let him! Take all the emotional bullshit out of this and the odds are in yer favour. You can do this. Just remember, it's a game o' chess, so fight smarter than he does."

Dempsey just nodded. He paced around the huge dressing room as if he were an animal in a cage. Aaron looked at him with concern.

"Hey, Jumbo, skip a bit o' rope and keep yerself warm after all that icing I did on ya," he said. "Jus' get into yer zone. Ye'll be fine." He tossed the jump rope over to his friend.

"'Ta," said Dempsey. He untangled the rope and jumped on one foot, then the other. He got into an easy rhythm and he tried not to think about what was to come.

The reality of it all didn't set in until all the lights in the arena faded to black. Only seconds before, the arena had exploded with sound and the energy of a thousand power lines sizzling and jumping at the announcement of the main event. Now, however, just moments later, you could hear a pin drop. In the silence, the thudding of Dempsey's heartbeat and the sound of blood rushing through his ears were ear-splitting.

Then a small light appeared over the ring and a long microphone cable was lowered from the ceiling. The ring announcer cleared his throat and spoke quietly, almost in a whisper.

"This is the CrazyBest Main Event and our final fight of the night. The winner of this main event will be the undisputed Absolute Best grappler in the universe! The first of our two competitors to enter this hallowed ground is a shoot-fighting specialist, fighting out of Japan, weighing at 17 stone 8 pounds, standing at 6 feet 4 ½ inches."

The announcer's took a deep breath. "Introducing Dempseeeeeeey Bellllllllllamyyyyy!" he screamed into the microphone.

The crowd exploded as Dempsey passed through the heavy black velvet curtain. The hot overhead lights cast deep shadows and made Dempsey look more like a Roman statue than a young man as he walked slowly down the pitch and into the ring. At ringside, Aaron leaned in close. "Remember yer training," he said in a low voice. "Remember yer strengths. We ain't gonna fight 'his' fight, right? Yeh ready?"

"Aye."

Dempsey pushed the top rope down and stepped over it rather than ducking under it. He did this for two reasons. First, it made him look larger than life and the crowd reacted like he knew they would – by screaming even louder. Second, he knew Toasty would be watching and he wanted to show just how huge he'd gotten. He bounced up and down on the balls of his feet in his corner as the arena went dark and silent for a second time. And now, the second opponent in this CrazyBest Main Event is Manchester's very own wrestling royalty, weighing in at 16½ stone, 6 feet, ½ inches in height, wearing black and gold shorts, Toasty Bonhammmmmmmmmmm!"

Toasty threw the curtains aside violently when his name was called and walked briskly down the ramp, his hands balled into fists. His bronzed face was weathered by all the passions of a predatory fighter. His Bonham blue eyes never left Dempsey's Bellamy blue eyes. . When he entered the ring, he walked right up to his nephew, dripping sweat from his methodical warm-up back stage. He wiped off his arms and slung the sweat down on the mat, one arm at a time.

"This is going to be a 30-minute shoot and I want to you to keep it clean," Maxwell the announcer said. "No eye gouging, strikes to the groin, head butting, or closed-fist strikes to the head allowed. Open-handed strikes to the head are permissible, as are closed-fist strikes to the body. If you are knocked down for more than a ten count, the match is over. If you are knocked down more than five times in one round, you lose by technical knockout. You can win by knockout, submission, or technical knockout. If it goes the full 30 minutes it will be declared a draw, but for heaven's sake I hope it doesn't …"

The announcer paused for effect.

"The missus is waiting supper and I might be knocked out meself."

The crowd laughed; the two fighters did not. They looked pitiless and fierce at each other and unamused by Maxwell's spoken liberties.

"Let's keep it clean, fellas," The announcer said, instantly taking the lightness out of his conduct. He suddenly knew his lightheartedness was not appropriate for the tension that the two fighters exuded. He left the ring, looking at Referee Hathaway with an admiring sigh, sensing it wouldn't be an easy one to referee. He quickly took his seat, relieved to now be on the outside looking in.

Dempsey put out his hand to shake Toasty's. Toasty just shook his head unwillingly and indifferently walked slowly back to his corner.

"So that's how you want to play it then," Dempsey muttered. His voice was inaudible over the nearly twenty thousand screaming fans.

The bell rang out loud and clear and every apprehensive thought vanished from Dempsey's mind. The crowd was still screaming, but it sounded faint and distant. Instead, Dempsey heard his own rhythmic breathing and the scratching sound his bright white wrist tape made when it brushed against his leg.

He knew things wouldn't go smoothly ten seconds into the fight.

Toasty charged out of his corner with purpose, his knees bent as if to shoot for a double leg takedown. Reacting instinctively, Dempsey by put his hands on Toasty's shoulders and pushed his hips backwards. He sprawled perfectly, but Toasty was feigning. Toasty hit him with a hard open palm stiff-arm that snapped Dempsey's head backwards as he scrambled to his feet. The blow landed flush on Dempsey's eyebrow. Instantly, warm blood dripped down Dempsey's face and into his eye, impeding his vision.

Dempsey shot in for a takedown of his own but was blocked. Backing up, he wiped blood from his eye and shot in again, like a mongoose going after a snake. Again he was blocked. Toasty expected him to shoot and was ready to sprawl every time. The only way to get the fight to the ground was with the element of surprise.

Dempsey went into the guard position and leaned forward, breaking away and kicking Toasty off. Toasty stood and went to grab Dempsey around his waist for a belly-to-belly suplex, but Dempsey drove him into the turnbuckle of the ring instead. As Dempsey tried to take Toasty down, Toasty grabbed the ropes.

"Let go of the ropes!" hollered the referee. Toasty cursed and released his grip.

Dempsey whipped out a stiff kick, slamming into Toasty's ribcage under his left arm. Grinning, Toasty ate his pain as he caught the kick. Ignoring the easy opportunity to take him to the mat, he stepped forward and pounded his right fist into Dempsey's solar plexus.

Bile stung Dempsey's throat and crept up his esophagus. He fought down the urge to vomit in front of twenty thousand people. This was not going to be a shoot between gentlemen, but he was okay with that.

He already had Toasty's timing down.

Toasty was a scrapper and a tremendous fighter, but he did everything full throttle. He made his way on brute force and heart. It was evident that he wanted to beat the will to win out of Dempsey before they went to the mat.

Unpredictability when fighting, just as in war, was always the best strategy, Dempsey thought. Toasty expected him to shoot, so Dempsey faked a takedown, and when Toasty sprawled backwards with his head low, Dempsey turned his body and swung his palm with an upward hook into Toasty's nose. It exploded with blood.

The crowd fell silent, and for the first time since the bell rang out in the arena Toasty was nervous. He staggered back. The referee stopped the action briefly to check the damage to

Toasty's nose. Toasty waved off the ringside physician, but the referee insisted.

"Oh yea, that's a break," said the doctor, looking Toasty seriously in the face. "Are you sure you want to continue?"

"Damn sure," said Toasty through gritted teeth, his bright Bonham blue eyes contrasted shockingly with the vivid red. Blood bubbled from his nose into his mouth and onto his chest as he charged in.

Dempsey got low and wrapped both hands around Toasty's waist, spinning him against the ropes. He let loose with a slurry of heavy punches, one of which connected with Toasty's liver. Toasty gasped and leaned against the ropes.

Like a baseball player sliding into the base, Dempsey slid forward and seized Toasty's ankle. He wrapped his legs around Toasty's thigh and brought him down to the mat. Swiftly, Dempsey stuck the toe of Toasty's wrestling shoe into his armpit and twisted him into a heel-hook.

The sound was sickening; it reminded Dempsey of the sound of tearing a chicken leg from its body. Toasty cried out in pain and for the first time in his life, Dempsey knew Toasty was vulnerable. He continued to put pressure on the ankle, turning it in an unnatural angle. Trying to break the hold, Toasty put the heel of his free leg on the back of Dempsey's thigh and pushed hard. The sweat on Toasty's leg made the escape easy. It was only then Dempsey realized why Toasty had warmed up so much backstage. He wanted his skin slippery, and his joints loose, for moments like these.

Toasty got to his feet quickly. When Dempsey tried to rise, Toasty drove his knee into the side of his head. The crowd reacted to the illegal shot with a collective boo, but the referee didn't seem to care. Toasty jumped on top of Dempsey and straddled his chest, hitting him with shot after shot, digging his knuckles into Dempsey's ribs and kidneys. When Dempsey tried to cover his ribs with his elbows, Toasty worked over his head and face with open hand palm shots harder than any punches Dempsey could remember.

Dempsey felt consciousness slipping and he turned his head away. Before his eyes closed for what would have been the last time that match, he saw Aaron in his corner. Aaron was calm and composed, mouthing something. Dempsey made out two words.

"Get up!"

Dempsey felt himself relax, oddly at ease with the situation. He now sensed little pain as punch after kick landed on his head and body. Putting his hands against Toasty's waist, he emphatically pushed him, Sumo-style, towards the ropes with everything he had. Toasty stopped swinging and tried to correct his balance, but it was too little, too late. Dempsey shoved him over and remained standing despite all it took to knock him down. The crowd roared with approval of this last-minute show of courage and power.

The incessant buzzing in Dempsey's ears finally stopped and he could hear Aaron over the crowd. "He's getting tired, he can't breathe through that nose. Shut him down! Shut him down now! He'll kill ya if he gets the chance!"

Toasty heard this too, and he charged forward, pinning Dempsey against the ropes. He doesn't seem tired, Dempsey thought. Dempsey's face hurt. He was exhausted and he wanted to end this as soon as possible. Toasty had one stubborn, heavy arm over Dempsey's shoulder and the other pugnaciously under his armpit.

"Tired eh?" Toasty laughed, and solidly butted his shoulder into Dempsey's chin, rattling his head.

Unpredictability is the best strategy, Dempsey reminded himself.

"You remember your ticket, Uncle?"

Toasty laughed, "Ticket? What the fuck are you on about?"

"You don't want to miss your flight." Dempsey replied.

Toasty shook his head back and forth and repositioned his arms, "I must have hit you harder than I thou…."

Dempsey grabbed Toasty's wrist. He spun Toasty against the ropes and stepped back, carrying their momentum away from the side of the ring. Turning like a swivel, he pushed his right leg across the front of Toasty's thighs and put all his weight on the opposite foot. Both men thumped down onto the mat. Struggling, they staggered around and returned to a standing guard.

Toasty threw a swift right-hand swing, but Dempsey ducked to miss it. With no sign of reluctance, he pawed Toasty's right hand down and popped Toasty with a quick jab to his face. Toasty stumbled, coming back again and again only to get blocked again and again, like an echo, by his tenacious opponent.

Dempsey set up for his big roundhouse kick, but Toasty was too quick. With a punt-like kick, he pummeled Dempsey hard in the stomach first, nearly bringing him to his knees. Wasting no time, Toasty tried to uppercut the big fighter, but Dempsey swerved just in the nick of time, missing it by the skin of a tooth. In a split second the playful light in Toasty's eyes darkened with surprise when he realized what was happening; his equilibrium suddenly shifted as he sailed into the air as Dempsey turned with him, arching his back and his feet into a textbook-perfect belly-to-belly suplex. They came crashing down with such force that they both thought they might fall right through the ring.

Dempsey landed like a ton of wet sand with his full weight on top of Toasty, forcing the air out of his lungs. Immediately he straddled his winded opponent. Dempsey's dead weight was too heavy for Toasty, so Toasty defensively brought his hands up, trying to drill punches into his massive opponent's head. Desperately, Toasty dragged his forearms up and across Dempesy's face, trying to shrimp and coil to his right, then to his left, but Dempsey squeezed his powerful legs snugly around Toasty's heaving mid-section like a boa constricting its prey.

Leaning forward, Dempsey placed his big palm flat down on the mat between Toasty's head and left arm. He grabbed the back of Toasty's head, rolling him to his left side and wrapping an arm around his neck. He was choking Toasty out, shutting off his vital blood flow to his heart and brain, and as much as he tried, Toasty had no chance of escaping. Dempsey's right ear was pressing so hard into Toasty's left ear that he could practically hear Toasty's thoughts. The roaring crowd's cheers were fading in and out. Dempsey was in the offense, but he was fading too. He needed to finish Toasty off soon, before he was running at a deficit too. He cinched his "head and arm triangle choke" another notch tighter, hoping to end the match.

Toasty's free right arm grabbed into the air, but there was no lifeline there to pull him out. He wheezed, barely managing to say, "Fuuuck."

Dempsey bore down with all his weight. Shooting his right leg over Toasty's body, he forced his knee deep into Toasty's abdominals. He was able to maintain a terrific base, but it wasn't necessary. Dempsey's head and arm chokehold was already cutting the blood off to Toasty's brain and heart.

Toasty was unconscious before he could tap. It actually happened so fast the referee didn't have time to intervene.

Dempsey let go of the choke, slowly got to his feet, walked to his corner and raised his arms in victory before collapsing in exhaustion onto the top rope. "The referee has declared Dempsey Bellamy our winner by submission," said the announcer as the referee raised the tired right arm of the spent fighter high in the air.

2

On The Same Side Again

Claudine arrived at CrazyBest about halfway through the matches. Prone to anxiety, she was intentionally late so she wouldn't have to watch her son brutally fight as much. She took her seat, but hardly had the intestinal fortitude to watch the bouts. It frightened her too much, especially with so many competitors coming away with gruesome injuries.

Now, with her son in the main event and fighting her brother no less, she simply could not watch another minute of the callous and fierce competitions. She felt too anxious and torn to watch the fight with the rest of the thousands of die-hard fans. Instead, she crept into the back and asked the security guard to take her to Dempsey's private dressing room. Luckily, the man recognized her and didn't utter a word of complaint. But even alone, in the quiet and unthreatening dressing room, Claudine was a ball of nerves. She didn't particularly want to see her son and her brother in a fight to the finish. This fight was like a volcano finally erupting, full of pressure and tension built up for nearly five years. *Would there be any winners in this battle?* Claudine hoped and prayed no one would be hurt too badly. She thought of Drew and what he went through in Germany and she felt her stomach knot up tighter.

After what seemed like an eternity, the match was over. Dempsey came back into his dressing room, covered in sweat and blood and clutching Aaron for support. He saw his mum standing there and smiled. Despite how battered he looked, the look on his face was one of elation.

"I won! I don't even remember what happened, but I won!" he said. Claudine gave her son a compassionate hug, being careful not to overwhelm his already overwhelmed body.

"Are you all right?" she asked, looking at the deep cut above his swollen eye.

"I feel like I've been hit by a train, but I'm all right," he replied. "How do you think it went, Aaron? Tell me mum and tell me too, because I can't really recall at the moment."

"It was one of the closest, most electrifying and impressive fights ah've ever had the privilege of watchin'," said Aaron enthusiastically. "Ah'm so proud of this kid! You're the absolute best in the world, son, and you deserve to be. You had way more goin' on inside yer head than anyone, except yer uncle, and the two of y'all damn well impressed me and gave the fans somethin' they won't see ever again. Thank God it was filmed, because no one would believe it unless they saw it with their own eyes. Ah think Toasty tried a few things he might not be too proud of, but you countered him and you damn well won!"

Aaron gave Dempsey's shoulder a cautious squeeze, careful not to touch any new bruises. "I believe your dad was in there with you tonight," he said in a calmer voice. "I'm tellin' ya, yer dad and yer dad too, Claudine, they were both in that ring! That's probably what saved 'em from killin' each other!"

A doctor came to the door and summoned Dempsey to be stitched up and examined. Aaron went with him, promising to bring themselves back soon so they could take a deep breath and unwind. It was all over, but there was no certainty where it was going to start or end with them and Toasty. Claudine smiled with a bit of uncertainty in her face as the two men left her to join the doctor. "Now just wait here, darlin' and we'll be back as soon as we can. Alright?" said Aaron.

"Alright, I can do that," Claudine answered back, trying to conceal how rattled she actually was, seeing her son so badly beaten up and not knowing if it was worth it or not, to him or to anyone.

About a half hour after CrazyBest was done and the building was emptying out, Dempsey and Aaron returned from being tended to by the doctors. Dempsey cleaned up nicely, but his face was swollen and stitched. The stitches were bleeding still and he face was bruised and distorted. He felt like a champion though. He was about to politely request his mum step outside so he could change into his street clothes when there was a knock at the dressing room door. It was Grant, but this time, he had a message for Claudine.

"Excuse me," said Grant, "Toasty sent me over here to fetch you before ya left the building. Would you mind comin' with me? He'd like a word. A calm one, don't worry," he interjected when he saw the apprehensive look on her face. "I think young Dempsey here beat the fight right out o' 'im. I think he's done fightin' for tonight"

"Mum, do you want me to come?" asked Dempsey, who was interrupted by the on-site medics who came back to Dempsey's dressing room to check on his stitches. One nurse scolded him for leaving before he could finish stitching his face.

"You're not going anywhere right now, mister," he said vehemently. "Not until we've got that cut on your face under control."

"I thought we were finished and there were all those lads in there that were just as bad off as I was. I honestly thought you were done fixin' me up," Dempsey bashfully pleaded to the nurse He had cold eyes like a shark, but they warmed up to him and he smiled slightly.

"Well, you have to let me finish this whip stitch and after that, if you convince me that you're alreet, I'll let you go. Yer eyes still look a bit dodgy, but we'll have a good look at them again after I finish stitching you up, now, alreet? So keep still and we'll make yer face right so yer mum won't cry when she sees ya," said the nurse seriously, then grinned. "I'm a big fan of yours, Dempsey. I can't tell you what an honour it is for me to stitch you up. But, you can't go anywhere until I get that done, alreet?"

"Don't worry," said Claudine. "I can handle it meself. You just relax, you deserve it right now."

Grant led Claudine down the hall to Toasty's dressing room. She knocked tentatively at the door.

"Hello?" she said as if she had the wrong door. Her face showed a faintly worried expression.

"Come in, it's alreet," Toasty said, swinging the door open. He looked even worse for the wear than Dempsey, but there were no medics in his room. "I asked everyone to give us a moment alone, this won't take long. Care for a bottle of water?" he offered, his face impassive.

"No, I'm fine," said Claudine, faintly worried, stepping quietly into the room. She watched her brother reach over and grab an envelope. She had no idea what he was doing, but Claudine was not going to try to initiate or dictate anything. She was expecting to hear how he was still mad about her book or that Dempsey betrayed him. Her family had tried to extend the olive branch to him for years and he refused to reach out and grab it.

Toasty, however, was calmly opening an envelope and taking out a piece of paper. He shook it out and read it.

> *Dear Toasty,*
>
> *What is it that I do that makes you still think of me as your enemy? We've been through so much together that I feel we should be friends. And of course, we are family. I guess you must like having me as an enemy, since you've been keeping it up for years, but I will not stop trying to change your mind.*
>
> *Love,*
>
> *Claudine*

"Well, I didn't know if you read any of those," said Claudine. She had written letters to Toasty over the past five years, but he had never responded.

"Listen, Claudine," said Toasty, heaving an impressive sigh and setting the letter down on his big knee. With all of his cuts and bruises from the match, he looked as if he had just lost a war. "I'm sorry. I'm ashamed o' meself for how terrible I've been towards you and the kids. I 'ad a lot o' issues to deal with, and there'll always be things I have to deal with because o' the choices I've made. But having said that, Dempsey beat me fair and square. I didn't give him an inch. I wish I did beat him, for the final fight o' me career. I'm officially retired now and truthfully, I'm lucky I'm even walking or thinking at this point. Me body's taken a hell of a beating and tonight was no exception, that's for sure. But that's not what I brought you in here to talk about."

Toasty got up and started pacing, looking everywhere but at Claudine. "I realize I've not been fair to you and I really feel like a complete guilty, selfish son–of–a–bitch 'bout how I've behaved towards you. I've not been able to think straight, especially since CrazyBest really started to get rollin' this past month. I wanted to talk to you before today, but I had to keep focused. The doctors told me that after CrazyBest, I absolutely need to stop fightin'. So this was me last chance and I didn't want to lose it. I'm not sayin' that stress is what cost me the Absolute Best tonight," he said suddenly, looking at Claudine. "Your Dempsey, hands down, is one o' the best in the world. I've tremendous respect for him and what he set out to accomplish as a lad, well, he did it. Your Dempsey stretched the life out of me tonight, but I tell you, it was an honour. Maybe I deserved it, eh?" he said with a bit of a laugh. Claudine just sat there, meekly smiling, but rather silent. She had no idea if her brother was going to be kind or cruel as he started to open up his feelings to her.

"I want me family to be a part of things with me again," he said, finally looking at his sister. "I wanted this before, but I guess it I had to really have it beaten into me before I would do anythin' about it. So, please, let's just carry on from here and forget the bad stuff, eh?"

Claudine recognized the look in Toasty's eyes. It was the same look he had as a child when he was apologizing for something really inexcusable, like tearing an arm off of Claudine's teddy bear. Even though he was so much larger than she was, it was clear that he was nervous. Now Claudine couldn't help but smile as she stepped forward and embraced her gritty younger brother. Her eyes welled up with soft, relieved tears.

"Oh, Toasty," she said, sniffling, wrapping her arms carefully around his bruised torso. "You can sure be a nasty headache and a heartache, as I know I have been to you, but we've never stopped lovin' you an' carin' about you. We want to put all o' this behind us too, you know?"

Toasty gratefully hugged Claudine back. "You're an angel, Claudine. I've treated you all like shite and if Dad or Drew had been around, they'd 'ave kicked me in the arse, but I just couldn't get past things, because I just couldn't. I couldn't bear to see you because it would've been painful. I just couldn't handle it so I avoided it, you, everythin' except the wrestling. Selfish, stupid thinking on my part… I hope you did manage somehow," he said. "You've got a right level head on your shoulders. But I think you've been strugglin' dead hard for a while and to that I feel right awful." Letting go of their embrace, he stared at the floor. "I'm ashamed o' meself for how I treated you. I wouldn't let the solicitors settle Dad's estate because I was punishin' you for what you said in your book. I know now that it wasn't your fault." A look of anger and obvious regret flashed across his face and he looked at the wall behind Claudine as if it had personally offended him. "I blame the whole thing on that bloody bitch Toni Orr and her fuckin' wimp husband Ernie. The bitch even contacted me about tryin' to make a movie about Drew, but I wouldn't even wipe me ass with her fuckin' offer and I told her so. And then tonight, the '*see you on Tuesday*' and her camera crew actually had the nerve to show up here trying to get interviews for some fuckin' celebrity sports show she manufactures."

Claudine's stomach turned and Toasty laughed at the look on her face. "Don't worry, I had them all thrown out. I wouldn't say she's got balls as much as she's just plain ignorant and thinks she can do as she bloody well pleases. Not at my fuckin' show she can't."

"Really? I can't believe it!" said Claudine hotly. "That is in really bad taste! She was probably tryin' to ruin the night for everyone and then get it all on film for one o' her vulgar shows. I don't know what I would have done if I'd have seen her. I might be in jail right now for attempted murder."

As Toasty laughed, Claudine thought back to when Toni had tried to convince her to get in on the movie deal. "Crikey, she's still goin' on about the 'Drew Movie,' is she? I hope nobody works with her on it. The Duffys dropped her years ago after I refused her, at least that's what they were sayin' in the tabloids."

"Yeah, well, who'd want to work with her, eh?" said Toasty earnestly. He leaned his shoulder into the concrete wall and sighed. "Well, enough about that, it's not a concern to me anymore--that bitch has gotten enough of me time already. There's more important things I need to say to you."

Toasty cracked two sparkling waters open as he continued, handing one to Claudine. "I know you probably already guessed this after everythin' I've said, but I stopped contesting Dad's will. I was being a bloody bastard and I should 'ave never ever kept your inheritance money from you. I was just afraid you were goin' to use it to try fightin' me on your book. Neither of us would have any money now if that'd happened; it would have all gone to the solicitors. Anyroad, I came to me senses right quick when I realized Demspey was going to fight in CrazyBest and I figured win or lose, I'd have to own up to this miserable, pathetic decision I made long ago, when I got it into me daft head to fight you on Dad's will. I just didn't know how to explain meself, how to make it right. I swore to meself that no matter what, tonight, after the show ended, I would try to put things right. So, what I'm struggling to say is, I have some money for you now, this minute," said Toasty, shrugging himself away from the wall. He reached over to a huge black nylon training bag on the floor and began rummaging through it. He stood up with an envelope in his hand.

"I should've given you this to you a long time ago, and to be honest, Claudine, I didn't know how truly bad it was for you. One of me wrestlers told me he ran into you working at the co-op and I couldn't believe it," he said, handing her the check. She looked inside the envelope and gasped as she read the tiny £35,000 written across the front of a cheque. It was more money than she'd had since before Drew had passed away.

"The house is still half yours too, by the way," Toasty continued. "That's in the will and it always will be a home to you and the kids. And, if you want, I was thinkin' you could come work on a small, part-time for me at IWF. Maybe you can work from home or come by the house a couple o' days a week. It's just a little job for you, probably won't pay for all you need, but it's there if you want it; doin' all the stuff that mum hated and never wanted you to do either, but like I said, it's there, if you're keen on it. Think about it, anyroad."

"But please, Claudine, with the money…" Toasty paused and crossed his arms, looking extremely uncomfortable. "I know you don't owe me anythin', but please, I'm askin' you to not mention this to Dempsey and Isabella. I'm absolutely ashamed o' meself as it is, for not gettin' this to you and makin' things right ages ago. I think it'd ruin things between us right now if your kids knew their Granddad left you this money and I'm only givin' it to you tonight… after you all went through hell trying to survive because you had no money when you really did. Does that make any sense and is that possible for you to do for me? I am so sorry, Claudine. I've been a complete selfish prick!"

She needed the money, but she needed her family together again perhaps even more than anything right now. Just then she felt like a winner; maybe not Absolute Best, but a winner in her own right.

"Yes, absolutely Toasty, for all sake's sake, let's do what you say and keep this between just us," she said. "Thank you for erasin' that cruel line in the sand. I just want to be happy again, you know, and this past hour has done that for me. I'll use this money to take care of things. I won't make a big deal of it by goin' out and buyin' stuff that make people, especially me kids, wonder if I just inherited a lot of money," she said with a laugh.

"Ta! Thanks very much, Claude," said Toasty, looking thoroughly relieved as he took a big gulp of his sparkling water. "Now, I think it's time to celebrate this reunion. Let's go have a good time at the after-party. I've got a splittin' headache, but I've got to go and make an appearance at least. Come out to it, will you? It's at the Edwardian and everyone's goin' to be there; it doesn't start for another hour, so we'll both have time to clean up. And try to get Dempsey to go. He's the new Absolute Best and it's time the world knows this."

"Okay," Claudine said with gladness. "I'll check with Dempsey and see if he's up to goin'. It's so fantastic to be talkin' to you again, Toasty."

The party took place at the Red Lantern Bar in the posh Edwardian Hotel in Manchester. In attendance, there were about two hundred guests mingling in the understated, but impressive, event room. There was a carefree air of everyone feeling welcome and validated. The hotel staff treated the fighters and their friends like celebrities and the fighters certainly were amongst the elite in professional combative sports. As part of the entertainment, Toasty hired an incredibly talented disc jockey, paid the hotel extra for staying late, and had the world class kitchen staff prepare some very tasty finger foods. There was an open bar with everything imaginable available to drink for Toasty's guests. Everyone was there: famous footballers, rugby league players, cricketers, singers, politicians, artists, celebrities, from the retired to the up-and-coming who's who, and, of course, Toasty's family.

Aaron enjoyed a few drinks of Johnny Walker Blue Label Whisky. After he was feeling good and a bit tipsy, he started really talking to Claudine, who was on her second tall glass of effervescent champagne.

"If any man ever tries to hurt you or Buffy ah'll kill him. Ah mean it, ah will kill him," Aaron calmly told her. The two of them were sitting at a high pub table in a quieter corner of the dimly-lit bar, far enough away from the DJ's speakers and all the music. They could hear and talk to each other somewhat comfortably.

"That's quite a commitment," said Claudine, 'shouting' as quietly as she could, "but I don't think anyone's comin' after me or Buffy! You, though," she said, gesturing to the spot on his arm where his big scar lay hidden by his button-down shirt, "You might want to watch out." She grinned.

"Yea," said Aaron, touching the spot. "Well, ah can tell ya now about this scar, 'cuz ah know ya better now." Aaron had been drinking and was feeling great, but he was still very serious this evening. He hunkered down in his seat, putting his elbows on his knees, whiskey glass in one hand. Fixing Claudine with a dramatic stare, he began his tale. "Ah was in the Special Forces back when ah was in the Army. It was real hard on me to see babies, young kids, mothers, even animals, who don't even know what the fightin's about and when they get hurt, or worse… well, it was just so fuckin' bad."

Aaron took a swig of whiskey, shaking his head emphatically as he swallowed unwinking at the stiff swish. Claudine thought of how much Aaron loved poor little Buffy and how hard it must have been for him to see so much suffering in his own life.

"That day with my arm, well, we got our orders to go inside this big buildin'," Aaron continued. "In there we meet up with enemy soldiers on the fifth floor and we start fightin.' Me and this enemy soldier end up fightin' our way over toward a big balcony and it is either him or me that's gonna get pushed over and fall like five stories down to the ground. One of us is going to die."

A few wrestlers made their way over to Claudine's table and gave her a congratulatory hug. "Your Dempsey's brilliant! He's the best!" they exclaimed. Claudine smiled, hugged them sincerely back and smiled at Aaron, as if to say, "Go on."

Aaron's eyes were far away, his expression pained. "There's guns shootin' and glass and debris flyin' all over. Ah got this guy on the ground and out of nowhere he pulls out this fiberglass knife and he stabs me deep in my right arm. He dragged that knife through my flesh like he was wanting to cut it right off. Ah could feel it go way in there and then ah couldn't move my arm at all and ah have glass all over me too. Ah think he figured he'd throw me over the balcony then, because mah right arm is already wrecked from 'im stabbing me with his fuckin' big glass knife.

A few more wrestlers came by the table. They respectfully acknowledged Aaron but seemed almost intimidated by him "So sorry to interrupt, mate, but we just wanted to congratulate you on a brilliant job of being Dempsey's corner man!" They reached out and shook his hand. He gladly shook it back and smiled at them sincerely.

"Thanks, y'all enjoy the fights tonight?" Aaron asked with interest.

"They were fuckin' amazin! Toasty didn't hold back and honestly, I didn't know who was going to win. But, when you think of Dempsey's size, even though he's only young, well, he had maybe not the experience of Toasty, but he had enough smarts to win against one of the best." This lad was slurring his words, but his sentiments were genuine and warranted.

The lad continued, not wanting to leave, but sensing the couple wanted to be alone. "Can I get you lot a drink? What ya havin?"

"We're alright, thanks. What's your name?" Aaron asked.

"It's Leo. Pleasure to meet you. Can I get a picture with you, Claudine?" asked the lad, with no sign of reluctance.

"Sure." Said Claudine, getting out of her high chair.

"Claudine, I just want to tell you how much me family loved growin' up watchin' your Drew. He was amazing. God bless him," he said, raising his glass up to the ceiling as though he was looking up to the heavens. "Your Dempsey's a chip off the old block. You must be so proud," said the young lad, sporting tattoos on his big biceps and caring his black leather waist coat on his arm. "Can I give you a hug?" the lad asked politely. Claudine stood up graciously and soon Aaron stood up too.

"Certainly. And thank you for supporting me family," said Claudine and the bloke left their table, putting his hands together as though he was praying for them. He was dearly affectionate for Claudine's family and it was nice to feel the fans' love again after all being ostracized by Toasty for so long. Aaron could see how it made Claudine feel so proud—he looked at her with starry eyes.

"Sorry about the interruption, again. Do go on, please," she kindly urged Aaron.

"Ya, so this guy had this big fuckin' fiberglass knife and he's gettin' the better of me. But then ah kind of went crazy, thank God, and somehow ah got this surge of strength and I threw the guy over the edge. Then the next thing ah know ahm inside the US Army helicopter. I'm like half conscious and the pilot's yellin' to me that a bomb went off inside the building and it knocked me out and then this doctor inside the helicopter is ordering me, like screamin' at me at the top of 'is lungs, 'Move yer fingers! Try to move yer fingers or yer gonna lose yer arm!' Ah keep telling him ahm tryin' and ah remember that I kept tellin' my fingers to move, but it took like two minutes fer my brain to get a message through to my fingers. Finally my baby finger heard my brain and it moved, just barely." Aaron twitched his baby finger ever so slightly. "Yup, it moved just that little bit just in time, or else they said ah woulda lost my arm, so thank God my baby finger's a good listener."

Claudine just stared at Aaron, who seemed surprised to have evoked this kind of benevolent curiosity from her. He stared right back, looking into her eyes. "Hey, darlin,' I see these guys keep passin' by and y'all keep givin' each other hugs. They just keep comin', these wrestlers and their hugs. It kind of bothers me, ya know?"

Like clockwork, Archie, another well-meaning wrestler came by. "Hey, Aaron. Great to see you," he said, in a strong Scottish brogue accent. "Your new trainee's quite the champ. And Missus Bellamy," he said, giving Claudine a hug. "Congratulations, ma'am. You've got a real family of champions. Your Dempsey's fantastic!"

Aaron slipped his arm around Claudine's little waist, sending shivers up her spine. "Thanks, Archie," he said, taking another sip of whisky. In a few seconds, they were alone again.

"Ah guess ahm kinda jealous. It's crazy that ah feel like this, 'cuz ah ain't allowed mahself to have strong feelings for any girl in a while... And not many girls impress me all that much, so it ain't too hard to control my feelings when they ain't there to begin with, ya know? And then ah meet you. You're real special, darlin'..." He sipped his whisky, but his eyes never left hers. It was as if he was searching for something. There was a stern cautiousness in his gaze, but she felt like could see past it into his eyes, into the depths of a warm soul.

Aaron took another sip of his whisky. He seemed to make his mind up about something.

"Let's go somewhere we can be alone, darlin'. I need to kiss you," he said. Something in the pit of Claudine's stomach started fluttering as Aaron boldly took her by her hand and walked her out down the hallway and around the corridor. They were standing in front of a locked door. The corrider was warm, and aside from the faint noise of elevator bells and murmurs of a distant crowd of a happy celebration around the corner, the hallway was quiet and out of sight, out of mind. Aaron led her slightly farther away to where a leaded glass window was and a huge, magnificent marble pillar blocked them even more from anyone's view. Outside the window, cars whizzed back and forth and Manchester sparkled in the night.

Aaron looked into Claudine's face and tilted his head slightly. Lifting his hand to her chin, he gently held it and pulled it up to his. Claudine felt her heart pound as he bent down and their lips met. Her knees went weak, just as they did when she and Drew first kissed.

3

Mum, I Do Believe He Loves You

"Mum, I got somethin' to tell you," said Dempsey as he walked through the front door of the cottage, Aaron just a few paces behind him. It was barely a month since CrazyBest happened and all seemed well.

"What is it?" called Claudine from upstairs. She herself had just gotten home from the co-op and she didn't want Aaron to see her in her sweaty, disheveled state. She stayed in her room, door slightly ajar, as Dempsey made his way up the stairs.

"Toasty offered me a place to live," Dempsey said, staying on the other side of the door so his mom would have some privacy. "Has he told you how he's havin' those new flats built for visitin' wrestlers and students?"

"Yes," said Claudine, peeling off her work clothes. "I saw the expenses in some of the books Toasty sent over." Claudine had started doing some bookkeeping and other paperwork for her brother since they had smoothed things over. She was very grateful for the extra work, which, along with her inheritance money which she was keepin.g quiet, allowed her to cut her hours at the co-op down to 20 hours a week. She actually had time and more importantly, was inspired to go to the gym now and simply enjoy mid-life. Now that she and her family were friends again, she felt like the weight of the world was lifted off her shoulders.

"So, he showed me one o' them today," said Dempsey. "It's got an attached garage and the flat's loaded with upgrades, like it's got a deluxe cooking island in the kitchen, a washer and dryer, the big walk-in shower and a free-standing bath, and satellite telly. He saw how much I liked his satellite telly and said he added it to the flat just for me. So, anyroad, it'll work out better with me staying there, I won't have to drive out every day."

"Sounds fantastic, luv," said Claudine. "Just let me jump in the shower and I'll be right down."

"Ta, Mum," said Dempsey. She listened to him walk back downstairs to join Aaron. It was not a big shock that Dempsey would not be staying for long; he had been on his own in Japan for nearly five years already. But Claudine noticed that Dempsey hadn't said anything about Aaron.

She stepped into the shower and let the hot water rinse away the salty sweat and ease the chronic aches from her job. Sometimes her lower back felt brittle from standing long hours on rock hard floors. She winced to think how much pain Drew must have been in. Claudine often thought of Drew, but lately she wasn't so sad when she did. Now, she and Aaron were courting and there was a romantic revival in her world. What a difference he made in her life. She loved having him at the cottage. Part of her – a big part of her – hoped he would stay, not just in England, but with her for good. She knew however, that he was only in England because of CrazyBest and that had wrapped up a few weeks ago. Dempsey and Aaron had decided before they even left Japan for the tournament that Dempsey would make England home again. After CrazyBest, he wanted to take a break from shoot–fighting, Aaron's specialty, and concentrate on professional wrestling. Everyone expected Aaron to be recruited soon by another fighter who needed a full–time trainer, since that was how he earned his living. When that happened, he'd move onto whatever country it was that the fighter lived in. Could he love life so much in England and with her, that he'd stay? The uncertainty gave her a pang in her stomach.

Claudine frowned, thinking about all of this as she massaged creamy conditioner into her hair. She was quite aware that Aaron was always transplanting himself to train fighters and his income depended on that, but one day he would find a place to call home, she assured herself. Japan was home for him for a while; now, it remained to be seen where his next home would be. If Claudine had anything to do with it, she would make sure his home was with her. Even though they had known each other barely a month, she didn't think it was a ridiculous idea, since they got on so well. But would anyone else, especially Aaron, see it the same way?

Mind racing, Claudine finished up and turned the water off, toweling herself dry. *Would her son approve of his trainer living with his mum in his late father's home? If Aaron did stay, would he become more than a guest in her home? Would anyone object to that?*

When Claudine tiptoed downstairs, without make-up and with her hair still soaking wet, she discovered that Dempsey was in the other bathroom having a shower. She was anxious to talk to Aaron alone, so she shyly faced him in the kitchen, hoping he wouldn't be aghast by her appearance.

"So Aaron, are you going to stay in England for a bit or will you be returnin' to Japan?" Claudine inquired tentatively, cinching her blue silk Japanese-style robe up and closing it around her chest with her hand a little tighter as she waited for his answer.

"Ya know, that all depends," said Aaron, not seeming the slightest bit put off by her appearance. "Ah'd like to stay in England fer a few weeks until ah decide what to do. Ah ain't gonna be returning to Japan for a while. Maybe ah'll get me some clients and train 'em somewhere else, who knows?"

That wasn't quite what Claudine wanted to hear. "Well, you are certainly welcome to stay here as long as you like, just in case you were wondering," she said, ringing water out of her wet, tangled ponytail.

"No, ah wasn't wonderin,' 'cuz ah knew you'd let me stay, darlin', and thank ya," Aaron said, smiling warmly. "Ah gotta be able to pay ya rent or somethin' if ah stay here, though. Ah gotta tell ya, some of the investments ah've got goin' on with my German stockbroker... He's been five for five with me on the deals ah've done with him. Ah'm investing the pay ah got from Jumbo with my guy, actually. It's one big lump sum and it's gonna be huge for me when it matures. Give it five years and ah'll be sittin' pretty, just like you, darlin'."

There was that "darlin'" word again. He said it to her many times and Claudine was thrilled to hear him call her that, but she still didn't know what to make of it. Was this something he said to girls in general or was it special for certain people? She had no idea. She would have to wait and hopefully find out that "darlin'" was meant just for her.

Within a few days, Dempsey was gone and it became just her and Aaron in the house. She appreciated his financial contribution every day, paying for everything from petrol to food to eventually rent, but what Claudine appreciated more than the money was how happy Aaron made her. As much as Aaron was physically attracted to Claudine, he also truly enjoyed her company. The more he got to know her, the better he wanted to know her. He wanted to know everything about her family, her history, and her most personal details. Which was why, one rainy night a few months later, Claudine thought to show him some of her artwork.

Rain relentlessly pattered on the stone window sills outside, but it couldn't reach Claudine and Aaron, warm and cozy as they were inside the sturdy and charming old cottage. She had just enjoyed a nice hot bath and she hugged herself with an excited shiver as she threw on her bath robe. She found Aaron in her bedroom, waiting for her with a glass of wine. Jazzy, upbeat music played quietly on the old leather FM Sony radio that had stood for years on her bed stand, even in her childhood bedroom back at her parents' estate. She pulled out, from the highest shelf in her wardrobe a shallow, a long, cardboard box of paintings and drawings. She carefully placed them on the floor and modestly began to present them to her lone, attentive audience. Aaron smiled as they sat on the bedroom floor with Claudine's entire artistic portfolio spread out around them.

"Damn, these are real good! Ya never told me you were an artist," Aaron exclaimed, carefully picking through the stacks of paper and canvas. "The way ya talk about your drawings, ah figured maybe you drew real good stickmen and rainbows." He held up a particularly detailed sketch of the donkey, Emily, in her pen outside. "Darlin', these are awesome. This kinda talent is a gift from God. Not everyone can do this kind of thing." He took a sip of wine, examining the detail in Claudine's drawing of Emily's face, right down to her soft nose fur and coarse donkey hair. "Why don't cha hang these up? Hell, why don't cha try an' sell some of 'em? Folks would pay quite a bit fer art like this!"

"Oh, ta," said Claudine, blushing. She hadn't shown her artwork to too many people in years and she was pleased that Aaron seemed to like it so much. "I've tried hangin' them up, but when I do, I start seein' everythin' that's wrong with them and I end up takin' them down. I've tried to sell them too, but everyone seems to go for the really good stickmen you were talkin' about and I can't seem to draw proper stickmen." Aaron laughed at her remarks, taking another draught of wine.

"I'd like to do more paintings and drawings, but I had to sell me draftin' table," Claudine told Aaron. "Drew got it for me back when things were, well… let's just say, back in the good old days. It was a beautiful; a proper antique, ya know, it was dear. It cost Drew plenty, but it was lovely, and it worked so well for me. I sold it though. I had to pay some bills. I did break down and buy a cheap three-legged easel to replace it, but I don't know if like the style of it. I can't lay it flat which I could with the old one. It was a proper drafting table and this new one is like a tri-pod… I don't know, I just don't seem to have the same chemistry with the new one as I did with the old antique one. It's like I have dreadful writer's block with me art now."

"Sounds like ya need to get a new *old* drawing table," said Aaron. "So, what do ya want to do with all this?" He gently stroked Buffy from her head to the tip of her tail as she decidedly placed herself with an air of belonging amongst the artwork on the floor.

"I guess Dempsey and Isabella will figure out what to do with what I do have one day," she said bashfully. "Maybe their kids will be the ones who find it all folded up in some old cardboard box and they'll want to bring it back to life by puttin' it up on their own walls. Or maybe it'll all get dumped in the bin."

"Darlin', you need to sell yourself more," said Aaron encouragingly, gesturing at all of the paintings and drawings on the floor. "Here's what cha need to do. Fer starters, yer gonna quit that shitty job stockin' shelves and being ordered around by yer rotten boss. Ah'm gonna help ya with money comin' in from my German investor guy, and that, along with the work ye've been doing at IWF, is gonna be enough. Ah wancha to get back into yer paintings and drawings. Then we're gonna sell your art. So, tomorrow, give yer notice at that stinkin' place and tell 'em yer finishin' up there."

He leaned in, looking Claudine intensely in the eye. She became suddenly aware of the fact that she was wearing only her robe, her hair still damp from her recent bath. "So here's the deal. Ah promise ah will help ya with money and get ya back into yer drawin' again, but ya gotta promise me that ye'll believe in yourself more. So c'mon, ya gotta say it fer me. Spit it out. Say 'ya promise,' and no filtering, no 'um' or 'ahhh' or 'gee.' Just do this fer me now, okay?"

"Okay, right then… I…"

Aaron looked at Claudine again, then picked his way around the drawings and paintings to perch on the end of the bed. "Here, c'mon. Sit down with me on the bed and do this for me. Then hopefully… we'll do some other stuff too," he said with a sexy smile.

Claudine followed Aaron's careful path to the bed and repeated his words. "I promise to believe in meself more," she said, without a lot of authority. She wasn't really sure if it was a promise she could keep. When Drew was alive, he only needed to smile proudly as he told people about his creative wife's artwork and they would want to have her artwork for themselves too. She didn't believe in herself the way Drew had, or the way Aaron did now. It seemed like an impossible promise for her to make.

"Maybe ya need some reassurance from me to help ya believe in yerself even more, darlin.' Let's chit chat and have another drink," he said, as if he could read her thoughts. Buffy jumped onto his lap as he poured a little more wine into their goblets. He massaged the little cat's soft, furry cheeks and velvety ears. He continued to talk with a sexy tone to his convictions.

"Listen sweetheart, ah ain't sayin' ah know what'll happen in the future, but ah promise to help you today," he said. "No matter what you do, yer never ever gonna change the past, so forget about it. And ya shouldn't be takin' the blame for everything that's gone wrong in yer life. Ya just can't do that anymore. It ain't healthy fer ya, ya know? You shouldn't blame yerself for yer husband's death. What, do ya think you put the morphine needle in his arm and shot it in? Nah, of course not, so don't be so damn hard on yerself. You need to stop doin' that, okay?"

Claudine nodded shyly. Both she and Buffy were under Aaron's spell and they listened to him hypnotically. "Now, ya can't control yer future any more than ya can change yer past. Ya can try plannin' things out, like Drew and y'all did, but things ain't in our control no matter how much plannin' ya do. Y'all did plan for the rainy days, and it's not yer fault those rainy days turned out to be monsoons. So give yerself a pat on the back for doin' as much as ya did. The mistakes and the blessings, the good and the bad and everythin' in between, ain't in yer control. It's all up to God. Do ya believe in God, darlin'? Do ya believe in a higher power?"

"Yes, I believe in God," said Claudine, "but I'm upset with Him sometimes."

"Why?" asked Aaron, almost annoyed. "Do ya think God's responsible for the choices ya made that brought ya to this place yer at right now?"

"Well, I think sometimes that if everythin' is out of me control like you're sayin', then why does God let things turn out so tragically? But then I go past that and think I've got no one to blame but meself. And that takes me back to how I should never have left Drew alone with his dad. I should have made sure I was with him all the way to the hospital. I don't blame God for that; I blame meself. And that's a painful regret that never goes away."

Aaron shook his head. "Darlin', ah can't see ya just leavin' yer husband there and walkin' away. Ya didn't know what was goin' to happen. But there's a reason for everything, and right now, only God knows why. It is not for ya to question what ain't in yer control. Ya understand?" asked Aaron as he stared at Claudine.

"Well, God *is* so powerful and I'm, well, I'm scared of him. Ya know, I've got that fear of God and I've surely disappointed Him even just now by tellin' you I've been mad at Him," stammered Claudine. "I know God sees everythin' I do, which was part o' me reluctance to enjoy meself in, well… it's hard to say this," Claudine hesitated.

"C'mon, darlin' and tell me," Aaron said, his eyes keen and sincere as he encouraged her to tell him.

"Well, it's dreadfully hard to say this. I've not really got a polished way of saying it. It's very, well, almost embarrassing." Claudine said uncomfortably.

"C'mon, tell me." Aaron said and patiently waited for her to confide in him.

"Okay, well, part of me was dead reluctant to enjoy, or maybe let's say, express meself in front of God when I was with Drew, in sexual ways..." Claudine took a large gulp of wine. "So when Drew and I, well, how can I say this, umm, made love, I knew God was watchin' and I felt, like ashamed. That's why Drew used to give me a glass o' wine to drink before we… umm…

which made me a lot less inhibited. I was dead shy with Drew at first, so a glass of wine was really, really helpful. I don't feel so anxious about that sort o' thing now… but umm back then…"

She took another sip of wine to steel her nerves. She had been meaning to say this for a long time and so far she wasn't making the impression she had wanted to. "I never really thought about bein' with anyone after me husband died, 'til I met you. I've a, ummm, well, a connection with you, Aaron, and… I never felt connected to anyone besides Drew, like I was under a fantastic spell 'im. It's like I'm under some kind of spell like that with you too," she said, staring hard at the floor now and feeling her face flush scarlet. "I guess you should know that, if you didn't already."

She felt Aaron gently put his hand on hers. "Sweetheart, I think ah'm under the same spell," he said in a soothing voice. "We have a connection like the Fourth of July and fireworks! Ah've never felt this way about anyone before. The unpredictable things that come out of yer mouth and the sound of yer voice, too. The little looks you have and the way ya carry yerself. Yer so different." He stopped, like he was looking for the right words. "Everythin' with ya is new for me; like, no one ever told me before that ahm a good kisser, until you. No one ever flossed my teeth for me before; now that's a damn first!" he said, laughing. "Ya rub my feet, ya cut my toenails for me, and these unusual things ya do drive me crazy for ya; ya fuss over me like ahm a champion. Life hasn't been barrels of fun for me, darlin' until I metcha. Ah love wakin' up next to ya and ah love how ya wanna take care of me. Ya have a real, genuine naïve side, and it makes me laugh 'cuz it's so sweet and innocent. Ah never knew someone like you really existed before I metcha. There's lots out there who pretend to care, but they don't give a damn. Not you though, and it makes crazy fer ya, darlin'! Cuz ya could be real jaded and bitter, but yer not. And ya know dammed well that I can't very much resist ya much longer!"

They had spent many nights together talking and cuddling, but they had not become completely intimate with each other before. Aaron looked over at her and smiled seductively, and she felt her body respond, without him even touching her. "Ah think it safe to say, darlin' that we're best friends," he said. "Ah look around and ah could just stay here forever." He carefully put Buffy off to the side of the bed and drew Claudine to him. She closed her eyes as his lips met hers and they moved into each other as if magnetized.

Claudine, usually a bundle of inhibitions, was finally ready to let herself go. Aaron felt the change too. He clasped one of her hands in his and held it over her head leaning into the headboard on the bed. He seized the other one and held it behind her back. Claudine wriggled, even struggled to break away, but he smiled and put more weight on her as if waiting for her to yield.

"Aaron, me arm," she said in a whisper, panting a little. She was not frightened at all in how Aaron's control over her absolutely seduced her, but she was overwhelmed with tantalizing anxiety. She could barely breathe, but she wasn't sure if it was because of his weight or her mounting desire for him. Aaron examined her face, releasing her arm slightly and continued kissing her, probing his tongue softly yet deliberately into her mouth. He bit her bottom lip hungrily. She kissed him back hard.

The kitten jumped off the bed, wanting no part of this play. Aaron sat up on top of Claudine, pulling off his T-shirt to reveal a chiseled torso riddled with scars. Claudine felt her breath catch in her throat as he pulled his sweatpants off too, then his black cotton boxers. Before she saw too much of his stunning body, he was back on top of her. Claudine thrust up her pelvis and he held his balance on top of her, locking his legs close around her hips like a body scissors in wrestling.

"Are you okay?" he whispered in his ear.

"Yes," she said and gently grabbed his wrist.

"Ya wanna fool around? Ya wanna wrestle?" Aaron whispered. He was more assertive and as she nodded yes he quickly clasped her hands again, locking fingers with her and navigated their hands over her head. Moving slowly now, his soft lips kissed down the crook of her neck. Gently he head-butted her, rubbing the top of his head into her chin and all around her jawline. He nudged his way into her already loose robe. Claudine accepted the weight of Aaron's body on top of hers, feeling the sensual needs in her heart and body growing greater and greater.

Aaron's strong leg-lock tightened and he securely held Claudine still. Passionately, he looked into her eyes as his soft lips pressed into hers. His hot kisses melted slowly and methodically, inch by inch, down to her breasts. Claudine's legs intertwined with his, hooking his ankles. He slid slowly inside of her; she gasped. They moved and rolled around, stretching, arching, and kissing as they made rolling, rhythmic love.

Pulling away suddenly, Aaron flipped Claudine over onto her stomach and again pushed himself into her. He kissed the back of her neck and in between her shoulder blades as she raised her hips up and down for him. Leaning forward, he put her in a chin lock from behind, biting her ear and sweetly kissing her cheek. They groaned simultaneously as he thrust himself gently into her. As they moved together their passion grew deeper; their momentum became faster. He leaned the side of his face on hers, grabbing her breasts as he thrusted himself into her. Without realizing it, Aaron was using so much force that he tightened his chin lock on her to keep his traction; accidentally choking Claudine so tightly that she almost passed out. Claudine had never been made love to like this before. When they were done, she felt oddly euphoric. Aaron lay on top of her and whispered breathlessly in her ear, "that was fuckin' amazing! Thank ya, darlin'."

She smiled, but tears rolled down her face and dripped onto the sheets.

"Darlin'? Hey, are ya cryin'? Ah didn't mean to hurt ya," he breathed, softly patting her messy hair down.

"I don't know why I'm so emotional," said Claudine, curling her body into his chest. "I'm all hot and bothered and I feel fantastic, but I feel like I got me ass kicked in a fight too. Don't get me wrong, I'm turned on, Aaron, and at the same time, I feel like me pride's been hurt. But I loved it. I don't bloody know what the matter with me is." She subtly shook her head and smiled, barely. The insides of her legs quivered and a few more tears rolled onto her nose.

"Don't cry! That was a wrestlin' match we both won, that's for darn sure. Ya turn me on so fuckin' much, darlin'! Yer beautiful." He pulled Claudine into him and they lay side by side, looking into each other's faces. Claudine tucked her knees up and folded her hands under her chin, but Aaron gently nudged her knees down and pulled her yet again closer to him. Buffy jumped back onto the bed and curled up above Claudine's head, where she promptly fell asleep.

The next morning they awoke, still lying next to each other in bed. Aaron kissed Claudine's forehead and stared into her eyes. His warm, inviting eyes and sexy, slightly asymmetrical smile made Claudine feel safe. She thought about how he had promised to help look after her. She remembered he wanted her to leave her job at the co-op. In her mind, it really was high time she quit her unfulfilling job and she was looking forward to getting back into her artwork and back into a happy world again.

Aaron turned his head on the pillow and looked at her with so much sweetness in his face that she felt completely secure. "Yer very special to me, Claudine," he said.

"I love you, Aaron," Claudine heard herself say. Then there was silence, except for Buffy's purring. Claudine felt suddenly hot and tentatively fretful.

"Erm, I'm not telling you that because I want to hear you say it to me," she defended slightly, "but because things happen and people get taken away from each other all the time. Sometimes you never see them again. Even though we are just sittin' here together and no one is goin' on a trip or anything, I just wanted to tell you how I feel about you."

Claudine could see the wheels in Aaron's head turning. "That's a real powerful thing to say, darlin,'" he said slowly. "Ah'm not sure what to say to ya right now. Ah wasn't quite expectin' that. Ah don't know what to tell ya right at this moment." He reached out and softly pushed strands of blond hair off her face. "Ya know, if God wants us to be together, then we will be together. Ah got feelings for ya, good ones, and yer the only person ah want to be with right now, just know that. Are ya happy when we are together? Were ya happy last night? Didn't we have a good time, or am ah the only one that thinks that?"

"Yes, I am very happy when we're together," said Claudine positively, but feeling more than a little disappointed. "I've not felt like this in ages and I'm dead grateful that I'm getting a second chance, you know, to feel this way again. O' course I always have a brilliant time with you, because you make me happy."

"Okay, then let's just leave it alone for now, darlin'."

Claudine felt deflated. She wondered what the hell just happened. *Was she just a fling for Aaron?* He certainly wasn't just a fling for her. The last thing she wanted was a fling. She wanted Aaron for keeps and he was treating their relationship like it was a day-to-day thing.

Aaron left for the gym and Claudine began preparing in her head what she would say to her boss about leaving work. She found it difficult to concentrate. She sat at the kitchen table with Mr. Wonderful dutifully sitting on the table with her. She was analyzing everything that had happened in the past few weeks. *What if Aaron was planning on leaving and that was why he wouldn't tell her he loved her?* She needed to talk to someone who was a good friend to them both.

Claudine ended up calling Dempsey, but he was rather uncomfortable with the topic. "Uh, well, I don't know what to tell you about Aaron, as far as your relationship goes, Mum."

"Have you ever heard Aaron call anyone 'darlin'' before?"

"Only you, Mum. But this is dead awkward for me to chat about," he laughed. He was good-natured and was trying to help, but it was a foreign kind of conversation for him to have with his mum.

"Well, can you tell me about any past relationships he had in Japan? I really need to know, Demps, and I'm sorry to be mithering you. But, if you can tell me anything, not to betray Aaron at all, but just tell me, so I don't end up spoiling anything," Claudine replied. Dempsey could hear a bit of desperation in her voice and he felt sorry for her. He didn't want her to worry needlessly by jumping to conclusions if he just told her what he truthfully knew about Aaron.

"I never saw Aaron be rude to any girl he took out for a meal or a drink in Japan and I never saw that he was too head-over-heels about any of them. I did know about him being involved with someone in Japan, but it didn't work out and he told me that after that bad break-up he had no desire to have another 'broken, sick heart,' as he put it."

"That's a bit of a relief," said Claudine. "Do you know anything about his... um... plans for the future? Do you think he'll be walkin' out o' me life soon?"

"Uhmmm, his future? Well, I don't know; is he trainin' anyone now? He'll go where he can earn money," said Dempsey. "Walkin' out of your life – I can't see him doin' that if he's happy. But at the end of the day, if he's not makin' money, he won't be happy."

"So you're saying that all Aaron cares about is money?" said Claudine frantically.

"Mum, Aaron is a good-hearted bloke and a good business man," said Dempsey. "I don't know what to tell you about him and you. Maybe ask Isabella; she's better with stuff like that. I don't really know what to tell you, Mum. I gotta go. Give Isabella a call, aye. I think she's better at this stuff than I am."

Claudine was even more perplexed after she hung up, but she took her son's advice and promptly called her daughter still working over in New York. Isabella picked up on the second ring.

"Mum! I was just thinkin' about you. How are you over there?"

"Hallo, Isabella. I'm doing well; it's good to hear your voice. Listen, can I ask you a question? Kind of a personal thing for me and I need some advice," said Claudine.

"Oh, o' course Mum, knock yourself out."

"Okay, well, here goes. With your dad, we could plan things; we did plan things. I mean, even if we had a huge fight, I still knew he would be there for me at the end o' the day, even if the fight went on for a few days, you know? We planned a life together, through it all."

"Did you and Aaron have a fight, Mum?" asked Isabella. She knew all about Aaron from many of Dempsey's letters to herand conversations with him when he was still in Japan. She also had heard plenty from her mum talking about him all the time whenever she called home from New York over the past month.

"No, not really," said Claudine, pulling Mr. Wonderful like a security blanket into her lap. "I just can't get him to talk about stuff, like plans for us, or where we might be in a year, you know? I have never met a friend of his, outside of Dempsey; I know so little about him, really, yet we're so connected. He said that it is none of his friends' business who his girlfriend is. But he doesn't really have any friends here. He seems detached, maybe so it's easier to just leave. And he says things one day like he wants me to meet his parents, yet he's never told them about me, because I asked 'im what they thought of me and he said they didn't know about me. I asked him about goin' to America to meet them one day and he got cross with me, like I was pressurin' him. I don't know if he is protectin' me or them or himself because he never tells me anythin'. I get frustrated and wonder if he's hidin' somethin', or perhaps he's embarrassed about me for whatever reason, maybe because I'm older than he is. I don't know, Isabella. He's never told me he loves me, but I have told him that I love 'im. Maybe I shouldn't have said anythin'. What do you think?"

Isabella was an excellent listener. After a moment, she said, "Well, Mum, I think Aaron is a different sort of person. He had a load of stuff happen to him in the war and he's probably dealt with a lot of more than we know anything about, but perhaps he's just protective of his feelings."

"Do you think he even cares about me at all?" said Claudine, stroking Mr. Wonderful's plush, luxurious coat.

"I think he loves you. I do think that, even though I don't know him and I really doubt it's an age thing," said Isabella. "Doubt he'd ever gotten involved with you if he was concerned about a five-year age gap. I don't really know him though, Mum. Maybe he's having a mid-life crisis. Not trying to be funny, but he might be, ya know? He might be shy of commitment because he has things he wants to do before he settles down."

"That's possible," said Claudine. "I hadn't thought of that."

"I'm not sure I'm helpin' you with anythin', Mum, but, at the end of the day, I do believe Aaron loves you, even if he hasn't said it with words," said Isabella encouragingly.

"Oh, Okay, ta," said Claudine. "So, what's goin' on with you?"

4

The Surprise

The next six months were some of the best Claudine had had in a long time. With Aaron's financial contributions and emotional encouragement, she managed to quit the co-op job, going into the IWF a couple times more a week instead. As winter faded and a bright spring began, she also started going over all of her old paintings and drawings, picking out her favourites and fine-tuning details here and there. She learned that she needed to make a convenient flipbook of photographs of her best work to take to art galleries and dealers instead of taking her actual drawings everywhere.

To make things even better, Aaron was slowly but surely coming out of his shell. He had started working with some of the wrestlers at the IWF, which was doing incredibly well. This kept him employed and inspired and he seemed more than content with his life with Claudine. He still hadn't said the 'L' word, but his actions spoke much louder than what he wouldn't say and Claudine often forgot about this awkward spot between them. But every so often, she wondered if he would ever *tell* her that he loved her.

Not that everything was smooth sailing. One afternoon in May, snuggled up next to him on the couch, Claudine lightly ran her fingers through Aaron's freshly- shorn hair, spelling his name with her fingers across his scalp. "A-a-r-o-n," she said in an almost childlike way.

"Oh, man," he said, suddenly sitting up. "She used to do that. Haven't thought about her in months…"

Claudine stopped, moving her hand to his shoulder instead. Aaron had never mentioned "her" by name, but Claudine knew he was referring to someone he had met in Japan. Aaron saw the look on her face and looked resigned.

"Ah guess it's about time ah told ya," he said, and launched into a full explanation. Claudine listened and didn't say anything as he told her about the girl who had brutally broken his heart in Japan. He described how he was street-smart and knew his way around Tokyo; this girl was just the opposite. An aspiring model straight from Romania, she was lost and struggling to survive in the Japanese metropolis when Aaron, her knight in shining armour, came along. He fell deeply in love with her and thought they had a real chance of having a life together forever, he felt that strongly about her. Unfortunately, Aaron was only a springboard for this girl. Once she was on her feet in this foreign land, she promptly left him for what she felt were more glamorous boyfriends, with more money and better opportunities for her to grow.

"She basically used me for everything. She took what money I had, she got me to protect her and I had no problem with any of that, because I loved her. But she lied about how she felt for me. She really was just treating me like shit. I was totally stunned when I found her with another man, other rich men, actually. They were going out to clubs and parties that she excluded me from. She liked being in that kind of racy world, obviously, because she wouldn't give these rich guys up to be with me. They were always little, scrawny, rich business men that she seemed to hang around with, saying they were part of the modeling business and I had no right to complain if I was truly supporting her. Well, I was supportive of her, but not when she's involved more with these rich guys than she was with me. She didn't give a damn about me, once she got on her feet. After that, ah didn't think the same way about love or women again and was certainly not interested in ever marryin' either," explained Aaron, his brow furrowed.

Claudine knew she was not like that girl. She so much wanted to be with Aaron, forever. *But maybe*, she thought, *that was the problem. Maybe Aaron loved this other woman because the other woman made him play cat and mouse.* "Would you want me… that is, to be with me more… if I didn't want you so much?" Claudine asked after a pause.

Aaron cupped Claudine's chin and tilted her face upwards. Even with such a serious look on his face, his clean-cut jaw, broken, bent nose and golden eyes were almost enough to distract her from her thoughts. "Darlin', ah'm tellin' ya to quit comparin' everythin' to the damn past," he murmured. "Yer thinkin' how ah'd rather pine for some girl who gave me the boot real hard in the nuts than return yer feelings for me, aren't ya? Don't compare yerself and our thing we got going on here," he said, brushing her hair back, "to somethin' that went bad in my past. Ah've never known anyone like you. Like, take yer way of talkin' in that British accent Normally it would bug me, ya know? But with you, ah'm like, wow, yer voice is damn sexy. Don't cha know that's how ah feel about ya? Can't ya see how special and important you are to me, you and yer family too? Hmmm?" confessed Aaron, but Claudine didn't react. "Hello?" Aaron asked, reminding her he was waiting for her response.

Claudine had pulled away slightly, retreating to the other side of the couch to retrieve Buffy and get away from his hypnotic gaze. "Well, how come, then, you haven't told your parents about me?"

Aaron sighed. "Sweetheart, for me, it's a private thing and ah don't care what people think. Ah know that's important to ya, but ah don't need approval from my parents or anyone about who I date. People aren't friends with me because of who my girlfriend is."

"But if summat ever happened to you here, I wouldn't know who to call. Or if you ever went away and summat happened to you, no one would call me to tell me anythin' and I would just worry me life away, never knowing what happened," she explained, feeling tears collect in her eyes. "I wouldn't even know where to find you. Sometimes I wonder if that is your intention. People just disappear sometimes. Like Drew, when he died, I had to go and find him and it turned out to be the worst thing in me life." She buried her face in Buffy's soft fur and felt the warmth of Aaron's hand on the small of her back.

"Yer over-reactin' cuz ah what happened to Drew. Just relax darlin'. No one can know what's gonna happen tomorrow and nothin' can change the past. Ya gotta live for today," he said soothingly. “We should just enjoy what we have in the moment. C’mon, why do ya worry so much, darlin’?”

“Oh, I guess I was just born this way and then I got years of practice,” replied Claudine stiffly, her words muffled by Buffy’s obliging body.

“Hey, cheer up,” said Aaron. He was amused by her comment, but knew she was upset. He gently rubbed between her shoulder blades, where he knew she liked it. “I got a surprise for ya. I’ll tell ya tonight, when I take you out for dinner. We’ll go train and then eat,” suggested Aaron, grinning as he got up. “I think yer gonna love my big news.”

Claudine soon forgot about her bad mood. As she got dressed for the gym, she felt more and more excited about Aaron’s big surprise. She knew Aaron could get silly by putting her in submission wrestling holds, and telling her clever jokes, but she couldn’t recall him ever saying he had a surprise for her; it seemed almost childlike of him. She made sure to pack a nice dress – a cute navy blue one made of a waffled fabric with a v-neckline – and some make-up in her gym bag so she could get herself presentable after working out.

At the gym, they trained chest, shoulders and abdominals in a rotation circuit. This was followed by a vigorous combination of sprints on the treadmill and speed pedaling on the stationary bicycle for ten minutes at thirty second intervals, with thirty second breaks. Aaron then insisted they do light cardio on the stair machine afterwards for twenty minutes, followed by another half hour of thorough stretching.

Aaron methodically made them both endure what seemed like the longest workout ever and Claudine could hardly contain herself. She felt impatience, happiness, and anxiousness all wrapped up in her tired body. *What was Aaron’s surprise? Maybe he was going to let her talk to his family over the telephone, or even better, to finally meet them.* She imagined it was going to be wonderful news, in any case, because everything was going so well between them.

“What cha think, maybe Italian food, darlin’?” Aaron asked as they were leaving the gym post-shower. It looked like Aaron had remembered a change of clothes as well; he looked sharp in his navy slacks and pale, apple-green dress shirt and he had a spring in his step even more than usual. It was nearing seven in the evening, but both of them were warm enough without coats.

"Sure, whatever you like. There's a lovely Italian place just down the street and they serve delicious homemade pasta and fresh seafood, too. I think you'll like it and we can even walk there," Claudine said, thinking they could run to speed things up. Her damp hair was in a fishtail braid and she was wearing a new blackest black mascara to make her lashes massively long and her eyes pop. She could tell that Aaron appreciated it by the way he kept sneaking side glances at her.

"Sounds perfect!" Aaron agreed. As they waited at a crosswalk, Claudine playfully asked Aaron to open his mouth up nice and wide. She tilted his chin down and looked inside.

"Oh, you poor, poor thing! I can see right down to your empty stomach. You must be starving and suffering," she declared. He laughed. He picked her up in a fireman's carry over his shoulder and ran across the street with her towards the restaurant.

The little restaurant was charming and authentic, with cheery yellow walls and black and white tiles on the floor. The host seated them in a booth near a window, where they could see the little red flowers in the outside window box.

"Can we get one of them bottles of Chianti?" Aaron asked the waitress when she came for their drink order. He was behaving very nonchalant, as if he had no big surprise at all. Casually paging through the dinner menu, he took his time ordering his meal and he carried on talking about nothing in particular. The suspense was killing Claudine. She wouldn't acknowledge Aaron's obvious stalling, although it was vexing her. She was having trouble concentrating, barely observing the vast menu as she whole-heartedly pretended to look it over. She kept bouncing her knees up and down under the table. She sipped on her glass of Chianti and hoped the alcohol wouldn't hit her too soon, but wanted it would take the edge off her mood. When the waitress came for their food orders, Claudine had to quickly scan the menu yet again and choose the first thing she saw that looked good – scallops in a white wine sauce – to avoid revealing that she hadn't actually read the menu, despite how long she looked at it.

Aaron's cavalier behaviour continued through dinner. The food came and went and Claudine began to worry. *Why was he being so coy? Maybe he didn't have such a great surprise.* It reminded her of people who made animals beg or do a little trick before rewarding them with a puny little treat. She felt like she was the animal waiting for its treat, maybe only to get a bite of a biscuit for all her patience.

They were now enjoying their tiramisu desserts. At least, Aaron was enjoying his; Claudine was stewing inside. She revealed this by demonstratively focusing on each taste she had of her sweet. "This is absolutely amazing. Such an airy sweet, yet so decadent," she boasted dramatically. Claudine pretended to savour the treat, taking the last small bites and letting them dissolve in her mouth. The waitress cleared the dishes away when Aaron finally rubbed his hands together, starting with a single clap.

"All right then," he said. "Ye've been very patient. I'm ready to tell ya about ma surprise."

Claudine studied him, staring at his intense face and cauliflower ears. She observed his bent nose, which had obviously been broken one too many times, and his meaty hands. She looked at him, all of him, and melted. She could not see one thing she would change. Ironic that only a moment ago that she was privately furious at him for making her wait so long to hear his big news.

"Now darlin', ah'll tell ya the plan ah have fer us," he said, leaning in a little. "We can do it, make the plan work if yer with me. Hear me out first before ya go gettin' all upset." Claudine's stomach turned as Aaron looked for the right words. She suddenly wasn't so sure that it was a good surprise.

"Okay, so it's like this. Ah have to go to Germany for a spell, to train these guys I met back at CrazyBest. Ah fly out Sunday. Ah've agreed to a nine-month contract with 'em and they've both got fights coming up, so ah've gotta start ASAP. They'll probably fight two times each in the next year. One guy has a fight in Brazil in a few months and the other guy, well, we ain't as sure he can be ready fer the first fight. We'll see."

Claudine was crestfallen. The last thing she wanted was for Aaron to leave.

"That's the first news, but don't be upset and don't worry about us, Okay, 'cuz everything is cool," he insisted. He moved over to Claudine's side of the booth, scooting in and running his finger up and down her cheek. He brought her chin around to face him and looked into her eyes. "Ah love ya, Claudine," he said. "Ah really love ya." He leaned in and planted a kiss on her mouth.

Claudine's stomach, which had been up in knots just a second ago, seemed to drop out of her body entirely. She leaned into him, tears forming in her eyes as she embraced him.

"Thank you for the surprise. I love you too," she said emotionally. "You know I love you, very much. Promise you will come back, from Germany, Aaron. Will you promise me?"

"Of course I will, darlin'. Let me finish, cuz ah can see yer already worrying about things. There's more," Aaron said his serious face back on. "Ah have loved ya for a long time. Hell, ya must have known by how we feel when we're together, not just 'cuz ah'm sayin' it now. Here's what ah think – ah think we should get married. Not a big wedding, just somethin' small when I come back from Germany. Okay? Ah have never felt about anyone the way ah feel about ya. Ah wanna be with you and yer family. Maybe now ya ain't gonna worry so much, 'cuz ya know ah love ya and ah want to marry ya. So, will ya marry me, Claudine? Oh, don't cry."

But Claudine couldn't stop the stream of tears flowing from her eyes as she threw her arms around Aaron's neck. "Yes, o' course I will marry you, Aaron. O' course I will!" She hugged him as if she couldn't let go. He squeezed back, eventually easing her back onto her seat.

"We need to be patient," he told her, "so let's plan to get married when ah get back, after the nine months. When ah have money in a few weeks from my clients, ah'll fly ya out to Germany for a few days and ah'll send money home to help ya out with things here, too. Ah figure we should save for airfares more than buying expensive diamond rings right now and ah wanna fly ya out to see me as much as ah can. We'll look at it all positively, Okay?"

When they got home after such a wonderful evening, Claudine found Buffy sitting on the couch. "Buffy, I'm getting married! Your Papa asked me to marry him," Claudine exclaimed as she kissed their little kitten on her tiny wet brick- coloured nose. Aaron just laughed and hugged them both.

"Now, Buffy, I must call everyone and tell them all the fantastic news," Claudine said as she picked up the phone. Dempsey, Isabella and Toasty were truly happy for Aaron and Claudine and the kids reassured their mum that nine months would pass by quickly, especially if they were flying back and forth in the meantime.

The next day, Aaron approached Claudine with yet another proposal over breakfast. Claudine was wearing an old denim sleeveless dress that draped just above her knees.

"Ya look like a sweet young farm girl back home in Texas," said Aaron as Claudine opened the door for Sally to go out. "Ah like that dress on ya."

"Oh, thanks," said Claudine, blushing. "I've had it for years."

"Darlin', I wanna talk to ya about somethin'," he said, his muscles bulging through his thin T-shirt as he reached across the table to grab the coffee. "Ah have a friend, ah told you about him, the German investor guy. He has been paying me two hundred pounds a month on something that started as a two thousand pound investment deal. They're stocks in natural gas and oil that they're drilling for in the Black Sea, north of Scotland. He's in with a German company that's doing the exploration; they're gonna start this new energy company and they need investors. It's not bein' traded yet, 'cuz it's still in the developmental stages, but by the time it hits the stock market it's gonna be worth a fortune. And we can still get in on it, at the ground level, but we gotta move on it, like, tomorrow. He said after a couple more days, the deal's done, closed."

Aaron took a sip of his coffee, his face serious. "My German guy, ah trust him. He's been doin' great things for me with my money. He knows the market and ah think we need to start makin' all the big money we can now, because the world's getting crazier all the time and we ain't got a lot saved. So, now that we're gettin' married and all, ah think it'd be a good idea for you to get in on it too, so we can start saving up for a future together. Ah know he can getcha at least ten to fifteen per cent, maybe more on your investment from German stocks; that'll take care of us if things get tough. And if things don't get tough, well, we'll just live even better. What d'ya think?"

Claudine answered cautiously. "I know that your investment has been goin' really well… I have some money, but I only just came into and it's specifically for payin' off me mortgage."

"Oh," said Aaron, stirring the sweetener into his cup. "What's the deal with that?"

"I had to take a lien out on this house ages ago," explained Claudine, toying with her fishtail braid. "The mortgage is due about a month from now, when the loan comes up for renewal. I can pay it off in full then and not get charged penalties for paying it off early; otherwise I'd have paid it off already. What a relief that will be to get it done, out of the way, once and for all, one hundred per cent. I don't want to ever risk losing me family home again."

"How much is yer mortgage? Do ya have to pay it in full now?" Aaron asked.

"Well it's just over £25,000 and I have enough to cover that, plus a little left over," said Claudine. "If I don't pay it off at the end of the term, I can get one-year extension, but crickey, I just want to get it over with, you know, pay it off altogether."

"Listen, ah know ye've been through a lot," said Aaron. "But if you pay off yer mortgage, ye'll be cleaned out. If ya can put that £25,000 into this investment instead, we'll be makin' a couple thousand pounds a month at least. With my investment, it'll be more like three thousand pounds a month. Over a year, it'll probably make thousands of pounds in interest and we still get the initial investment back. And I'll help cover the mortgage payments in the meantime. We can do a lot more together than we can independently."

He looked at Claudine and his face softened. "Ya say ya never want to be poor again and this is a good way to make that happen. Ah think this is a damn good idea, but it's up to you, darlin', and I can't blame ya if ya wanna be cautious, but I really believe we can make money with this. Paying off yer house ain't making ya money, sweetheart. It ain't costin' ya a mortgage payment every month, that's true, but like I said, it ain't makin' ya nothin' either by payin' it off." Aaron said.

Claudine got up and puttered around the kitchen, thinking hard. She put some dishes in the dishwasher, refilled the animals' water dishes, and wiped down the counter before sitting back down.

"Aaron, you know what I've been through and you know how I am now and why. I believe in you and everythin' you have told me. You tell me that in less than a year we'll be husband and wife. You know I love you with all me heart, so what's mine is yours, Aaron. I know you've helped me plenty over the last six months with payin' for things. You did that quietly, never wantin' me tellin' anyone." She reached out and touched his hand where it rested on the table. "So, takin' it all into consideration, I will invest me money with you. We're goin' to have a great life and when we're relaxin' and enjoyin' it, it will be because of you."

A big grin cracked Aaron's usually serious features and he grasped Claudine's hand in his. "Darlin', things will keep being amazin' fer us, but we can't do it all without money, so thank ya fer trusting me. Thanks fer everythin.' Ah ain't gonna let cha down, ah promise," he said. He scraped his chair back and got up to give her a hug. Holding her in his arms, he gazed longingly into her blue eyes.

"We're gonna be so happy, darlin'! We're gonna have it all, with each other," he said affectionately.

Before Claudine knew what was happening, Aaron was kissing her with so much emotion and sensitivity that she felt taken aback. Her whole body tingled in response to his touch as he lay on top of her. He tenderly gathered her hair at the roots with his hand, where her plait started, pulling her head to his Their kisses flowed from each other's mouths. Their tongues twisted together and she gently bit his lower lip.

Claudine curved her body into Aaron's big, strong hands as he caressed her. They moved all over her with a purpose. One hand kept hold of her hair while the other guided her hand down to his waist. Smiling, she pulled her hand free and eased his sweatpants down below his round buttocks. He let her slide his pants down, moving his hand back up to Claudine's breasts and rubbing them through her dress. She hadn't bothered to put a bra on that morning and he was taking full advantage of the fact. He squeezed her breast with his thick hand and brushed her nipple through the thin cotton material with his thumb. He kissed her face and earlobe, breathing deeply into her ear.

She felt a shiver go up her spine. Aaron tended to her body in different ways and intensities all at once. Even as he brought her to her feet, she felt like she was floating on air. He turned her body towards the wall and he slid his hand up her dress. He let go of her hair and grabbed her wrist, impassionedly twisting her arm back behind her so it was tolerantly sandwiched between her back and his rock-hard abdominals. He leaned them both into the wall and he made love to her.

They moved from standing against the wall to lying on the chesterfield in the front of the television. She mounted him with her legs hooked under his to give her even more closeness to him. They made intense love for several minutes, sweating and glowing, breakfast growing cold on the table.

Soon Aaron was back on top of Claudine and she was facedown, lying on her right arm. Aaron lay flat and heavy on top of Claudine. He kissed her passionately on the side of her head as he put her in a rear chokehold, thrusting himself into her repeatedly for over a minute with all his strength.

When he was done, he kissed Claudine tenderly. She lay lifeless on the chesterfield.

"Are you okay, darlin'?" he asked, breathing heavily and sweating.

"Barely," whispered Claudine, whose throat was so constricted that she was scarcely audible.

"That was amazin'," breathed Aaron.

With her eyes shut, hair messed, and her body panting and perspiring like she'd been in a fight, Claudine did her best to nod her head in agreement. Aaron adoringly patted her hair, smoothing it down off her sweaty face. Tenderly he worked his way around her body, rubbing her deltoids with his big hand and stroking the soft, wet skin on her biceps.

"Darlin,' ya got more fight in ya than some of these Brazilian Jiu Jitsu guys ah train with. Yer a tough one! Ya don't know how much that turns me on, 'cuz yer so innocent and tough all at once," Aaron told Claudine. She smiled, still sprawled out on the chesterfield, enjoying the impromptu rubdown. Even though she felt so turned on and sensational by Aaron, she thought he was almost too powerful for her when they made love. He didn't hurt her with his incredible love-making, but she felt defenseless during it too. The bottom line was that she loved how alive he made her feel.

Before long, it was Sunday and Claudine was at the airport with Aaron, getting ready to say goodbye to him. The past few days flew away so fast. Aaron and Claudine had taken care of the investment paperwork on Friday; Saturday they drove out to the farm to see Toasty and Dempsey and now it was time for Aaron to go.

Claudine thought airports were either really sad or really happy, because people either had to say farewell to someone they loved or they were full of joy, greeting loved ones. This, unfortunately, was not one of the happier airport moments. Inside the cold terminal, Aaron hugged Claudine lovingly.

"This is gonna be the worst part of the whole trip, saying good-bye to you," he said into her ear.

Claudine clung to him. "Please, please be careful," she pleaded, and tears filled her eyes. "I've had bad luck with people I love goin' to Germany."

"Nah, don't go thinkin' like that, sweetheart," he said, brushing her tears away. "Remember, we're only an airplane ride away and we have our mobile phones and email too."

Claudine could not stop the tears from rolling down her face. "Shhh. Ah gotta go," he said as he shushed her lovingly and wiped her running nose with his hand. "Please don't cry, darlin.' Hey, let me tell ya this. Ah can count on one hand, only one hand, all the people in the world ah love, did you know that? And yer one of those people. Who woulda thought that a guy like me, who nearly lost his right hand, would be so blessed today?" he said as he held out his hand, fingers wide apart. "Yer one of my five fingers," he said with a bit of a smile, "and I love ya. I love Buffy too. Look after her and look after yerself, okay?" He kept wiping the tears away from her cheeks like windscreen wipers wiping away rain. He kissed her affectionately, with sadness in his eyes; Claudine was not the only one upset.

Finally, Aaron slowly turned and walked through airport security. He looked at her just before he disappeared through the doors and blew her a kiss, smiling his asymmetrical smile.

5

Love From Your Messy Projekt

For the first couple of days without Aaron, things were all right for Claudine. They texted nonstop and spoke to each other a few times a day. "It's important to me that ya knew how yer doin' and I can't help but miss ya, darlin,'" he said. "Don't be impatient with me for texting and calling so much, all right?"

"I would never be impatient with you," Claudine said. "I feel the same way. It won't be too long before we see each other again, thank goodness."

"Ah'm just waiting on the first instalment of the contract money," said Aaron, "and ah'll fly ya out here. Can't wait to see ya, darlin,' ah miss you so much already."

After a few days, the frequent texting and calling back and forth dissipated slightly. Claudine tried to busy herself with work at the IWF, driving in more often than usual to help out onsite and be near her brother and son, but it was hard for her to keep focused.

About two weeks after Aaron got to Germany, he left Claudine a message on her phone. "Hey. Ah called your home phone so ah can leave a longer message for ya," he said. "Yer probably at Toasty's or somethin'. My damn cell phone's gonna get cut off soon, ah have to switch to a German phone instead and it doesn't have international callin' or textin' I'm tryin' find a long distance plan that has that and isn't gonna cost me a fortune. I might end up getting' a land line. But we still have emails, so check yer emails if you don't hear from me. One of mah client's hurt his hand, so he's history, and the other guy ain't gonna be ready for Brazil, so that cuts into my makin' the money I was countin' on, but ah think ah'm gonna be trainin' a young American celebrity over here who's makin' a movie. Ah ain't at liberty to say too much yet, 'cuz it ain't for sure that ah'm going work for him, and he's real private, but he saw me trainin' mah clients and said he wanted me to train him too, so we'll see. Darlin,' ah'll call ya later, but remember to check your emails. Kisses for you and Buffy, love ya!" and he kissed into the phone twice which was his trademark way of saying good–bye to Claudine.

After the cell phone service was cut off, Aaron was rather diligent about sending emails. His written words were different than his spoken ones, where his Texan slang was heard and enunciated in them. She wouldn't hear his beloved drawl for a while, as he never did get a land line. But his letters were there for her to reflect on always and she read them whenever she felt lonely. His first email to her read:

> *Darling, did you get my message? My cell isn't working over here now but that's okay, we've got email still. You know, I think I'm gonna make you my projekt? You got so much potential! Wait till I get home, the things we are gonna do together, we'll be so proud of ourselves and have a great life again. Can't wait to see you. Keep up the good work at the IWF and with your paintings. Our money is invested now and it looks good. Everything is good here but I miss you and Buffy. xoxo Aaron*

Claudine loved how he spelled 'project' as 'projekt' and she loved her new role in his life. She tried to keep her chin up and keep working, going to the gym, and spending time with her family. They often asked about Aaron, especially Dempsey, and Claudine was sorry that she did not have more information to share. She wrote to Aaron almost every day, telling him about what she and Buffy were up to, but after a couple of months of getting his cell phone service cut off, he didn't respond very often or in the ways he used to.

It was getting harder for Claudine to look at her email inbox. Every morning, it was torture not to see anything from Aaron. She worried a lot about him and she worried about their relationship. The emails she did get were very unwanted spam, aside from the occasional beautiful note from Isabella. Claudine did, however, get a monthly statement from Aaron's investment broker and from the exploration company they invested their money in. These also turned out to be unwelcome because the information was not encouraging. Rather than making money, it looked as though Claudine was actually losing some of her initial investment. Monthly disbursements were so insignificant, barely worth a few cents at the moment. She wrote the investor and got a rather dry email back reminding her that any investment involved financial risk and that he expected the amounts to go back up by next quarter. Claudine was a ball of nerves, but she tried as hard as she could not to think about it too much. She believed things would be better next quarter.

Aaron's next email came about two weeks later.

Hi Darling,

Sorry I didn't write sooner – been hectic here. Maybe soon I'll have the money for a ticket to fly you here, but money's tight right now. You've seen the investment emails from the exploration company, so you can see I'm not getting any money from that. I'm so sorry about that, my friend says it'll turn around soon. But no one predicted it was going to take such a dive.

I'll be signing a contract with the movie star I told you about, so I'll be in Germany area a while still. I'll be getting paid by the movie company so I have very different contract than I thought I was getting with the movie star, but it's still good. Stay positive, remember your potential and remember I'm always with you. Miss you. Kisses xoxo Aaron

Claudine immediately wrote back to him:

Dear Aaron,

I feel lousy. I miss you. I go back and forth with worries that something has happened to you like Drew, because I don't hear from you for days. Maybe you've just forgotten about me and have found someone else. I write you all the time but you don't respond. This is the first email I've gotten from you in so long. What has become of you?

Anyway, everyone is well here. IWF is going great. Toasty and Dempsey are planning another CrazyBest and they want to start running tours in Europe and Asia, but we're not sure when that all will happen. It is hard to believe that nearly a year ago, Dempsey and my brother were getting ready to fight each other and I met you. I will try not to hold it against your movie star client, whoever he is, that he is taking you away from me (ha ha) but seriously, I hope he is looking after you and I hope you are truly fine. He's got the best trainer in the world! Please write soon!

Love, from your messy Projekt

Again, Claudine didn't hear form Aaron for a while. She wrote to him plenty of times, but she heard nothing. She was getting especially nervous because the money she was supposed to be getting from their investment was not looking very promising. The world economy seemed to be rather gloomy. When the time came for her to pay off her mortgage, she was forced to take the one-year extension, agreeing to pay monthly installments instead of the lump sum she had dreamed of making. With her job at the IWF she was able to get by, but she was having so much trouble focusing at work that she was making embarrassing bookkeeping mistakes here and there and Toasty was getting frustrated with her.

Three weeks later Aaron finally responded to Claudine. Their email exchanges read like this:

Darling,

I'm so busy now. We're gonna be in Switzerland for a while. I'll get you a ticket and money next month and we'll have fun! I have to run now xoxo Aaron

Claudine was getting fed up with this routine. This was starting to eerily remind Claudine of what had happened with Drew; it made her shudder when she thought about the parallels. When Aaron failed to call, or even write, when Dempsey won CrazyBest the second year in a row, Claudine's emails started getting more desperate.

Dear Aaron,

Are you still my fiancée? Are we still best friends? I am pretty sure you said we were going to get married, but maybe I'm imagining you said that. Did I imagine it? I asked you in one of my many emails if you found someone else, but you didn't respond. Is there a problem with money, maybe? If the company you're working for hasn't paid you any money, you shouldn't be working for them – that is what you would tell me!

If you want to see me, I could try to pull the money together from my end. I am not trying to be demanding, but I wish I knew what was going on. Feels like I have been through this before.

Love from your bewildered Projekt

P.S. In case you hadn't heard, Dempsey won CrazyBest again. I bet he would like it if you called to congratulate him.

Aaron responded to Claudine's email about a week later.

Hi Darling,

Am I still your fiancée? Hmmm, let me think about that. LOL, of course I'm still your fiancée and of course I'm still your best friend. Just been so busy, AGAIN, but I'll email you when I can.

I love you, Projekt. Don't worry so much, okay? And tell Dempsey I'm proud of him. I'll give him a call when I get a chance. Still don't have a phone.

Xoxo Aaron

Claudine's hands went up to her face as though she was warming it on a cold day. The short email from Aaron was so uplifting that she smiled a big wide smile and tears came to her eyes. She promptly emailed him back, profusely thanking him for his love and hoping he was having a successful trip. Her final sentence was *"As usual, I miss you Aaron and I love you always and all ways, xoxo Claudine, your special p r o j e k t."*

As Claudine struggled with her emotions and her finances, time passed by one agonizing day at a time. Aaron had now been away for ages and had not written anything to Claudine since his email when he told her he was 'of course still her fiance and of course still her best friend.' Claudine had started applying to jobs that sounded interesting outside of the IWF, ones that had to do with artwork mostly, and the job rejection emails she was getting did not help to improve her low self–esteem.

Three months after Aaron left, Claudine got an email from the investment company.

> *Dear Ms. Bellamy,*
>
> *Thank you for your investment with Honnecker. It is with great sadness that we inform you that the board has voted to dissolve the company...downturn in the global economy...restructuring of our assets...regrettably strict regulations, taxes and legal setbacks due to water rights... This decision to dissolve and restructure does not come lightly... Any and all investments in Honnecker at this time have regrettably been stalled ...*

Claudine felt a wave of panic grip her. The words on the screen were suddenly difficult to see, swimming in a sea of blinding light. Hastily she grabbed her phone and dialed the customer support number at the bottom of the message.

After half an hour of stammering and trying to understand the representative's thick German accent, Claudine understood that Aaron's "German investor guy" had been let go. The investment company, which Aaron had promised was a surefire money-maker, had failed before ever making it to the open market. Their money at Honnecker was just a drop in the bucket and so many others lost their investments there too. Many invested more than she had. But it was all she had and now, she felt abandoned and doomed.

Claudine did not go into the IWF that day. Instead, she got back into bed and listened to the several angry but concerned messages Toasty left on her answering machine, asking her why she hadn't come in. *What would he do if he found out what she had done with her inheritance?*

The next morning, an email from Aaron appeared in Claudine's inbox.

> *Darling, I'm real sorry that I don't have money to send to you. I'm sure you've already gotten that email from the investment company. I don't know what to tell*

you. And my contract money is tight and I need what I get for my own legal problems here. I'm sorry.

I've got a lot of personal family shit going on that only I can deal with. I don't want to talk about it. I'll get it sorted eventually but right now, it's impossible for me to marry you. There's nothing you can do to help.

This is real difficult for me to say and for a long time I've wondered how to tell you this. In fairness to you, I wish you wouldn't keep asking to come see me. There's nothing for you here. It is complicated. You deserve better than this, but that's all I will say. I have a lot going on and right now I need my freedom to move in a different direction from you. You dwell too much on the past and uncertainty of the future and that isn't healthy for you. But you don't let things go, Claudine, and it's not going to help either of us right now. I'm okay with uncertainty because it's up to God, not you or me. We have different echoes at moment. I love you but not in the way you want me to love you. Like I said, it's complicated. Just live for today and count on yourself first before anyone else. If you find someone to take care of you, I understand, but learn to take care of yourself first. That's the best advice I can give you. I wish you the best of luck.

Aaron

Claudine felt as though there was suddenly a crushing weight on her chest, threatening to break her heart into a thousand pieces. *How could Aaron have done this to her?* She just couldn't understand any of it and she couldn't find him to ask him what the hell was going on. Feeling dizzy, she leaned back in her chair and closed her eyes. There was no one to talk to about what a fool she had been. Her only solace was to send Aaron a volatile and emotional email.

Dear Aaron,

You are an outright liar and a coward. You don't even have the backbone to tell me why you want me to move on from you. You played me like a bloody banjo, right up to the little kiss you blew to me at the airport before you said goodbye to me. You just left me hanging here. I quit my job because of you. Everything is more important to you than I am, obviously. You completely shut me out. You are the one who proposed to me. You are the one who made all the promises to me about everything, including my inheritance money. Now I'm out the money to pay off my mortgage, I'm out of a full-time job and my heart is broken. It's all because of you. I'm just an old carcass to you. That's how you treated me. You broke my heart. I want you to know, even if you don't care, your cruelty has nearly crippled me, financially and emotionally.

It sounds like you have already moved on from me so I will too. Yes, I will move on from you as fast as I can. When I pick up the pieces this time, don't dare come back and tell me you sorted things out and you're ready to start a life with me again. You obviously never really wanted to in the first place, so I suppose I shouldn't flatter myself that you would ever want to in the future. You are obviously bad for me, so don't contact me again.

Disappointed,
Broke,
Sick,
Heartbroken,
Used,
Claudine

She sent it off to him with the click of a send button. Now it couldn't be taken back. Even though it was only 8:00 p.m., she decided to turn in.

6

Why Wouldn't People Want To Remember The Good Times?

"Mum's the one who painted herself into a corner here. I'm not going to enable her. She needs to figure this out. She's had five years to make a plan, Bella. How did she let it get to this point?"

Dempsey and Isabella sat in his car, driving back very late in the night from the Manchester Airport, the back seat loaded with Isabella's suitcases and gifts from America. With their matching dark curls and fair complexions, the siblings were strikingly similar to look at, though they weren't of like mind at the moment.

Isabella had been in New York for the past year and a half, performing in off-Broadway plays and working wherever she could to improve her acting skills. Before that, she had been at Carnegie Performing Arts Academy, learning everything she could about being a part of the stage, from building it to legally defending it to making it come to life before an audience. At last she was coming back to England to live at home again. "I'm trying to get me own stuff goin' with Toasty and invest money in doin' our own pay-per-view shows and I might want to buy a place of me own too," Dempsey continued. "I've got a lot on me mind right now, you know? Maybe Mum needs to get a job and stick with it! She was doin' fine working for Toasty, but then she just up and stopped comin' in and he had to hire someone else." He banged his big fist on the dashboard. "I'm not a bank. I'm always lendin' her money for petrol, car insurance, phone bills, and now this, by the Christ."

Isabella stared her brother down. "I give Mum money for little things, but that's all I can afford to do right now. When I get on me feet, which I'm slowly doing, I personally will pay you back, Dempsey. Is that okay? I know you have the money. Won't you help out? Please?"

Isabella shot Dempsey a sideways glance that reminded him unnervingly of Louisa, their grandmother. "Dad, Toasty, and Granddad have all helped to give you a name and it's gotten you noticed. You have a respectable career now and you have Uncle Toasty to work with. Who is there for Mum? She's forty-three years old now and she's got nothin'. She's had the shit kicked out of her the past ten years, Dempsey. No one is helpin' her by openin' any doors. Her career as a mum, which gets very little credit these days, won't get her a job. She's just wanderin' about, getting belittled and rejected because she doesn't fit in. She told me she didn't want to go back and work in a shop anymore, but she couldn't go work for Toasty at the moment either because it makes her too sad. She told Toasty that and asked him if he could lend her some money. He was annoyed with her, saying it was an insult that she found it all sad, when it gave the family their livelihoods. It ended up in a big row, and she said she just needed a break, and could he lend her some money. For some reason, he wouldn't. And when she called me, it was right after that."

"She said she doesn't want me to be shocked when I get home and see her after all this time. She said she's havin' trouble paying the mortgage and makin' ends meet. She told me she didn't fall out with Toasty and she didn't blame him, but she's not workin' 'im or for anyone at the moment. I gather the mortgage is supposed to be paid off by now and she' not got the money, unless you help her," Isabella said.

"Well, it's a shame for Mum, but she can't just expect things though. I know Toasty has big plans and I told him I'd help him. He's expanding the promotion while the business is up and trying to buy investments while the economy is down. When the economy picks up, his investments will be worth a fortune. And I want to be a part of that," declared Dempsey.

"Well, Mum would like to go to university, get a degree and become a school teacher. Plenty o' people are goin' back to school while the economy is down. The wrestling is doing well though, from what you've just said. Can't you just give Mum a break and hear her out. If you took care of her, just while she goes back to school, and paid for her schoolin' then she'd have a fulfilling career that she'd be proud of. Or maybe you can help her pay off the cottage. Helpin' her with either one of those would make things a lot better for her and all of us, actually. I wonder if she asked Toasty to pay off the cottage and he refused her. Maybe that's why she stopped working for 'im. I don't know, but I do think she's intimidated by Toasty and maybe a bit by you too, maybe that's why she hasn't said much to you," Isabella said.

"Well, that's kind o' out o' the question to pay off the mortgage, if ya ask me. I can't do that. She had a job with Toasty, then she stopped with that. She just sort of gave up on everything. He never mentioned they fell out, but he said he was disappointed in her for some reason. I don't know what that is. We did naught to her and she just turned herself away from us. I go over now, just to see Sally, but Mum is dead quiet. It's not like we say anythin' bad to each other, but she's just really distant. Maybe you can snap her out of it," Dempsey said. His tone was impatient. "Supposin' you had to start at zero, Dempsey, without someone sharin' the load with you. What kind of job would you be able to get right now if you weren't wrestlin', Demps? Would you be an outstandin' graphic designer or a smashin' engineer? Probably not, so perhaps you'd end up sellin' memberships at a gym and makin' enough quid to just get by."

Dempsey looked uncomfortable, but Isabella kept talking. "No one has it dead easy right now, Demps, so I'm sorry that you seem to be the one holdin' the solutions to Mum's problems in your lap… And just so you know, it's probably best you don't go tellin' Toasty about Mum and the cottage situation. He can be right hard on her as it is."

"Well, I wasn't plannin' on mentionin' any of this to Toasty, for your information," said Dempsey defensively, grabbing his protein shake from the cup holder. "He'll find out eventually, but don't come accusin' me when he finds out and gives Mum a stern lecture. And maybe that's what she needs. It's time Mum got a job and quit with this stuff about how she made a career out of being a mum and a wife. It isn't helpin' her now and she needs to make a new plan. I'm sorry to sound so cut and dry, but we're grown up now and dad's been gone for years! It's not practical to say, 'Hey, Mum, go to university for four years and become an arts teacher so you can have that career you've been dreamin' of. Right, that would put her in her late forties and who's to say she could even stick it out that long–she has a load of trouble stayin' focused and she'd probably not be able to manage to earn much of a living on the side in the meantime, so who'd support her? Me! That's who. And it was dead irresponsible of her to just stop coming to work for Toasty. She basically just called him and said she wasn't coming in for a while and that became permanent. She didn't say what happened. She just stopped everything."

Dempsey suddenly looked at Isabella as if he had just thought of something. "Why doesn't Aaron help her? He needs to step up to the plate as well. I'll ring him up over in Germany and have a word with him."

Now it was Isabella who looked uncomfortable. "Well, I thought you knew that Aaron and Mum are kind of done and Mum's heartbroken. She's kept it quiet, but they've been done for a while now, as far as I can tell. They didn't fall out and I gather he just gave her some rubbish email about how she deserves someone better and he wished her luck. What a prick. I think that was about the time when she stopped comin' to work at IWF, so now you know," she said to Dempsey, who looked shell-shocked.

"So just consider, Demps, that Mum feels incapable, unwanted and hopeless right now. She has no one. Only us."

Dempsey swallowed. His face was white now, but his jaw was still stubbornly set. "I can't lend Mum any money and I feel bad for her about the cottage and shitty circumstances right now, but I can't do it…I didn't know she and Aaron were done. That's too bad, but I can't help that either… Maybe in a few months I can do something for her money-wise, but not right now, or I'd have to put the brakes on everythin' I've been plannin' for me own future. I will help Mum later, when me plans with Toasty are in place and I've got me own house. Mum and the animals can come live with me. I think she's just gonna have to sell the estate."

"You are impossible! Never mind, I will figure somethin' out for Mum, cuz she's not bloody sellin' her house," snapped Isabella. "I guess you have bigger problems than I thought."

There was an awkward silence that lasted several minutes as Dempsey weaved his way through traffic and got closer to the farm. As they pulled up in front of Dempsey's flat, Dempsey turned off the car and heaved a sigh, putting his hand in front of Isabella to stop her from getting up.

"I will pay off Mum's loan, whatever she owes on it, so she never loses her cottage," he said heavily. "I will do that for her and for you, Isabella. I don't like to fall out with you or Mum. You will have to help me get this sorted out tomorrow at the bank and we'll surprise her. She doesn't even know you're back, so it'll be like a double surprise," he said, patting Isabella on the shoulder. The angry look fell from her face and she threw her arms around her brother.

"You're a good man, Demps. Thanks," she said into his shoulder.

They got out of the car and Isabella looked impressed as she saw the flats erected at the side of the estate.

"Wow, this is brilliant, Dempsey! Granddad would be pleased, I think, to see all this. It's amazing," she praised. She breathed in the air and looked around in the night. The lights from inside the house lit up the gardens in a subtle way and it seemed like the surroundings were polished like the powder on the skin of a plump, concord grape. The dogs ran out, a new Rottweiler named Betty, and Jeep, the old Bull Mastiff. Jeep seemed to have some renewed youth in him with the pretty new Rotty in his company. Grant, the big Scottish wrestler who was now a permanent fixture at the Bonham Estate came out to the car to help them bring the bags in.

"Good to meet you, Isabella. I remember you when you was just this big," he said, indicating she was only a toddler when they last met, "but you might not remember that." He laughed. "Will you be staying here with us? I see you've got your bags here, or are you going 'round to yer mum's?" he asked.

"I'll be goin' to me Mum's in the mornin' but it's too late now. I didn't want to inconvenience her, much as she'd be mad at me for not going straight home. You won't say anything to her, will ya? She'd be so tired and I know she's been, well, not full of life lately. Anyroad, she doesn't know I'm even here yet. Our Dempsey and I are goin' round in the mornin'. I need to find Uncle Toasty and tell 'im not to say naught." Isabella admitted.

"Oh, your Uncle Toasty drove up to New Castle to look at the Metro Radio Arena and visit a bird, I think, but ya didn't hear that last part from me," he said, with a wink. "He won't be back 'til later tomorrow. He'll regret he wasn't here now, though, but he didn't know. He's told me how proud he 'is of you, with all your plays you've appeared in on Broadway," said Grant. His deep Scottish brogue couldn't hide his own pride for being in Isabella's company. Grant was such an admirer of her whole family.

"Oh, I'm glad to hear that. I've not seen Uncle Toasty for years, but I know everything is good now, so I can't wait to see 'im. We'll just tell 'im I got in tomorrow. That way he won't feel bad and me Mum won't find out either." She smiled and hugged the dogs, spying Jersey the Siamese cat sitting on the window sill.

"Jersey, you fat cat, get over here!" Isabella called. Jersey met her halfway and then stopped. She ran over and swooped him up in her arms, kissing him on his fat fawn colored stomach. "Let's all go in, shall we? And we can leave me things in the car. I've got everything I need now!" she said and went into her Granddad's house like she'd never been away.

The next day, first thing in the morning, the Bellamy siblings headed to town, straight to their mum's bank and Dempsey paid the loan in full. Dempsey called his mum up on his mobile on the way out.

"Hello?" said a faint voice on the other end. Dempsey was surprised. He realized he hadn't talked to his mother in a while and her tired, frail voice made guilt well up in his stomach.

"Hi, Mum!" Dempsey said. "I've got two huge surprises for you! I'm headed over right now."

"That's great," said Claudine trying to sound less depressed than she truly was. "I'll see you soon. Love you." He heard a click as she hung up the phone.

When they got to the house, it was around eleven in the morning. Cicero, the rooster, was crowing as they drove up the dirt and road. He never crowed at sunrise as far as anyone knew, but he crowed away the rest of the day, sometimes while standing on one leg. When the kids came in the door, Sally the bull terrier who was nearly deaf, rushed to greet them, hobbling a bit in her old age. Dempsey had to duck his head and nearly turn sideways to fit through the door, just like his dad used to do. He picked Sally up and bear–hugged her for a long moment, playfully biting her soft ears. They had their special thing, like

Isabella had her thing with Mr. Wonderful and Claudine had hers with Buffy.

Claudine, at first, was nowhere to be seen. The kids soon discovered her still in her bed clothes, stuffing a load of clothes into the washer. She appeared to be hurrying to tidy up the house before Dempsey arrived. The curtains were closed throughout most of the house and it was dark and sad inside, like Claudine. Isabella, who hadn't seen her mother in nearly two years, was shocked at her appearance. There were some silvery white hairs shining in her mother's dirty blonde hair and she had dark crescents under her eyes. She looked tired and bedraggled, as if she had been crying.

"Bella! My God, I didn't know! Oh my heavens! You're home! I knew you were due back soon, but I'd 'ave prepared better if I'd a known. Never mind… Come here, sweetheart!" she said, drawing her daughter into a loving hug. Dempsey gave his mom a hug too, and Sally laboriously jumped into the mix to be part of the conversation. An overwhelmed Buffy fled in a scared protest amidst the wonderful calamity.

"Mum, you look like you've been cryin'. Are you alright?" Isabella asked.

"Yea, I'm fine," said Claudine. "It's so good to see you! Here, let me put the kettle on and I'll just change into some proper clothes. Hang on, I won't be a minute."

While their mum dashed up the stairs, Dempsey confided in his sister. "Mum looks not too fancy, you know like she usually does. I'm glad we didn't pop round in the middle of the night—she would 'ave been dead tired. It's a shame," declared Dempsey.

"I didn't want to look too shocked, but I am concerned. Mum never looked so sad, even with Dad and Granddad. I really think your help couldn't 'ave come at a better time," whispered Isabella.

The kettle began to boil and Isabella prepared the tea pot, stirring the boiling water over the tea leaves in the old china tea pot, full of little chips, hairline cracks and tea stains. Claudine appeared, slightly out of breath, smoothing her limp hair back.

"Oh, ta Isabella. Let me help you. Do ya want honey? Milk?" their mum asked.

"Yes, please," said Isabella, pulling out chairs for them to all sit. Claudine thoughtfully put a worn-out tea strainer over each cup and poured tea into each cup, then stirred into each cup a spoonful of honey and a healthy splash of milk.

"Mum," said Dempsey, putting a big hand on his mom's now bony shoulder, "You know you can talk to us. We're here to help, if you need it, like. Ah, well, I just want you to know that."

"I look that bad, do I?" said Claudine despairingly, holding her two children's hands. "Ahh, well, to be honest and straight with you both, I'm rather confused about pretty much everythin'. I've never felt so bad in me life, actually. I feel like a misfit and I wonder if I'm losin' me mind because I get so forgetful. I can't remember if I did what I thought I did, like, did I lock the doors? Did I feed the animals? Did I buy print paper? Because I can't find where I put it, a whole bloody package of paper! - Or I think about how I must have said the wrong things in a job application or worn the wrong dress and throw the dress in the bin, then take it out the next day because it wasn't the dress. And I hate me hair so I'll cut it with cuticle nippers in the bathroom and then wonder why I did it, but I can't just go out to the bin and bring it back like the dress. And I'm so tired all the time, but I sleep all the time too. Everythin' is so off with me and it seems permanent. If it's permanent, then what's the bloody point? Is this it for me? And if I lose this place, me animals, that's it then. I give up. If I lose this, then I lose what your dad left for us, what his dad left for him."

Claudine was crying now, tears coursing down her face as she continued. "And I start thinking about way back to Drew in Germany. I should never have trusted that bastard Karl to get him to the hospital! Why did I trust him? Why? Why? And I trusted Toni when I should've seen her comin' from a mile away. She pretty much made a mockery of me and me whole life. She repeatedly lied to me, so why didn't I absolutely insist on seeing a rough draft of me book? Why did she want to hurt me so much too? Why do people get their delights off hurting vulnerable people?"

Picking a kitchen rag, she threw it across the room in anger. Sally jumped up and scampered off after it and brought it back. Claudine, in her tears, smiled and patted the sweet dog on her head, taking the cloth and handing it to Dempsey to throw for Sally. "She's missed you, Demps. And I wish that damned Aaron would have just levelled with me about why it couldn't work between us," she continued ranting as her children watched her, not saying a word. "That's not unfair to ask. His 'it's complicated' explanation was a bloody cop–out. To think I was that stupid to believe he ever cared. What's wrong with me? How can I be so naive about everything? Outside of me family, I don't even have a single friend around here. I don't know what happened to Aaron, I've got no bloody job, I don't fit in anywhere and I've got no useful skills! I've made so many bad decisions and terrible mistakes! I'm a bloody disaster!"

Claudine broke out sobbing. Dempsey awkwardly patted her back while Isabella hugged her and held her as she cried. "Nobody wants to be around me," Claudine continued in phlegmy gasps. "I don't blame them! I'm a complete misfit. I'm forty-two years old and I've got nothin' to show for meself! I'm a burden to everyone and I don't contribute anythin' good to any of you! I'm such a disappointment to everyone, meself included! I really am!"

"Mum, that's not fair to you at all," said Isabella fiercely. "You are not a misfit and you can't keep takin' the blame for everythin' all the time. I get upset when I hear you be so hard on yourself - it's not healthy for you. You were taken advantage of by some dreadful people, but you're not the bad one!"

For a few moments, the only sounds were Claudine's gasping wet breaths and Sally's worried grunts.

"Mum," said Dempsey, "I think I have something that'll make you feel better.

Claudine turned her bleary eyes on Dempsey. She looked so exhausted and sad that it nearly broke Dempsey's heart. "We've just come from the bank," he said, smiling at her. "You officially and completely own the cottage again."

Claudine blinked. "What do you mean?" she asked, wiping tears off her blotchy red face.

"Dempsey paid it off," Isabella said, proudly patting her brother on the shoulder.

Claudine gasped. With the missed payments and penalties, the loan had been over £25,000; she had a stack of bills on her desk to prove it.

"Now you won't be so sad, eh, Mum?" suggested Dempsey hopefully.

Claudine looked at her son and tears spilled, once again, from her bloodshot blue eyes. She hugged him tightly, bawling as he held her and Isabella smoothed down her hair. Sally tried to get in on the huddle and finally broke it up, knocking Dempsey away so she could sit in his lap. Isabella laughed. “Saving the cottage was a very noble cause for you too, wasn’t it?” she asked the happy old bull terrier.

“Demps,” Claudine said once she had finally regained her composure, “I’m so ashamed that you had to do that for me, but I can’t tell you how much that means. I promise I’ll try harder to find some steady work and keep looking at the bright side of things. I’ve just … gosh, I feel so bad all the time. Half the time I can’t even get out of bed. I’m actin’ just like me mum used to,” she said with a half-hearted laugh.

Indeed, Claudine often wondered if this is how her mum felt when she couldn’t leave her bedroom for hours, even for days at a time. The kids went to bring Isabella’s luggage in while Claudine sat in the kitchen for a moment on her own. Silently she thanked God for her remarkable children, for their immense generosity and success and happiness, and she thanked him for her life, too. She hoped God understood why she was crying; she wasn’t ungrateful for her life, just overwhelmed and sad. Her heart felt like it had been punched and stomped, like a cauliflower ear in its early stages of hardening and it hurt. It felt as though she was getting quite the cauliflower heart and although it wasn’t totally hard and thick, it was becoming rather beaten up.

***

The next day, it was already well past noon when Claudine opened her eyes. She had been lying there, dozing and dreaming that Aaron was lying in bed beside her. No one could take these memories away from her and she wasn’t crazy for thinking about them so much, she insisted to herself. It was a comfort to think about them. Why wouldn’t people want to remember the good times?

Buffy was snoozing next to Claudine’s head on the pillow. Claudine grabbed her and pulled her in close. Buffy wanted no part of this and wriggled free, but she didn’t run away. Instead she sat next to Claudine’s face and purred. Diligently, she licked her mummy’s face with her little sandpaper tongue.

Even though a massive weight had been lifted off her shoulders when Dempsey generously paid off the big lien on the cottage, Claudine was wondering when the days of her jumping out of bed and feeling absolutely amazing and excited would be back again. She walked into her bathroom and took a look at herself in the mirror. "Yikes! Ugh!" she said out loud. She looked like a corpse, too thin, with deep, dark circles under her eyes. She just shook her head a bit in disgust and took a brisk shower, cleaned her bedroom, and moved the furniture around in it. She hoped it might somehow give her a different outlook.

Feeling better, Claudine went down and put the kettle on for a cup of tea. She found a note from Isabella, saying she'd be back later. It was three o'clock. She found Buffy waiting in the back kitchen, running around with her little tail straight up in the air. It was a bit bushy and it made her even cuter as she ran her ritual of figure eights around Claudine's legs while anxiously awaiting her tin of Kitty Feast. Mr. Wonderful was already up on the table, demanding his dinner with loud meows. Claudine mixed heavy cream and a bit of boiling water with the canned Kitty Feast, stirred it up with love, and put it on the table.

Claudine watched Buffy eat, thinking of the day they found each other, as Claudine liked to think of it. Almost unrecognizable now, Buffy was fatter, healthy, and clean, with exotic speckle and stripe markings. Her stomach was pure white except for a little light brown patch in the shape of a heart. Claudine thought this was very appropriate, since Buffy was a genuine sweetheart.

A memory popped into her head of a lazy evening spent lying on her bed with Aaron, just relaxing and looking up at the ceiling. She remembered turning his head towards her and whispering in his big cauliflower ear, "I have a secret to tell you." She had paused so he would look at her.

"Okay, what's the secret, darlin'?" Aaron had asked sleepily.

Claudine had continued, "Well, I think that if you and I were to ever give birth to a 'kitten', it would be Buffy." Aaron had burst out laughing and hugged her affectionately. "Darlin', only you could think of something like that," he laughed.

Claudine shook her head now, trying to shake the memory from her mind, and unenthusiastically turned on her computer. There were no replies from the many jobs she had applied to. She spent the next few hours building a new resume and then sent that in to all kinds of random companies that needed help from people with her job skills. Although she did this several times a week, lately there were no responses at all.

It was now nearly seven in the evening and she was thinking about going back to bed when the phone rang. It was Isabella, calling on her mobile phone.

"Mum, I'm up at Uncle Toasty's with Dempsey and me mate, Mary, and I thought maybe me I'd bring her 'round to see you tonight. Do you want to go out for a nice Indian meal, or Chinese?" asked Isabella.

"Oh, I was just about to go to bed," replied Claudine.

"Seriously, Mum? It's only half past seven," said Isabella with amazement.

"Well, if you're with Dempsey at Toasty's, then you're a good hour away. It would be half past eight by then," Claudine said slowly. She really didn't want to go out now. She just wanted to go to sleep.

"Piggin' heck, Mum. We're drivin' cars, not walkin'! We could be there in twenty minutes."

"I'm in my pajamas and literally I was about to climb into bed. I just don't feel like goin' anywhere tonight. I'm sorry, but I hope that's alright," said Claudine, who in fact had never gotten out of her pajamas that day, except to shower.

"No, that's really acceptable, Mum, unless you agree to let us do this tomorrow then," said Isabella playfully. "It'll be fun! We'll pick you up for your tea and go for Indian or whatever you want. I want you to meet Mary! We want to tell you about the documentary we're makin' on Dad. It's a labour of love and it is goin' to make you very proud."

Thanks to their frequent emails, Claudine had heard all about Mary. Isabella had met the girl in London before she had gone to America. She had even flown across the ocean to go visit Isabella while she was on Broadway. They would forge ahead in life as best friends. Mary was a young, entrepreneurial lady in her early twenties who wanted to make movies; Isabella was a young enterprising actress who wanted to make movies and star in them, too. They were a match made in heaven and Mary was the only child to the very wealthy retired rugby star Dino Tsillas, a wrestling fan who was friendly with Dempsey and Toasty. He was also the bloke who found the lads for Dempsey and Aaron to spar with before the very first CrazyBest WrestleFest.

With Dino's encouragement and backing, Isabella and Mary had decided to work on a documentary about Drew's life. This would tell the real story once and for all; Isabella hoped it would clear her father's name after the disastrous *Blank Canvas* book and the predictably dreadful film by the same name that Toni was *apparently* still working on. With the young girls' determination and creative imagination, along with Mary's father's connections and financial help, Claudine had no doubt these two young ladies were going to become heavy hitters on the entertainment scene.

"Oh, it will be nice to finally meet Mary," said Claudine cheerfully.

"That's the spirit!" said Isabella. "So get some rest then, Mum, and I'll see you tomorrow. Don't go to bed early tomorrow though, alright?"

7

When The Food Gets Here, It's Going To Be Good

Trying to look nice for her daughter and make a good first impression on her daughter's important new friend, Claudine made an earnest effort to spruce herself up the next day. After her shower, she put her make–up on and curled her hair with a curling iron. Her old stand–by dress was originally a mid-calf length dark grey cashmere number with half sleeves; in its day it was flattering, comfortable, and professional-looking, but now it was so stretched now that it almost went down to her ankles. It was also getting a lot of pilling around the underarms and bust, but having sold so many of her nicer things over the years, Claudine didn't have much of a selection anymore. She knew Isabella wouldn't care, but she hoped Mary wouldn't notice it was past its prime

It was nearly three o'clock when Claudine made herself another pot of tea and sat down to read the daily newspaper. She found a note on the kitchen table that Isabella left for her. It read: Mum, check your stars!

She read Taurus for Dempsey first, Aquarius for Isabella next, and then her own, which was Cancer. It read: *It's time to get back in touch with a ton of friendly acquaintances you will want to be closer to.* Getting everyone you like in a room together will help foster new friendships and strengthen your own self-esteem. Why not go out for dinner with them? She was about to read more when she heard a cacophony of noises from the rooster crowing to the donkey braying and the dog barking, Claudine knew her daughter was driving in. She heard the car doors slam and excited talking as the two girls came up the front path leading into the house.

"Hallo, Mum! I want you meet me mate, Mary. Mary, this is me mum! Can I make me and Mary a brew, Mum?" asked Isabella as she spooned instant coffee into cups.

"O' course, Isabella. Kettle's still hot. It's lovely to meet you, Mary, and me stars say it's a good thing too." Claudine said, shaking the young woman's hand. Mary was a short, curvy girl with a small waist who looked vaguely Greek. Her skin was pale and her thick, dark, curly hair was shiny, long and beautiful with reddish highlights. It was pulled up in a ponytail, causing a cascade of curls to fall pleasingly down her back.

"This is Sally, she's delighted to meet you too," Claudine said as the dog greeted Mary.

"And I'm, ahmm… happy to meet you," said Mary, shying away from Sally. "I've heard so much about you from Belle and my dad was your husband's biggest fan. I met your brother Toasty and your son Dempsey yesterday. They are very nice."

"Tell me about the new documentary. How's it coming along?" Claudine asked the girls after they had settled down, enjoying their hot drinks.

"When the food gets here, it's going to be good," the girls giggled simultaneously.

"What does that mean?" inquired Claudine, with a perplexed grin on her face.

"Well, " began Isabella, "you know when you order your meal at a restaurant and you're really hungry, even starvin', and it seems to be taking them forever to bring it to you and you just keep drinking water, watching and waiting, and everyone else at your table is hungry too? Well, no one really knows what to say after a bit and it goes dead quiet. That happened to us when we went out for Chinese and finally one girl broke the silence and said, "When the food gets here, it's goin' to be good!" Mary and I just looked at each other and laughed. It was true, what she said, but we were laughin' because it seemed like such an unhelpful but hopeful thing to say. So now when we are chompin' at the bit for somethin' great to happen, like with this documentary, we wait and wait and we think, when the food gets here, it's goin' to be good," explained Isabella.

Claudine grinned again, less perplexed, but still not quite sure.

"I guess you had to be there," said Mary kindly to Claudine.

"We do have a lot of good interviews lined up," said Isabella. "We'll be goin' all over the place for it. Let's see, there's Ireland to interview the World's Most Muscular Man, then over to Scotland to talk to the World's Strongest Man, because Dad trained with them both; and then we are all flying to Samoa to film our interview with the High Chief Haku Peter Anoai. Toasty arranged for Demps to do a couple of shows there too, and scout for new wrestlers to bring back up here. It'll be a fantastic couple of weeks down south."

"That sounds wonderful," said Claudine. She had just noticed Mary was turned awkwardly at the table to stop Sally from putting her head in her lap.

"Mum, you know Mary has never owned an animal before?" said Isabella, noticing the same thing and called Sally away. "She thought she was allergic to them, for her whole life, but since she's been round to Toasty's yesterday and today and been with all the animals there, includin' the horses, her allergies haven't flared up at all, not even once. She thought she was deathly allergic to animal hair, so maybe she's just not allergic to our animals."

"That's true. The only pet I had growing up was a fish," said Mary. "Me mum, who I don't speak to anymore, but anyway, she told me that cats gave people diseases they get from eating mice and rats and dirty birds. Is that true?" Mr. Wonderful, right on cue, jumped on the kitchen table and began licking the butter in the ceramic butter dish.

"Bloody hell!" exclaimed Mary, her dark brown eyes growing wide. "It is not him jumping on the table that scares me, because I've already seen all that at Toasty's with his cat Jersey. It's the bloody size of your cat. Belle, you weren't exaggerating about your mum's cat being over two stone. He's massive!" Mary looked around, scanning the floor. "Where's the other cat? Belle said you had two cats."

"Buffy? Oh she's resting upstairs probably; she's had a busy day already. Being shy takes a lot out of her," explained Claudine. "But what a champion she is. She rescued me from a rainstorm. She pulled me with her little strong jaws, into her car, and drove me to the doctor. The doctor didn't do much, so Buffy took me home, fed and washed me, and she's been looking after me ever since that day. She's the daughter Aaron and I never had," said Claudine very matter–of–fact, with only a hint of mirth in her eyes.

"Belle, is your mum serious?" Mary whispered. Isabella didn't help much because she was so straight–faced and accepting of these statements, but she finally cracked and started laughing.

"No, she's having you on, Mary. Me mum and her boyfriend rescued Buffy and now she treats that kitten better than she treats me! I never got deluxe kitten food when I was a baby!"

Mary still seemed rather confused by the conversation and couldn't keep Sally from jumping up on her. "Oh, you've got a face only your mother could love!" Mary told Sally as she tried to keep her composure and not let the sweet dog frighten her.

"So, Mum, I know we're a bit early, but are you ready?" said Isabella. We are taking you out today for Indian and we want to do some clothes shopping as well. I'll get you some new things for your job huntin', or just some new things for no particular reason. Maybe you can work for Toasty again, even though he's hired a new bloke to take over all that monotonous office work you were doing. I don't blame you Mum, if you don't want to do that, but if you had to go back, I think Uncle Toasty would find something for you. It might make you feel better, or not. Maybe it would make you sad too… I don't know. But I do know we're taking you out to buy some new clothes and some things for your kitchen." Claudine started to open her mouth to protest, but Isabella looked at her sternly. "Sorry, no negotiatin'. Do your fat cats and fat dog need food? We will get that for them too; I wouldn't want to come here and find they ate you because they are ALWAYS hungry and you're always feedin' them. What's your obsession with having all the animals around here fat?" Isabella said, needling her mother with a laugh.

In the end, Claudine was coaxed out the door and the girls enjoyed a lovely day of extravagant shopping, delicious meals, and terrific fun. As the afternoon drew to a close, Mary asked the Claudine and Isabella if they had time to drop by her studio.

"My dad would love to meet you," said Mary to Claudine. "Like I said, he's a huge wrestling fan and he's already met Dempsey and Toasty a bunch of times."

"Oh, sure," said Claudine, "and me stars today said I was supposed to foster new friendships or something like that, right Belle?"

"Yes, that's right. I'm glad you're paying attention Mum. You still read your stars, right?"

"Yes, I do, luv," Claudine laughed. It was fun to be in good company and she felt rejuvenated with the help of these bright young girls; she felt like she was a few years younger, even. She was odd letting her daughter buy her new clothes, make– up, and shoes, but Isabella had insisted, saying she had been doing well for herself lately.

"My dad has his own studios down in London, near Croydon and one here, in Manchester," Mary explained as she drove. "They're for different things, like he rents office space to businesses in Croydon, but he has massive studio space set up at Thronos Productions here in Manchester, so if someone wants to make a movie, his studio is the place for them to go. He's always picks out good properties. He also has four playhouses: one in London, one in Liverpool, one in Birmingham, and another here, because he lives up here now. And this is our Manchester studio, the Thronos one that we're pulling into now," she said as she leaned outside of the car to speak with the security guard. The guard's blue jacket had Thronos Productions embroidered onto the pocket in white Greek-style letters. Under that, in simple capital letters, was the name Brent.

"Oh, hallo there, luv!" said Brent, who had a grey moustache and a grey head of hair to match. "It's a bit late to be comin' in to do some editing, but I can't tell you kids what to do, can I now? Make sure you check in on your dad. He's still inside working. He might appreciate you noticing how hard he works, luv. You kids these days never have enough time to say…"

"Right, thanks for being the point of the pencil, Mr. Chisholm. See you later!" replied young Mary, and without hearing any more of Mr. Chisholm's unsolicited advice she soon drove off through the gate, over the speed humps and into her parking stall. The sign at the front of the stall said *Mary Tsillas, Producer*.

They got out of Mary's Volkswagen Golf and walked around the grounds, tightly bundled in their coats, as Mary proudly described her father's establishment. "This building here, it's mainly for administration and records; that hanger over there is where we do a lot of the stage building," said Mary, pointing to some of the buildings dotting the vast area. "There's been a load of carpenters and painters in there lately. Some company is working on a big film, so it's been busy in there. It's brilliant how they put the things together, like a town, and then when the film is made, the town looks like the real thing."

She turned back around and headed them towards the administration building, running ahead to open the heavy door. "This door is over four hundred years old and once belonged in a Welsh castle," she said, running her fingers over the front. "Me dad saw it and he absolutely had to have it. And then he ended up putting it here at our studio. I think it was a little 'house–warming' gift to himself. Me dad and I have our offices on the fourth floor, c'mon."

They walked toward the lift and Claudine admired the handsome building as she followed the girls inside. The floors were granite and in the middle of the lobby floor was a huge marble centrepiece resembling a throne. "Thronos is Greek for throne," Mary repeated. "Me dad is Greek; me mum is French."

The lift took them slowly up to the fourth floor. Claudine saw beautiful paintings and nicely framed posters all along the walls down the hallway nearing the offices. "This is our hallway of fame and your Dempsey's picture is right there," and she pointed to a signed photo taken of Dempsey and her father outside Donny Roach's gym. Claudine noticed half of Aaron's body was in the edge of the photograph. She didn't say anything, but remembered it was taken around the time when she first met Aaron. He and Dempsey were training at Roach's Gym, getting ready for CrazyBest.

"Mum, tell Mary about that portrait you painted of Dad. You know, the one that loopy fan stole from the town hall in Wigan, when Dad was getting an award there," insisted Isabella. "Me mum is a brilliant artist," she told Mary proudly. "She loves to draw and paint things. Me mum's drawings seem to… to have a soul, like they're alive. When she was our age, she was goin' to go to university to study art and literature. She is really good, but you'll probably not admit it now, eh Mum? You'll go all shy. But trust me, Mary, she's a fantastic artist."

"Well, thanks, Isabella," said Claudine. "That is nice of you to say about this old crow. I do love to paint… I started workin' on a new one a few weeks ago, of Buffy, but I've put away for a bit. I just can't get into it and besides, findin' a job is me priority now. I'd go see Toasty about work, but I couldn't bear to let 'im down again. I'd rather let down someone who means naught to me, basically, than let Toasty down. I can't seem to commit to anything, so little jobs here and there might be what I can live with at the moment."

"Don't worry about it now, Mum. You'll sort it all out. Right now, just enjoy the day and come see Mary's office. It's gorgeous," said Isabella, taking her mum by the arm to see what all the fuss was about.

Isabella and Claudine followed Mary down the long hallway. As they were walking, a door opened at the end of the hallway and there stood Dino Tsillas himself. He turned and stared out his window, looking into the night. He seemed to be stuffed in a light blue oxford dress shirt, unbuttoned at the top to accommodate his big neck; navy trousers that skimmed his muscular legs; and black canvas combat boots. The odd professional attire (particularly the combat boots) didn't do much to distract from his cauliflower ear and broad, crooked nose; Claudine had a feeling he might be more at home in loose fitting working-out clothes. His dark curls matched those of his daughter, but with grey highlights instead of Mary's red ones. Below his dark brown eyes were thick greying eyebrows that reminded Claudine of caterpillars. She couldn't help but notice he had curly hairs sticking out of the top of his Oxford shirt too. None of the men in her life, from her father to Aaron, had very much body hair.

"Oh, hallo, Dad! Old Gingersnaps Chisholm said you were in, but I wasn't sure because I didn't see your car outside," said Mary, greeting her father with a causal hug. "Oh, you know Isabella, eh Dad? And this is her mum, Claudine Bellamy."

"Pleased to meet you, *Claudia*," said Dino, holding out his tanned, beefy hand. "And nice to see you again, as always, Isabelle. I love that name. I've a sister named Isabelle. She's back in Greece now though. Come on into my office, all of you. My car's parked in the back. I was just looking at it from my window."

The small group walked into the office, which was large enough to be a conference room and had ceiling-to-floor windows overlooking the property. As Claudine was admiring the view and Dino's light blue Bentley, Dino turned back to her.

"You know, I was a huge fan of your Drew. And I loved your dad as well," he said in a reverent voice, as if he was talking about the Pope. "He did plenty for wrestling and sports in this country. Your whole family did."

"Thank you," said Claudine. "That means a lot."

"No word of a lie," said Dino, suddenly looking much more at home to Claudine in his professional attire. He seemed quite comfortable in the role of being an executive, even in a dress shirt and dress pants that looked at first out of place on him. Claudine realized it was just that she hadn't seen athletic men dressed up in an office before. She had seen Drew dressed up, but it was at a big gala or for a wedding, but never in an office. Her father was always dressed, but never quite as corporately as Dino. It made Claudine wonder how *executive* Dino Tsillis was. "Your family has a first-rate wrestling product that I would love to see exploited properly and I say that with respect, luv. Your family runs a good wrestling show, the best in my opinion, but no one really sees it outside of England these days. I would love a chance to promote it worldwide. I think, with the connections I have, that your Toasty'd be impressed; your son too, for that matter. I'd like to talk to your brother about it, actually." He arched his back and rotated his head on his big neck, as if he was cracking it, before sitting down in his handsome dark green leather office chair. Gesturing for the rest of them to sit, he smoothed his thick hands across the top of his gleaming cherry wood desk.

"Well it is something to think about, but let's not bombard Isabella's mum with all this business talk, eh Dad?" said Mary. "It would be great if we all could get together for a Sunday tea, maybe at one of me dad's restaurants. Let's try to do something soon."

"Sure, I could set summat up for you and me brother and Demps to meet," suggested Claudine. "What kind of restaurants do you own?" She was feeling sweaty all of a sudden in her cashmere dress. She wondered if it was a little warm in the hall, or if this was the start of the infamous hot flashes that Toni absurdly diagnosed her with years ago. She hoped it wasn't an anxiety attack; she had nothing to be anxious about, but she felt a touch claustrophobic for some reason.

Isabella, who had made herself busy in a corner of the office as she prepared them cups of tea. She walked across the big office with a silver tray of mugs filled with tea. "There you go, Mum, just how you like it, with cream and honey. And for you, Dino, tea with cream only, and Mary a tea with sugar only, and for me tea like me mum's."

"Oh, ta, Isabelle," Dino said, grabbing the delicate porcelain handle on his cup of tea with his thick fingers. Claudine noticed that his fingers would not fit through the teacup handle; it reminded her of her dad. She always thought big, thick hands were a sign of character.

Dino saw Claudine looking at his precariously held cup and let out a chuckle. "Remind me, Mary, to buy American tea cups when I go there again. They make big cups there with handles that fat bent fingers like mine can actually hold. I look like a gorilla trying to hold these. This cup looks like it was made for a little woman, or a raccoon even," said Dino. Claudine laughed, and Dino looked pleased with himself.

"That reminds me, Dad, I think you'd truly get a laugh out of Claudine's animals," said Mary animatedly. "She's got a cat that weighs two stone, easy, and a bull terrier, another cat, a donkey, even a rooster all living at her house and the best thing of all is I didn't get sick from being around them! No wheezing or itchy eyes. I'm right as rain, as you can see. Isabella thinks maybe I'm not allergic anymore. I swear I didn't get any bad reaction," said Mary as she saw her father's face frown in disapproval.

"Well, be careful, Mary. We've never had any animals as pets before because of your allergies. Quite frankly, I've never owned a moggy in me life. No use for them really, unless you have a rat that needs catching. But, if you didn't get sick, that's good, luv. Just keep your medicine handy all the time. I don't want you getting ill."

Dino straightened up, still holding his teacup handle with two fingers. "Well, luv, I've got some more work to do, so I'll see you all another time. It was an honour to meet you, *Claudia*" he finished, looking at Claudine and smiling. She didn't mind that he got her name slightly wrong. It actually made her laugh.

As Claudine and the girls retreated down the hall, her thoughts turned to Aaron. All of a sudden she couldn't stop thinking about him. She missed him very much. Deep down, she still believed he was coming back for her. One day, when whatever was bothering him went away, he would return to her and she would welcome him back with open arms.

8

WANTED: ENERGETIC WOMEN

It was a foggy February morning, but it was warm inside Claudine's cottage. Buffy and Mr. Wonderful were on the bed and Mr. Wonderful was trying to give Buffy a thorough face-washing, but she kept thinking they were kick-boxing and was giving Mr. Wonderful some powerful back leg punches. He just carried on washing her face like a patient parent. Claudine sleepily watched this scene, pretending that Drew was lying in bed beside her.

The telephone rang before Claudine even stepped out of bed. It was Isabella. "Hallo, Mum!"

"Good mornin', Isabella! How are you?" Claudine said in a scratchy voice.

"I'm smashin'! Are you still in bed?" teased Isabella.

"Errmm, what time is it?" Claudine searched around for the watch that Aaron had bought for her, but Buffy had knocked it off her night stand, which she often did when at night she was playing.

"Half past ten. Your mornin's nearly done. I was up early and I should 'ave got you up with me. C'mon then, up and at 'em!"

"Oh, well then, I better get to it or get up and at 'em, or whatever it is, scoffed Claudine with a smile.

"I'll take you somewhere right pleasant Mum, for a couple weeks, when this is all finished," said Isabella, who was leaving for Samoa the following day with Mary and Dempsey. "Maybe

Spain or Greece for a fortnight, eh? I'd take you over to Ireland with me now, but that's only for a day or two, and that wouldn't be much of a holiday. We'll get it all sorted out for a nice place for us to have a proper holiday."

"That's a nice idea, but I'll have to see if I'm suddenly workin' by then. I might not be able to go, but we'll see. That's so nice of you, luv! Thank you," said Claudine, playing absently with Mr. Wonderful's tail. "How close to finishin' the documentary are you, do you figure?"

"Well, I'm not sure, a few months away still, I think" said Isabella. "We're just getting started, but it's absolutely gonna happen, the way we want it to be. I've got some film stars from America, some footballers, and a prince from Dubai – Dad and Toasty wrestled at his son's birthday. I have them yet to do." There was a short pause. "You will be proud o' this, Mum, and I think everyone else will be too. There've been a lot o' lies and rumours goin' around about our family, thanks mostly to that horrible woman Toni Orr. I can't wait to set the record straight."

Claudine felt tears coming to her eyes. "Thank you, Belle. I know your dad would be really proud of you. The whole family is impressed with how you've taken the bull by the horns to get this done. You have a lot o' proper style and direction, Isabella."

"You've got proper style times ten, Mum," said Isabella. "I'm sorry things have been so rough for you lately, but I see things are slowly turnin' round, don't you think? We just have to stay positive and keep tryin'."

"I'm sorry too, but it's to you and Dempsey that I am sorry," said Claudine, who was full-out crying now. "I should have been lookin' after things better, somehow. I know Dempsey was disappointed in me when he had to pay off my lien on this cottage. I'm really embarrassed that I haven't even got the money for cat food. I don't even have enough money to buy a bloody box of hair colour from the chemist." Claudine's words were starting to come out in gasps, but she kept talking. "I don't know what to do. I am overqualified for moppin' up gymnasium floors and for cleanin' toilets and I am underqualified to work in an office. I get laughed out of the boutiques and furniture shops by judgmental shopkeepers who think I have no bloody business bein' in their shop, even though when your dad was alive, he and I would spend a fortune in those same places. Do I really look that out of touch now? Am I that out of sorts?"

"No, no, Mum; try not to get discouraged. You sounded so happy when you were half-asleep," said Isabella. "Do you need me to come home; make you breakfast?"

"No, thank you, Belle, I'll be fine," hiccupped Claudine.

"Well, maybe this will make you feel better," said Isabella. "I talked to Toasty about having you do some work for the IWF again. Things have been going smashingly here, business is really expanding, so even though he had to hire someone full-time, it looks like there is still some paperwork that you could do right from home. You'd just have to come in and pick it up once a week, or maybe Dempsey could drop it off for you. That way, you'll have some kind of income while you wait for somethin' more permanent."

"Thank you," said Claudine, dabbing at her face with a tissue. "That's a huge help, Isabella. I should be able to manage doing some paperwork for 'im here at home."

"There's another thing too," said Isabella slyly. "Erm, well…I'm just throwin' this out there, Mum, but Mary's dad, Dino, asked me this morning if you would consider havin' a day out with him. He said he'd take you to a rugby game and out for a meal. It's up to you. What do you think?"

"Hmm. Well, does he know I kind of have a fiancée?"

"Ya, well I told Mary about some of it, but Mum… I hate to break it to you, but it's been nearly a year since Aaron left and three months since you got that horrible email from him. I think it would be good for you to get out of the house and do something fun. What do you think, do you want to give Dino a chance?"

Claudine bit her lip, thinking. "If it's just Dino and me going on a proper date, I'll have to take a pass at the moment, Bella. But, I wouldn't feel that uncomfortable if maybe all of us got together at Toasty's for tea or went out for a meal. He's a nice enough man, he's doing plenty to help you and he seems to want to do business with Toasty, but I don't think I'm ready for anythin' with anyone yet."

Claudine sighed and looked out of the window at the grey sky. "Deep down inside, I keep thinkin' Aaron will come back," she said, her voice cracking a little. "We were engaged, you know? It's not like we were just pen–pals. It's odd, but meetin' Dino yesterday only made me miss Aaron more. If Dino and I could just be friends for the moment and see how that goes, that would be terrific. I wouldn't want to lead anybody on. I hope Mary understands."

"That is completely fine with me and I know it's fine with Mary. She didn't want her dad askin' in the first place, but he called me anyway. I completely understand how you feel."

"And please don't worry, Mum," Isabella said in a softer tone. "You've got your house, us, the animals, and somethin' will come up for you that deserves you, whether that be a new job or a new lad. I can feel it. So keep well, eh? Maybe do some drawin' today or do some exercisin', eh? Doing those things always help you feel better. I love you, Mum, I'll let you go now and remember, Dempsey and I'll be gone tomorrow for a fortnight."

"I love you too, and thanks. I'll see you later and I want you to have a good safe trip. T'ra," replied Claudine.

Claudine put down the phone, wiped her face off, and stretched. As her shoulders popped and her back crackled, she remembered how Drew used crack her back for her, cracking her little neck with his strong but extremely gentle hands, putting her back in alignment so her headache would go away. He never hurt her, not even once. Claudine knew Drew never intended to leave her like this. He never would have wanted her to feel as sad as she did these days, yet here she was.

Looking outside, Claudine decided to take her daughter's advice and go for a jog. She got her worn-out running gear on and put her stiff trainers that she hadn't worn in months on her feet. Starting her old familiar running route, she warmed up with a brisk walk before breaking into a jog.

It was a five-kilometre outdoor run, which was an easy feat for her once. She used to run it every other day without fail for years. Like Isabella said, it always made her feel better after the run was done. Outside it was drizzling, just the kind of weather she loved to run in. There was a lingering burning tar smell in the air; someone was probably patching up a hole in a roof. She loved that smell too. It took her back to her father's farm, where he used to mop hot tar and oil on the barnyard roof so rain wouldn't leak onto the wrestling ring.

Claudine hadn't exercised at all in a few months, not since Aaron had sent her that fateful email. Today, she felt like she was trying to run a hundred miles knee–deep in mud. With tremendous difficulty Claudine finally reached the halfway point, at two and a half kilometres. Then, breathing heavily, she turned around and walked back home, sweating and wheezing. Rain trickled down her face in rivulets and dripped off the end of her bedraggled ponytail. Disappointed as she was in her out-of-shape physical state, she still felt a sense of accomplishment that she at least got to the two-kilometre mark. She would do better next time, she promised herself.

As she got closer to home, walking down her cottage road, she heard her donkey Emily braying and Cicero the rooster crowing. They were brilliant living burglar alarms; they went off when anyone was coming up the road, even if that 'anyone' was Claudine. She greeted them as she walked up to the house's back garden and in through the unlocked back door.

Claudine took off her trainers and gulped down a big glass of water while she looked for her horoscope in the morning newspaper, her ponytail dripping a little water onto the kitchen floor. She didn't see anything really special there for her stars today. Love and money are coming your way soon, read the horoscope. Enjoy it, you deserve it. *Bollocks*, thought Claudine.

Her eyes moved onto the classified advertisements. She read the job offers and saw an advert for fitness instructors. "*Wanted*," read the advert, *ENERGETIC WOMEN for fun new SYNCOPATION fitness franchise.*" There was a telephone number to call for more information.

Claudine tore that section out of the newspaper and put it next her telephone. The usual things she had inquired about for employment all seemed to be unfulfilling, short–lived and paid a pittance. She figured she had nothing to lose by calling the *Syncopation* number.

When she dialed the number, an answering machine picked up immediately. "Thank you for calling Syncopation, America's number one fitness franchise and now, England's newest fitness franchise," said a cheery female voice. "We are looking for instructors and students to help launch our fitness phenomenon here in the United Kingdom. Please leave your name and number in your message. We will call you back soon. Thank you for calling Syncopation. BEEEEEEEEEP."

"Hallo, I'm Claudine Bellamy and I'd like more information on what is involved in becomin' a proper instructor. I actually have some experience in fitness… when are classes available and where are they? I would like to go to one and give it a try."

And she read off her mobile number and home phone number for someone to ring her back.

***

At about nine thirty the following morning, Claudine got out of bed and called the Syncopation number again. This time, someone picked up.

"Hey, this is Glenda. Can I help ya?" said an American female voice.

"Good morning. My name is Claudine. I called yesterday about the advertisement for your classes."

"Oh yes, Claudine Bellamy, I remember," said the woman in her relaxed American accent. "I'm Glenda. Are ya familiar with us, with Syncopation at all? Maybe you've seen our website?"

"No, but I will visit it. What's the web address?" Claudine asked. They began talking about fitness, choreography, women's group fitness classes, and franchises. It sounded structured, perhaps a bit too organized for a tentative and unsteady girl like the present-day Claudine, but it sounded like so much fun at the same time. She was still curious. She had to find out more.

"I'd like to at least try one of the classes. Are there any in the Chester area?"

"Let's see. I don't think so…still checking here. Just bear with me while I look… no, not at the moment, darn it. We have some down in the London area. Are ya anywhere near there?" Glenda asked. "I'm sorry, I'm not familiar at all with your country and I've been here nearly a month. I bet London isn't even close to where y'all are, is it? I'm not sure where anything is, outside of London and this office, which is in Manchester."

"Oh, that's too bad. I'm not close to London, but I'm somewhat close to Manchester; I live in Chester," said Claudine.

"Don't worry, we might still be able to work something out," said Glenda. "I'll say this about the Syncopation Corporation. It's owned by an amazing woman, the same one who started it all up thirty years ago in Chicago. She was with a dance company originally, then she started her own workshops and it slowly took off from there. We've expanded into Canada and Australia and now we're gonna crack the European and British markets. I've been running my own Syncopation studios in Little Rock for more than ten years. I helped quite a few of the other franchisees get started back home and I guess they like how I did it so they asked me to look after the European leg of things. I see amazing potential here in England, 'cuz it's a small area with a real big population and lots of interest in fitness. It will be awesome when it gets running full speed.

"So sooner rather than later, there should be a franchise opening in Chester, or near there. Maybe you could even open it. We're expanding. If ya do want to move ahead with us, you'll want to get yer own Syncopation Studio and teach, like yoga, aerobics, hip-hop, jazz dancing, and cool stuff like that. That's all part of Syncopation."

Claudine pondered this for a moment. "I've always loved gymnastics, but it was pretty much just me brother and me teachin' each other circus moves. I also did a lot of weight trainin' with me husband, who was a professional wrestler."

"Oh, wow! Professional wrestling is getting real big over in United States. What does your husband do now?"

"Oh, he passed away about a few years ago. He was rather young when died from a wrestlin' injury, over in Germany," explained Claudine, trying hard not to reveal too much of herself. It was better to keep it short.

"Oh you poor thing! I am so sorry," said Glenda, sounding genuinely sad for Claudine. "I really don't quite know what to say, except Syncopation is wonderful therapy and that isn't just some sales pitch."

"That's good to know," said Claudine. "There is one thing, though. I never really thought about havin' me own studio as a business and I have absolutely no money to start anythin' up. I just borrowed money from one of my kids for coffee and cat food, actually."

"That's rough," said Glenda. "We can help you with some things, but you'll need money to start your franchise down the road. A lot depends on what your rent is. The American instructors are training women here to become instructors right now; I'm here helping them with finding locations and setting up the business end of it. It takes time and money and dedication, like any business. If ye'd like, I can drive to Chester tomorrow or if yer in London next week, we can hook up then. I could meet with ya over a cup of coffee, or tea, if ya prefer? Would ya be interested in that?"

"This does sound interestin'," admitted Claudine. "Out of curiosity, what does a franchise cost to own?"

"Well, it'll only cost about two hundred pounds for the initial franchise fee and that includes training," said Glenda. "We've cut the price way back so we can get Syncopation started over here as quick as possible. Depending on what rate ya get for liability insurance and rent, well, it'll likely be at a couple thousand pounds at least to get ya up and running. You'll need things like a sound system, the music, mats, weights – we will help ya with all of that. We know we'll get our money back real fast and we know we have to spend money to make money at this initial stage.

"We can't say it'll be easy to get started; it's new, so there's a learning curve fer all of us. Right now we're willing to do a lot of creative housework to make this work over here, 'cuz it'll do real well here once it gets going. It's got all the essentials to take off big time!"

Claudine knew she didn't have two pence to rub together and that a few thousand pounds would be difficult to come by. But nevertheless, she agreed to meet Glenda in Chester. It was only a conversation, after all.

A few days later, they met at a little diner in central Chester. Claudine parked on the street it and headed on foot to the centre of town, walking quickly to get out of the fresh, brisk air. When she got there, she walked around to see if anyone looked like a Glenda. Claudine hadn't thought to ask the woman what she looked like, so finally she dialed Glenda's mobile number.

"Hello?" a woman's voice said behind her in an American accent. A moment later, the same voice echoed through her phone receiver. Claudine turned to see a tall middle-aged redhead with sky-blue eyes directly behind her holding a mobile phone to her ear. She looked a bit like a sixties movie star.

"Well, hallo," said Claudine. They looked at each other and started laughing.

"Glenda," said the redhead, holding out a slender, pale hand.

"Claudine," said Claudine. "Very pleased to meet you."

Glenda's hand was as warm and velvety as her voice; she made Claudine feel at ease at once. In the crowded café, they managed to get a table that a few older ladies were vacating. Glenda immediately launched into an explanation of her Syncopation vision for the UK.

Glenda confessed that when she started her first Syncopation classes in Little Rock, Arkansas, she had been in a bad place. Fresh out of a divorce, she was in her twenties and had just given birth to her third child. "I gained a ton of weight, half 'cuz I was pregnant again and half 'cuz I was just plain old depressed," she explained. "My husband fell out of love with me and fell in love with someone else. Then he left me for that someone else. I needed to lose some weight and start feeling better about myself, so I started taking classes in the Little Rock location. It was in a big plain, old empty auditorium, with only about five women and me, plus the instructor in the class. We kept it going and then I ended up becoming an instructor and eventually taking over her franchise. Thanks," she said to the waiter as he set a heaping Ploughman's salad down in front of her.

Claudine munched on her grilled vegetable sandwich, listening to Glenda's fabulous life story. "Gradually, I got a few more people coming in and trained a few to become instructors," Glenda continued in between bites of salad. "My classes were good because I had a babysitter, so a lot of women could get a workout in and a free babysitter for an hour. They could dance and laugh and get in shape and not worry about their babies fussing. Those babies hollered a lot at first, but after a while, everyone got into a routine, even those lil' babies."

Claudine was enraptured now. She could see how something like this could unfold. Glenda saw this and continued with enthusiasm. "I got more and more classes and more money saved and then I bought the building - the old auditorium, plus the land it sits on. Then I started to rent the place out for other things, like meetings, movies, judo, yoga classes; there's tons of space in it, but the Syncopation is still the meat and potatoes there, mostly from the steady attendance from the military wives who live out by my big old studio in Little Rock.

"Then, a few years ago, I saw my old cheating ex again in Little Rock," Glenda said with a smirk. "He literally bumped right into me and he didn't even recognize me. In fairness to him, it had been a long time," she said with a laugh. "Anyway, once he remembered me, he played the nice guy, you know, happy to see me and wanted to go have dinner, blah, blah, blah. I asked him where 'she' was and he said 'she' was history, long ago."

"You mean you hadn't seen him in all that time?" asked Claudine.

"Nope. He took off to Omaha, Nebraska and I stayed in Little Rock. He has some family still in Little Rock, but we never kept in touch 'cuz he was quite the deadbeat." She shook her head, her red locks swaying. "Anyway, to make a long story short, my kids, my Ford truck and I survived, and now my daughter's an instructor there too. She runs things for me when I'm on the road. I make about three hundred dollars a class these days, with a full class, which for me is about twenty people, and we run six of them a day, so that's about eighteen hundred dollars a day and they run all week, but only four classes on Sundays. I admit if I had to pay rent, or buy a building now, it would be harder, but not impossible."

Glenda smiled at Claudine, who was enjoying a bite of sandwich with a contemplative look on her face. "There are lots of women from Syncopation like me, who have made a great life and living from it. I pay my instructors $50 per class that they teach. Some of them teach five classes a week, some teach twenty classes a week. And lots of them have their own permanent jobs on top of teaching their classes. If they ever feel they wanna branch off into their own place, I help them and that's another rewarding part of my job now, so I'm real grateful for how it's worked out for me."

Claudine put her elbows on the table and laced her fingers together, resting her chin on the tops of her hands. She imagined what it would be like to make $1,000 a week, even with the exchange rate. She fervently wished that there was a franchise already in Chester where she could work, instead of trying to scrape together money to buy her own.

"I'm gonna to tell ya a few more things, Claudine. I feel younger than ever, seriously, and I'm not worried anymore about finding a guy to take care of me or to spend my time with. If it happens, great! But, I can afford to be fussy and particular now, so I only want a real man. Is there such a thing as a real man?" she said. "I don't stress about being on my own anymore. If I wasn't so happy, maybe I would think differently. I've learned some things the hard way, but I haven't got many regrets. I love my job and I don't really answer to anyone, as long as I'm being honest and respectful. It's no big deal that I'm single, because I have so many really good friends now. So, I am not lonely and I am not alone."

"Well, I'm lonely and I'm alone," said Claudine sadly. "That all sounds so wonderful, what you've told me, but how can I make this happen, since I have no money and nothin' to bring to the table?"

Glenda finished up the last bite of her salad, chewing slowly. "We'll try to figure something out," she said. "Let's getcha training and see how ya like it; ya might have to keep working away at other things and just keep saving until ya have the money to get it going, if it's something ya want to do. But I think ye'd make a great instructor. Ya seem well-qualified, with yer background in sports an' fitness! I'll take that," she said to the waiter as he handed them their check.

"No," said Claudine, "let me pay for my sandwich at least."

"Absolutely not," said Glenda, handing the waiter her credit card. "This is a business lunch and I can write this off on my taxes in United States. I'm here to seek out super nice and super fit women to teach Syncopation, so the least I can do is treat y'all to lunch."

On the drive home, Claudine wondered how she could make it work. The idea of becoming a Syncopation instructor appealed to her, but she felt like it was out of her reach. She needed money and she'd have to memorize routines. *Was she capable of memorizing routines?* She decided believe in herself and to give it a fair try. She also decided not to tell anyone else for the time being.

At home, Claudine got herself undressed, washed her face, flossed and brushed her teeth. She slipped on an old soft T–shirt of Drew's, a pair of pajama bottoms, and climbed into her chilly bed. Under the bed sheets she tried not to move too much, since each time she moved, a swath of cold sheets greeted her warm body. She finally got comfortable lying straight, face up with her hands folded across her chest like a corpse in a coffin. Her feet felt frozen, but she couldn't be bothered to put socks on them now that she was all tucked in.

She lay there in this position, eyes open and stared into the dark at her bedroom ceiling. Images of Dempsey and Isabella as babies flashed through her mind. They were so cute; Dempsey had had blond hair as a baby, but Isabella had dark curly hair like Drew from the very beginning. Drew was such a proud father. Both times when Claudine was in the delivery room, he came in wearing a flimsy blue hospital smock, blue paper slippers, and a blue face-mask the nurses insisted he wear. The smock was the biggest size the hospital had, but it positively did not fit him. All Claudine could see of his face were his big, beautiful hazel eyes, so concerned, and his long thick eyelashes moving up and down as he blinked.

How had things gone so terribly wrong for Drew, who was such a good man? He was too trusting, she thought, but she wouldn't have wanted him any other way. She missed everyone and she felt like she had no one, even though her children were staunch supporters of hers.

"God, I've made so many mistakes and bad choices," she said out loud. "I keep makin' 'em, too. I wish I knew what to do. I can't stop thinkin' about how I messed everythin' up and I don't know what the right direction is anymore. I pray I won't convince meself that I am so unnecessary and burdensome to my family that I do something crazy. Please help me to find where I am supposed to be. Please help me forgive meself for leaving Drew's side. I want to move on from this sadness and hopelessness, I really do. Please help me make this despair go away, God. Amen."

Buffy hopped onto the bed. Instead of taking her usual place on top of Claudine's head, she nuzzled her way around Claudine's chin like she was burrowing. It tickled Claudine's neck and made her laugh. Buffy was determined and got under the bed clothes. She nuzzled her way under the covers right down to where Claudine's cold feet were, curling up right in between them. Mr. Wonderful made himself right at home on top of the bedclothes as he shouldered himself into Claudine's ribs.

9

I'M OLD SCHOOL

For the next month, a motivated Claudine had an inspired point of view for the first time since Aaron had cut off contact with her A Syncopation package arrived in the post from Glenda. It contained DVD training demos with notes and more information about becoming a certified Syncopation instructor. Every day, after doing a few hours of job applications and IWF paperwork, Claudine practiced and practiced the routines in her front room or even out in the back garden where Drew used to train. Not only did she find them interesting, she seemed to have a knack for them. Claudine was learning more specifically than she ever knew before what muscles would be working during the different movements in each of the routines. Day by day, she improved her technique for every movement from how to turn her head to remembering to point her feet and toes. Finally letting go of her inhibitions when it came to things like rolling her hips or shimmying her shoulders made the dancing feel natural to her. She became very cognizant of how important it was to learn how to also be a good teacher and then be that good teacher. She paralleled it to a nurse a good bedside manner.

She felt her attitude about life brightening from the day she met Glenda. Deep down, when she got past the anxiety about not being a perfect teacher. She remembered her father saying there was always more he could learn when it came to his catch wrestling. Her father, a master of submission wrestling, and his words from long ago motivated her to just keep trying to be better as she learned her routines. Time would tell if it would also rub off on her in life beyond Syncopation. How bright her life could be then. Wouldn't striving to be a popular and good instructor be even more rewarding rather than being the perfect one?

Claudine was learning to pace herself for the one-hour classes as well. There was a warm-up routine, then a few songs to get the heart rate up, a few more songs to get it working at higher intensity. After that came a cool down, stretching, core routines, arms, legs, and a final song with more stretching to bring it back full circle. The students could burn as many as 600 calories in just under one hour, depending on how they applied themselves in the sixty-minute class.

To Claudine, these workouts were more than just exercise: they were a brilliant form of physical, mental, and emotional therapy for her stressed-out mind. The music and the routines were choreographed, mostly to songs from the present day. There were jazz, blues, hip hop, rock and roll, rhythm and blues, funk, soul, country, and even symphonic tracks in the routines. It was easy to start feeling good once the music was playing.

As a supplement to her individual rehearsals, Claudine made the one-hour drive to Manchester once a week to attend Glenda's Syncopation classes and workshops. Glenda was training groups of regular students, but there were also many women who were interested in becoming instructors training there. Because of Claudine's financial situation, Glenda was letting her take the classes for free in exchange for help setting up the room and demonstrating different exercises. Some days during rehearsals, if she was more frazzled than usual, Claudine could not remember her queues in time to the beat of the music. Sometimes she could not remember her routines at all. She'd chasse' left instead of right; box step forward instead of back. She'd be mad at herself for not getting things right every time, but regardless of that, after her Syncopation rehearsals, she always felt so much sharper and happier for the rest of her day. Glenda was an excellent, patient teacher, and she took a genuine, personal interest in Claudine.

One rainy and chilly afternoon, as she was in the middle of a Syncopation practice session at home in her front room, the phone rang.

"Hey, Mum!" Dempsey's voice said on the other end of the line. "I'm back home now; just got in with our Isabella from that Polynesian tour. I love it there. We need to take you there sometime - they'll treat you like a queen. It was beautiful weather, the food, the people were all fantastic!"

"Hello, stranger! Good to hear your voice. I've missed you. Sounds nice, like real paradise," panted Claudine, wiping beads of sweat from her brow. "I'm glad you liked it so much."

"Are you alright Mum? You sound, I don't know, maybe like someone was chasing you?" asked Dempsey.

"Yes, sorry, I just finished a workout," said Claudine.

"Oh, good, That's very good. I'm glad you are doin' that again," said Dempsey. "Listen, I won't keep you, let you get back to your workout, but I've got a surprise. Can you come by Toasty's for tea? I'm makin' me curry chicken with rice and diced potatoes, carrots, peas, those Granny apples, raisins, onions. I know how you like it, with all that stuff in it. And it's easy to make loads of it for all the new guests that are stayin' on at Toasty's. Isabella already promised she'd pick you up. So come round tonight and remember to bring Sally."

"That sounds really nice. I'll start getting ready now. Can't wait to see you and meet these new guests. If they're Samoaan, they'll be big lads. Yer Granddad would 'ave loved seein' 'em. Anyroad, I will start let you go and see you soon. Thanks, love ya! 'Tra"

"Love you too, Mum. T'ra!" Dempsey replied back.

Isabella called almost as soon as Claudine put the phone down.

"Hi, Mummy. I missed you!"

"Oh, hello Bella. Good gracious, I missed you too. I really did. I'm so glad to hear your voice. Seems like ages. I literally just put the phone down with Dempsey," said Claudine. "I felt so lonely while you all were gone. Glad you and Demps are back now, even though I heard it was paradise there…must be hard to come home to rain and wind like we're havin' today. Dempsey said he absolutely loved it. " asked Claudine.

"Oh, Samoa is absolute paradise. It was just beautiful," said Isabella rapturously. "The High Chief was so good to us and he treated us like we were royalty. Honest…he treated us like we were part of the Monarchy," laughed Isabella. "And we got some beltin' interviews with him too. When we talked about wrestlin', we were all speakin' the same language, even though he doesn't speak much English and I definitely don't speak Samoan. The High Chief's daughter is a princess and she is so beautiful. She does Polynesian dancin' and she tried to teach me and Mary, but we couldn't do it like she can; it's gorgeous watchin' when she dances and the High Chief played his ukulele. Then the fire dancers came out and the bongo drummers started. It was a big celebration for us and we got plenty of it filmed too. And Dempsey wrestled there and we got that filmed too. He was the foreigner in the ring, so the fans booed him. It was dead funny to see, ya know, cuz he's always the big hero everywhere he wrestles up here. So he took that as an excuse to wrestle like a villain. He did a good job, I must say. Anyway, Mum I promise to take you there one day."

"Maybe, if that's something we can manage without too much pain and sufferin' beforehand," said Claudine and she laughed. "Perhaps for me forty-fifth birthday you and Demps and I can go to Samoa. I would absolutely love to go there with you, when everything is better for everyone. A trip with you would give me somethin' to look forward to for sure. Anyway, Demps said you're going to pick me and Sally up and bring us round to Toasty's."

"Right, I'll be there soon! Give me an hour, right? I'm so excited to see you, Mum!"

"Same here," said Claudine with a smile. "I'll see you in a bit. You're a sweetheart Isabella. T'ra." said Claudine.

"You're a bigger sweetheart, so there," said Isabella and she quickly put the phone down before her mum could counter back.

At about four o'clock, Isabella pulled up to the cottage in a silver Ford Fiesta Toasty often lent out to visiting wrestlers. It was a standard with manual gears, so it made for a less than smooth ride, with Isabella pulling the clutch in and out while talking with a lot of hand gestures.

"Are you usin' kangaroo petrol?" Claudine asked as Isabella jerked through the gears, nearly making her mum sick.

"Crickey, you're as bad as Uncle Toasty with getting' car-sick. It's not me drivin', I can tell you that; so it must be you two," said Isabella as she hiccoughed through the gears. "So, how're ya doin' these days? Ya look great, have ya been workin' out more? 'ave ya been outside? Ya got some lovely colour to your face."

"I am feelin' better," admitted Claudine. "I'm just workin' on a little summat and I will say that it does involve a lot of dancin' about, an' watchin' the telly. You can let Uncle Toasty know that's what I get up to all day, watch telly an' dance about the front room. I'm sure it'll stir up some sort o' controversy."

"Tell me more, Mum," begged Isabella. "What are you up to?"

"No, no, I can't say just yet," Claudine teased. "When I get it right, I'll tell you first, before anyone else. It's just a bit of inspirational movin' about, let's put it that way, that I'm workin' on at the moment."

When mother, daughter, and dog pulled into the farm, Toasty came out to greet them wearing a flashy, custom-made stunning silky-sheer leopard-print dress shirt and a gold chain around his neck. His hair was gelled up into its usual short spikes. Claudine looked at him with trepidation as she got out of the car; sometimes, she was still intimidated by her brother. Not always knowing for sure whether to hug him or not, she held out a hand. He scoffed.

"What's that? Don't be cheeky. Give us a proper hug," he said, wrapping his sister in a loving bear hug. He lifted her right off the ground, leaving her feet dangling for a moment before he set her back down.

"Now, let's see - I hear if I offer you a glass of red wine, you won't turn me down. So, can I offer you a glass of wine?" he said slyly as he herded his sister in the house.

"Where did you hear that? Not that I'm disagreein' with you," said Claudine with a laugh. Barely in the door, Claudine could already hear laughing and talking, but not all the voices were recognizable. The friendly old mansion was full of life today, just as her dad and mum would have wanted it to be.

"Your Dempsey said ya had a few glasses o' wine with Aaron whenever he came round to see you an' then ya really came into yer own," teased Toasty.

"Dempsey, what are ya talkin' about? I wasn't fallin' down drunk or anythin' like that!" said Claudine bashfully to her son, who was laughing as he handed her a round goblet of burgundy wine. "We were only watchin' tele an' relaxin' with a sip o' wine." She tasted the wine and nodded her head to indicate it was delicious-tasting red wine; she playfully disputed her son's claims

"No one said you were fallin' down drunk, Mum, but when you relaxed a bit, you sounded really quite cute. I heard you'd laugh dead loud, impersonate people, and skip about like a March hare in front of Aaron and Demp. I was glad to hear you were havin' some fun and letting loose," Isabella said as she handed her mum a tall-stemmed goblet of chilled white wine. Now she was holding and sipping away at two drinks. She smiled. It seemed like all was right in the world for them today.

"Speaking of Aaron, did you ever hear what happened to that Yankee bastard Maybe he's not a bastard, but he's a bloody tosser, fuckin' off the way he did, leaving you engaged to him but makin' a right bollocks of it all? Did he go to a Bolivian prison or is he some sort of secret spy-agent mystery man working for some royal dynasty in Napal now since he fucked off into nowhere land without any reason?" asked Toasty sarcastically as they walked into the dining room. A loud and laughing Toasty seemed to indicate the wine he was drinking was helping him come into his own as well. Claudine didn't bother to answer him but she was slightly amused at his sly comments. Her many little sips of red and white wine were already making her feel as ease. She didn't know herself what became of Aaron but Toasty's sarcasm towards him didn't seem undeserved. Thinking about him at the moment didn't make her feel anxious. Maybe she was starting to get over him.

In the huge dining room, around a long cherry oak table, Claudine saw the familiar face of Mary, alongside of Dempsey and Isabella. All looked stunning with their fresh tans from paradise. She recognized Dino standing near to them, leaning his hand on the captain's chair in front of the table. He was talking to the huge Samoaan men. The Samoan giants were standing near the radiator by the big double glazed window overlooking the green gardens. The newcomers looked nearly identical, except one had long hair and the other had short hair. Both were dressed in big woolly sweatshirts, track pants, and Polynesian sandals and they looked right at home playing with the dogs and holding the cats on their thick, wide shoulders. They smiled and showed impressively healthy teeth as white as coconut meat.

Dempsey approached his mum and took her goblets of wine out her hands. "Let me crack yer back, Mum," he offered, as he gave her a big hug from behind. She had her arms folded and he lifted her up off the ground and in a quick, gentle motion squeezed her. Her back made a noise like ice cracking.

"Ohhhh, I felt that, Mum. You needed an adjustment," said Dempsey, proud of himself.

"Ahhhh, that felt good, Demps. Ta" said Claudine gratefully as she rolled her shoulders up and down, reflecting he had adjusted body her wonderfully. She felt like she was straight and upright again. She picked up one of her glass of red wine, leaving the other on the table momentarily as Dempsey started making introductions.

"Mum, this is the surprise! Look who we brought back with us from Samoa. The big wrestlers came closer to Claudine. "This is Leilani. 'L' for *long* hair, right? And this is Sui–ee – 'S' for *short* hair, that way you can remember who is who. They look alike pretty much, except for their hair and Leilani is the older brother in their family. They're gettin' used to our British accents, but they don't understand why our rain is so cold," laughed Dempsey. Claudine shook hands with these gentle giants.

"They like the cats so much because the cats kept them warm and I'm still doing great with the animals too. Not a single sneeze or watery eye. It's like a bloody miracle!" said Isabella, as though she had accomplished something in not getting sick by animal fur. Claudine laughed as Mary came up to say hello.

"So, what do you think of the teddy bears we brought back from the Islands? "Aren't they scrumptious?" Mary whispered to Claudine.

"Mary has fallen for Sui-ee; they're courtin', but she doesn't want her dad to know, not just yet, eh?" said Isabella quietly into Claudine's other ear. "Her dad would think it was too soon; ultra-conservative, he is."

"They seem very nice, Mary," said Claudine sincerely, giving her daughter a look of pleasant surprise. Dino appeared then, carrying a fresh glass of golden-coloured wine.

"Claudine, you have to try this," he said, handing her a glass. "It's all the way from America; Michigan Reisling, actually. Great white wines there, one of my wrestler friends turned me on to it..."

Claudine graciously took the glass, even though she was still working on her first two glasses. Claudine remembered she had not accepted his invitation to take her out for a day at the

Rugby match and then to dinner. She hoped the evening was not going to be uncomfortable for either of them when Dino winked quite deliberately at her, twice in a row. She wasn't sure how to receive his winks. She awkwardly sipped out of both of her glasses of her wine.

"Thank you, it is absolutely delicious," she said. "It's your first time to the farm?"

"No, not by any means; I've been out here a few times now," said Dino. "Was first here many years back, when your dad was still wrestling. I brought a couple big, powerful lads out to train with him. They'd been with him in the ring 'bout an hour, then they ran off, yelping and a whimpering, with their tails between their legs. I wouldn't have believed it, if I hadn't seen it with my own eyes," he said with a laugh. "I didn't really believe a man of your dad's age, because he was getting' on in years at that time, could beat one of these young lads, let alone both of them."

"He was tough, that's for certain. He was one of those who truly forgot more than most people remembered when it came to his wrestling," said Claudine, smiling.

Dino gestured over to Dempsey, who was engaged in disjointed but enthusiastic conversation with Sui-ee and Leilani. The language barrier was an obvious obstacle but they were managing comfortably.

"I wasn't surprised when I saw the same thing happen again with your son, Dempsey. I met him and his trainer at Roach's Gym, and they were looking for big blokes to spar with, for the Absolute Best championship. So, next day, I bring some of my hardest bouncers in and before I know it, your Dempsey has 'em tapping out, screaming '*uncle*' and crying for their lives. They didn't even get a single punch in, neither of 'em." Dino laughed again, shrugging his big shoulders. "It was bloody amazing how easy he beat 'em. It wasn't just those first two I brought down, but all of 'em I recruited every day for a fortnight for him to spar with before CrazyBest. I was impressed and I'll tell you that for nothin,' luv."

"Yes, he takes after his grandfather and father," said Claudine. "I couldn't be prouder of him."

"In my day, I was a tough bugger too," said Dino, puffing his chest out like a gorilla. "I would have liked to have given wrestling a try, but rugby was where I ended up. It's what my passion was. And I can't complain, I've done good by it. So, tell me, whatcha do these days fer passion?" he said with a sly smile and another hard wink.

"Well, I love to paint and draw and when Drew was alive, I really loved trainin' with him," said Claudine. "I always looked forward to it. It never seemed like work, even though we worked out dead hard most of the time. I might like to get back into somethin' like that again. Here's to hoping," she said and put her two wine glasses in the air, tasting splashes of both.

Dino, however, didn't seem to take in a single word she said. "The first time I camc out here, I saw you, actually," he said, stepping a closer to Claudine. She noticed he didn't drink to her little effort to make a sociable 'cheers.' She leaned back away from him as he leaned forward towards her. She was sort of intrigued by him, but she couldn't help but feel shy around his bolder actions.

"I had this Bulgarian bloke with me, who was into the Greco-Roman style wrestling. He was working on the docks and I noticed the cauliflower ears on him. I asked him if he played rugby, or maybe boxed, and he said it was from his amateur wrestling days. So he asked me about your dad, if I knew him, like. I said I did. I ended up taking him up to meet Billy. They got to talking and then doing some wrestling. You were so small then and you kept coming out of the house with angry messages from your mum. Do you remember any of this, luv?" he asked as Claudine shook her head to indicate she did not recall it.

"It seemed like hours had gone by, and I'm being straight with you when I tell you that your dad and this bloke were still putting holds, when you came out again and said, 'Dad, Mum's throwing your wrestling boots and all your gear out the bedroom window and she says she's going to set your wardrobe on fire if you don't come in the house and help her.' And then she came out the house and, dainty as she was, she marched up to us and gave your dad a swift swat on his arm. I told her right then and there that I knew she was mad as a bee trapped in a bottle because we'd been keeping Billy so long. I told her my name and said what a pleasure it was to meet her and that we'd only be a few more hours. I was kidding with her like, but she swatted your Billy again and went back into the house. Well, I just roared," said Dino, who was beside himself again with laughter, just at retelling the story. "It was bloody funny; I'll tell you that for nothing, sunshine! God, what a fun lady your mum was! Do you remember now?" His face was red and his dark brown eyes were watering from laughing so hard. He gasped and caught his composure after a moment of jovial demonstration.

"Vaguely," admitted Claudine. There had been quite a few episodes like that between her mum and dad, that Claudine remembered bits and pieces of. Unfortunately, she couldn't remember Dino ever being up at her dad's house. She wished she could have heard her father and mother's thoughts about this Greek man. She felt like he might have been fun for her father to wrestle about with on the mat in the barn. She couldn't imagine her mum being too charmed by him, however. Her Louisa was just too reserved to ever make a lot of conversation with the colourful characters who came upon their open house. Aside from the ones who lived on the estate, like Lobo the old mechanic and Kevin the welder. Besides, Louisa Bonham was too busy working in the IWF office in the upstairs of the house; and worrying everything from the wrestling business to the politics of Britain to the economy of the world. Claudine was lost in her thoughts about her mum and dad when she heard Dino asking her a question. I said, did your mum do that often, come out and swat your dad? Did she say anything about me when you were all back inside the house? Do you remember what she said, your mum?" Dino asked, hopefully.

"Sorry, I can't remember," said Claudine, wondering herself.

"Well, anyway, that was me first time up here. And that was years ago. Not a whole lot has changed and I see there's still loads of the animals running amok. Do you keep any of the animals for a profit?"

"What?" Claudine asked. She thought she had misheard him.

"Do you sell any of the livestock for beef, poultry, eggs, wool, mutton – you see where I'm going with this luv? Your brother Toasty could make them cost–effective to keep if he had a few of them slaughtered now and again, to pay for their feed and maintaining of the whole lot," Dino said matter-of-factly.

Claudine looked at him, shocked. Dino looked back at her and put on a face like he was a teacher talking to a difficult student. He opened his eyes wide and expectantly. "You see, sunshine, if you take two or three of them when they're ready for slaughter and sell them for whatever you can--"

"I know what you mean, but we've never ever, ever killed any of our animals," Claudine interjected. "They give us milk and eggs, a bit of wool, but we only sheared the sheep a couple times, like it was more Toasty's and my idea…and the cow, she gave us some milk, but she had it for her calf most of all. We did love the fresh cream from her. And we had goat milk too. But, we grew up with 'em, like they were our pets, cuz they were, they still are. They're our friends. We'd never eat them, that'd be cruel." She gave Sally, who was sitting next to her, a protective pat on the head for emphasis.

"But I've had roast beef and steaks out here with Toasty before and I see your family having chicken curry tonight," pointed out Dino. "So how can you be so cheeky with me? Bit of hypocrite, aye?" he asked, grinning slyly, like he had her beat. He gave her another hard wink.

"We don't kill our animals," insisted Claudine. "That's not why we have 'em here on our farm with us. Our animals are a part of our family!" She was getting annoyed.

"Hey, Dino, look what Uncle Toasty sent over for you," said Dempsey suddenly, taking Dino's goblet of wine away and sticking a nice big frosted mug of cold Irish cider, filled right up to the very top, into Dino's hand instead. Sally gave Dempsey a playful lick and Dempsey got down and pounded his fists on the floor. The dog responded in kind and in a few moments she was all wound up, jumping up and down from the chesterfield and around the room like she was a puppy again. Dino watched with a mix of surprise and disapproval.

"Well, sunshine, if it's fish you prefer, then I'll take you out on me yacht and maybe do a bit of fishing," said Dino, raising his eyebrows up and down twice as if he was offering her a major treat. "I've got a massive sailboat too, you know, and we can float about in it while I explain the ways of world to you. They say the world is our oyster, or is that being cruel to oysters?" he laughed and then gave Claudine a nudge on her arm and another wink. "I'm only joking with you, sunshine. Don't know about you, but I feel bloody great tonight!"

In a moment, though, his mirth was gone. "When you see me putting up those sails and navigating my Vanessa - that's the name of me boat - you'll see wrestlers aren't the only fish in the sea," he said meaningfully. "I hear you've a boyfriend who's almost a wrestler, that trainer lad. Tell me, how much money does he–"

Luckily Claudine didn't have to answer, because Sally, who was still very wound up and playful chose that moment to jump right up on Dino, spilling his cold cider ale all over himself, even on his face. "Bloody hell," he yelled, setting the glass down on the nearest flat surface and shaking cider off of his hand. Mary, laughing hysterically, rushed out to grab a towel from the kitchen.

The evening did get better for Dino, though, after he managed to scope out a seat next to Claudine at the long dinner table. She listened as Dino told her about his ex–wife and how much she loathed rugby, but didn't mind all the money it brought in and the celebrity lifestyle it gave her. He talked about his many tattoos and how getting each one made him even tougher, and how he got his first one, £1,000,000 in greenish-black ink tattooed on his right forearm after he made his first million pounds many years ago. Claudine didn't get in a word edgewise, but she didn't try to; she had had a few glasses of wine and it was nice to relax and let someone else do the talking. Dino was a real character and he seemed to enjoy being a part of things. The only part that really kept Claudine at a distance from him was his body odour. She almost relled herself when she caught a whiff of his pungent body odour that smelled like strong sweat and onions. She wondered if his velour track suit was making him sweat more. She was curious to know if Toasty, Dempsey or Isabella smelled it as well.

"So, luv," he said after he had talked for a half hour straight, "I started to ask you earlier about your boyfriend, but I thought I overheard Toasty say he was not really in the picture anymore. He's gone overboard, has he? Is he AWOL, MIA?"

"Oh, Aaron?" said Claudine. "He's gone 'abroad' to Frankfurt, or Switzerland, now. He first went to Frankfurt a few months back to train some lads who found out about him through CrazyBest." Dino listened and Toasty tuned in too, as Claudine, who had enjoyed at least three glasses of red and white wine went on about how Aaron's cauliflower ears made him look like koala bear and how he fed their little kitten protein shakes off his finger. Both men thought this was nauseating.

When the evening came to an end, Dino overheard Claudine asking Isabella for a ride home. "Toasty, Dempsey, Isabella," he said grandiosely, “It would be my honour to drive your Claudine home. I can be trusted to get her home safely.”

“Thank you, that’s very kind,” Claudine said, catching a sincere look from Isabella. “It’s just a ride home,” she muttered in her daughter’s ear. “It’ll be alright. But you’ll be home soon, right?”“

“Well, Mum, I was actually going to stay here and drive to Mary’s flat since it’s closer to here than the cottage is. We’re workin’ on the documentary first thing in the morning” said Isabella. Uncle Toasty said it was fine with him if I stayed. I was gonna sleep in your old bedroom. Is that alright?”

“Oh, of course, luv. I’m kind o’ touched that you’ll be sleepin’ in my old bed. It’s pretty comfortable in there,” said Claudine with a smile.

“So, does anyone object to me taking Claudine home?” asked Dino, raising his voice over the side-conversations going on.

“That’s fine with me,” said Dempsey, as he and Toasty exchanged meaningful smiles. He quietly said in his mum’s ear, hugging her, “I’ll babysit Sally, Mum, if you don’t mind. I don’t think Dino would want her in his car.” They fondly bid the pair farewell and watched them walk out into the cool night, but it wasn’t raining anymore.

Dino opened the car door up for Claudine and helped her in, even reaching in and buckling up her seat belt for her. Claudine looked back over to the house and saw Dempsey, Toasty, and Isabella casually leaning their backsides on the slate windowsill, pretending not to watch. She suspected Dempsey and Toasty would be smirking with boyish silliness and Isabella would maybe just have her fingers crossed. She knew they would all be hoping it could turn into something more, but she tried not to read into it too much at this point. There were things already about Dino that she wasn’t sure if she could like, such as his awkwardness around animals. When he called her ‘sunshine’ it didn’t thrill her the way it did when Aaron called her ‘darling’. It was just a drive home she reminded herself, nothing more.

Dino got in to the driver’s seat and fastened himself up. Then the pair began a quiet and acutely uncomfortable ride back to Claudine’s, because of the silence. Dino, who was normally so chatty, was silent for once, and the only time Claudine really said anything was when she was giving Dino directions to the cottage.

As hard as Dino had tried to make himself appealing to her that evening, Claudine couldn't help but think about Drew and Aaron and how much Dino was not like them. She missed Drew so much right now; she missed his big thick torso, his meaty hands, his sweet smile and beautiful hazel eyes, and his absolutely wicked sense of dry sarcastic British humour. She had been completely herself with Drew, more than anyone else in the world. He would have had a picnic with Dino by pulling pranks on him, making him into his friend. Aaron, who was also so different from Drew, but still was very much on the same page she was on, but Dino was not on that same page. Dino just didn't seem to connect with her.

About halfway through the drive, Dino noticed Claudine pulling on her seatbelt where it met her collarbone.

"Is it not fastened proper, luv?" he asked, nearly slowing the motorcar to a complete stop

"No, it's just a bit tight around me waist, so I'm loosenin' it a touch from up here," said Claudine, pointing to her collarbone.

"You've got to keep it secure right down in front of your pelvis, luv, and your shoulder too, but it shouldn't be tight around your tummy. Let's take a look," offered Dino, reaching towards her.

"No, this is fine, yes, I've got it, thanks," said Claudine in a rush. She immediately thought of how she never heard her Drew or her father use the word 'tummy;' it was always a 'gut' or a 'stomach' in her family. Or how the headmistress at school would tell her and Toasty to sit on their marshmallows instead of their buttocks or bottoms. It made her grin a bit.

As Dino pulled up to Claudine's home, he started to act nervous. "Thank you for a lovely, lovely evening," he said. "It was really, really lovely, except for the animals and all the fur on me clothes. But even so, Claudine, I can't remember when I've had such a really, really, good, lovely time and I'll tell you that for nothing," he said as he parked the car. "As a gentleman that I am, let me get the door for you and I'll escort you to your home safely, as I promised everyone. I'm a man of my word and a gentleman."

"Oh, you're all right, Dino. I can see meself in from here," said Claudine. The path up to the house is a bit dodgy, especially at night.

"No, no luv, I'm old school, as I'm sure you are," insisted Dino. Claudine wasn't sure if that was supposed to be a compliment or not.

"Well, I have a few noisy, protective farm animals, so just never mind them if they make a fuss," Claudine warned Dino. "I have a donkey, Emily; a rooster, Cicero; and a hen, Henrietta; and some more animals inside the house. Emily the donkey and Cicero the rooster really love Karaoke nights in town; they've been known to stagger home spiffed from all the ale after a good night of singin' for prize money. It's hard for Cicero though, since he has to get up early, right at the crack of noon," she said, looking sideways at Dino.

Dino looked at her with a baffled expression. "You're having me on or are you being serious? I can't bloody tell with you or your family, when your bloody joking or not, especially with your bloody animals. You stay put," he said and he got out of the car, rolling his ankle slightly on the uneven dirt road as he walked around the front of his Bently.

"Oops," said Claudine to herself and pretended she had not noticed as he opened the car door for her.

When her door was opened, Claudine could hear Cicero the rooster, as if on cue, crowing. Claudine smiled and took it as a sign from Drew.

"I beg your bloody pardon? You weren't kiddin' when ya said yahad a rooster. You're like Pippi Longstocking," exclaimed Dino, taking her hand and helping her out of the car. "'ave you got a pet monkey as well? Let me 'elp ya with gettin' things in order 'round here, luv. This's a piggin' animal farm."

"Well, actually, you could help me get a job," Claudine blurted out as she started toward the door. "Oh, I shouldn't have said that. I've got a bit of work through Toasty and the odd little job here and there. But I'd like to find a nice, secure job in top of what I do for Toasty that pays well. I need to come up with money for somethings straight away. But everything here at home is just where it should be, nice and disorganized. Home sweet home, eh?" She suddenly wondered if Dino could really help her get a good job that paid well, just for a little while, with all of his connections. She needed to come up with money to buy her Syncopation franchise and have for rent money for a studio once she found a place.

"Listen Claudia or Claudine, whatever the bloody hell it is. Sorry luv, I get mixed up, I'll come round tomorrow an' we can talk about it more," she heard Dino saying as he followed behind. "What sort of office skills do ya've? Oh, never mind, I'll jus' come round tomorrow an' we'll get it all sorted. We can have a meal in town. Make a proper day out, eh?"

He spoke as Claudine hurriedly walked ahead of him to her front door. Dino stayed right behind her, vocalizing about the importance of networking. She was trying to get ahead so much she had no idea what he was on about. All she could hear was him saying, "Networking! Networking! Networking!" She just wanted to get inside and see her cats.

She turned around to Dino as she reached her front door. He was directly behind her. "Well, I have a job interview tomorrow, so I'm not sure what kind of day out we can have, but–"

"Who's it *wiv* , luv?" Dino interrupted. "I can pu a call in t 'em an' make sure they treat cha proper, an' not give ya the bullocks treatment, alreet?? Ah know, cuz truth be told, I've done it myself to loads o' people who I've interviewed. Made my mind up not to hire someone b'fore they even sat down. I've can be a rum bugger sometimes, eh?" Claudine wasn't sure if Dino was a bit drunk, because some of his words seemed slurred, although his driving had been perfect.

Claudine was fumbling for her keys to fit in the front door lock when Dino cornered her in the doorway. He put his hands on the top of her shoulders and attempted to turn her around.

"Er, umm, the job, umm, I'm not sure who it's with, I think a staffing agency," stammered Claudine, still trying get the door lock to open when Dino successfully turned her around. "I'd have to check me email, umm, to see who it's with and where it is."

Dino closed his eyes and leaned in as if to kiss her, so she darted her face over to the left. "Maybe you could write me a letter of reference, or recommendation. That would be all I'd need and you wouldn't have to trouble yourself with drivin' all the way out here from Birmingham."

Dino opened his eyes. In the dark, they looked as black as coal. "It's Manchester where I live now, silly girl, but tell ya what, luv; I'll do both. And I'd be honoured if you'd le' me end this smashin', lovely evenin' with a kiss. Give us a kiss, eh?" He started closing his eyes and leaning in again.

"Well, see, about the kiss," said Claudine, who was now caught in some sort of hug with Dino without knowing why or how she had gotten in this position. The smell of his oniony body odor hit her again and in all this awkwardness, she immediately wondered if Dino wore deodorant. "You see, Dino, well, I've still not moved on from Aaron; not at all, actually. He was me fiancée before he left for Germany, and well, I just am not ready to be kissin' anyone else right now. He's always on me mind, well, either him or Drew. Wow, it's getting late. I hope you didn't think this was a date. Oh, heavens I didn't mean for that to rhyme, Well, I best be getting in. But thank you so much, Dino. You got me home, safe and sound; I'll ring the kids up and let them know."

Dino, who had given up trying to kiss Claudine, laughed and let her go. "Ya don't know 'ow cute ya look, gettin' all piggin' nervous. I know, I know you've talked about this Aaron bloke all night, an' I've been warned an' told by everyone that you're not really interested in anyone else right now, but I will get you for my own, no bloody mistake there. Once that happens, you'll never want anyone but me. At he end o' the day, he's not a patch on me, an' I'll tell ya that fer nothin'!

"Let me take y' out fer a meal tomorrow, jus' t' give ya a nice break, an' I'll see if I can 'elp ya wiv findin' work," he said to Claudine's back as she finally turned herself around and turned the skeleton key in the lock. "I'll come round fer ya in th'mornin'. Do ya like Italian food? Do ya 'ave any food allergies?"

"No, I don't have any food allergies at all, although I am allergic to vacuums," she said as she narrowly slipped in the door. Unfortunately, he managed to come through the door too, pushing it wide open.

"Never 'eard o' allergies to vacuums," he said blankly.

"Never mind; I should let you be on your way, as you've got a long road ahead of you tonight. So, ermm, I will get Isabella to call you in the mornin' to give you me email address, or I will get yours from her. We'll sort it out, umm, but I'll let you go now and thank you so much for the lift home." She was trying to ease him back out the door.

"Luv, this 'as been a magical night," said Dino, taking her hand and pulling her back outside the doorway with him as she was pushing him out. He pulled up her hands to his mouth and kissed her delicate wrists, then he pulled Claudine in, putting one hand on the back of her head. Before Claudine could protest, he was kissing her right on her lips, trying to slip his fat, warm, sticky tongue into her mouth. His breath smelled of alcohol and his scratchy chin hairs chafed against her skin. She put both hands on his chest and pushed him away, wiping her mouth with the back of her hand.

"Sorry luv…, no, I take that back… I'm not really sorry for stealin' a kiss from you," said Dino, winking at her affectionately. "I'll see ya tomorrow, luv." He strutted back to his car, looking remarkably like Cicero the Rooster with his cocky gait. Claudine quickly got in her house and solidly closed and locked the door behind her, shaking her head in disbelief.

Buffy cautiously peered out from underneath the chesterfield. Claudine, still wiping Dino's kiss off her lips, kneeled down to greet her. The little cat immediately smelled her face inquisitively and then scurried out from under the chesterfield, darting straight up the stairs. Buffy's stomach was very low to the ground as she ran away, disappearing under Claudine's bed.

"Oh Buffy, come on now. I would never kiss anyone back now, except for your papa," Claudine said to her hiding kitten. She lit the gas fire and then turned on her computer. She waited for her email to open. She checked it for the address of the job interview. She copied it down on a piece of paper to take with her tomorrow. She also forwarded it off to Isabella, asking her to forward it to Dino. Once that was done, she lay down on the big brown velvet chesterfield that Drew had custom-made at one of the big chesterfield shops in Manchester in their glory days. She fell asleep waiting for Buffy to come back down.

10

The Right Girl For Me

The next morning, Claudine was still sleeping on the chesterfield. What a wonderful slumber she awoke from. She was quite warm, still in her coat and still wearing the shoes she wore last night.

Claudine felt Buffy above her head, preening her warm little body. Mr. Wonderful was solidly sitting in the crook of her arm, sound asleep. Slowly, Claudine got up and put Mr. Wonderful, mostly still asleep onto the chesterfield next to Buffy. She walked to the back kitchen to put the kettle on. Feeling rather overheated, from being asleep in front of the fire and having the cats sleeping on her while she was still in her winter coat, she promptly went outside to visit Emily. She had just finished giving Emily a nice brushing when a car pulled up. It was Dino's pulling up in a huge BMW sedan.

Why the hell didn't Cicero crow? pondered Claudine as she saw her rooster casually and crowless, strutting around the side of the barn. She darted back inside the cottage, panicking over her appearance. Buffy, who had been on the kitchen table waiting for her breakfast, leapt off and ran straight up the stairs to hide under the bed. The little cat sensed something was out of sorts this morning.

In an instant, Dino abruptly rapping the brass knocker at her front door. Claudine rushed over, sliding and nearly doing the splits to keep herself from wiping out on her Syncopation DVD case lying on the Oriental rug. She lifted her leg up and down, making sure she hadn't pulled her groin and unlocked the front door. Dino pushed his way in, as if to help her get it open. "Morning luv! Bit early, but you know, seize the day," he said. At the moment, Dino reminded Claudine of a friendly dog that kept coming into the kitchen.

"*Carpe diem*, my foot," Claudine retorted.

"Oh, I see you know a bit of French, eh? I speak a bit of French, you know, from my former wife speaking it," said Dino amicably. "If you need any help with your pronunciations, or any other French things involving the tongue, just give me the nod and I'll teach you all I know." Dino laughed as though he had just told a brilliant joke.

"Isn't *carpe diem* Latin?" Claudine asked, still hot in her winter jacket.

"No, sunshine, it's French. Like I said, me ex was French, so I know all about the French language. Not so much written, but spoken, I do know that. But it's funny you'd think it was Latin. That language hasn't been around for ages, luv. It doesn't exist anymore. But never mind, I still think you're dead clever." Dino gabbled on. He was suddenly more vexing than she thought two minutes ago, when he was just a friendly dog.

"No, I'm pretty sure *carpe diem* is Latin, not French. And Latin still very much exists, just English is the dominant language in the world now," retorted Claudine.

"Listen, luv, I'm Greek and I know all about the English language, and French and what I really want to talk about is how 'bout I fix us a nice cup of coffee while you go upstairs and clean yourself up? I've been up since five a.m. and already read the paper. Go on now, there's a good girl, eh?"

Eager to change out of last night's clothes, Claudine took a deep breath and started up the stairs. "If you want, you can get caught up on all the gossip with the farm animals outside," she called down. "They're terrible gossips, but they only speak Latin," Claudine called out from the stairway.

"Oh, I never gossip - it's a nasty habit!" he called back without a trace of his own sarcasm or appreciating her own sarcasm.

"Whatever," mumbled Claudine. She brushed her teeth and washed her face, put a little makeup on and changed into a simple light blue cashmere jumper with a hood that Isabella bought for her. "He's not for me! He's not for me!" she repeated to herself. Finally she sighed and shook her head slightly as she headed back downstairs.

When she came back into the kitchen, Dino gave her an obvious once-over, staring blatantly at her chest. Claudine sweater was so basic and hardly form-fitted dress, was very uncomfortable with his staring.

"I got the big moggy off the table," he said.

"Oh, that's Mr. Wonderful; he's part cat, part superhero and he's always allowed on the table," said Claudine.

"Oh? Really? Well, anyway, luv, tell you what, instead of me making us a brew, let's go out and find a place that serves all–day breakfasts. I'll get you some food supplies for your kitchen, shall we? I've cleared out my whole schedule today." He looked about at all the clutter and disorganization with distaste; it almost seemed like he didn't want to eat anything prepared in her rustic kitchen. "You're missing quite a few kitchen essentials, as I noticed while I was having a root around for a clean cup. We definitely need to reorganize for the sake of efficiency. Ever heard of K.I.S.S? Keep it simple, stupid," Dino chuckled. "I'm keen on micromanaging and keeping things in order. In a home, *micro-managing* is as important as *networking* is to business. Micromanaging saves time and money, and I'll tell you that for nothing."

"Getting back to my cat, Mr. Wonderful, being on the table," Claudine sighed loudly, "Well, I feed him and Buffy on the table because Sally the bull terrier will eat their food if it's on the floor."

"Then, tell the hound 'no'! You and your family need to train your dogs to behave and let them know who the master is," said Dino flatly. "We are king of beasts. That saying didn't just invent itself, you know. And if you started to see it that way, then you won't have the moggies on your table and doggies jumping about."

"The animals and I all have equal shares in the company, eh, Mr. Wonderful?" said Claudine, as she swept Mr. Wonderful off the floor and put him back on the table. This time, Dino did laugh a bit.

"Well, sunshine, let's go get you some breakfast," he said, staring again at her breasts. She put her coat on and quickly buttoned it up to her chin.

Dino took Claudine all around Chester that day. At his insistence, they stopped at several home goods stores after breakfast. Many times, Claudine told Dino it was not proper for her to be accepting so many gifts from him, but he ignored her protests and continued shopping. He charitably picked up some useful items for her, including a new toaster, but always the ones or colours that he liked best. If Claudine said the blue one, for example, he would say the red one was better. He also seemed fixated on stocking up her cleaning supplies, spending several pounds on disinfectant, wipes, and brushes.

"I have got vinegar, baking soda and lemon juice at home that I put in spray bottles and clean with that," said Claudine. "I do clean, ya know?"

"Bloody hell, luv, that's going to do nothing but make a pasty mess. You need these things to make your home clean and sanitary. And I'll tell you that for nothing. Now just let me get these things for you. Maybe you'll enjoy cleaning once you see how nice you can make things look." Dino said, trying to be helpful. Claudine didn't argue. She remembered when she used to buy cleaning supplies when Drew was alive because they made her house smell nice. After much opening and smelling of cleaning supplies, including things like laundry detergents, fabric softeners, washing-up liquid, sudsy hand cleaners, shampoo and conditioner, etc. Claudine agreed to let Dino buy her a shopping buggy full of new smelling products to clean her home with. She felt happy. It seemed to make Dino happy too.

After shopping, Dino took her to her job interview. A friendly recruiter welcomed them soon after they entered the office. "Hallo, I'm Susan," she said brightly. "Pleased to meet you, Claudine. Come this way, to our conference room."

"Did you have a chance to call anyone here about me?" Claudine asked under her breath as she walked past Dino to meet Susan.

"Didn't think you needed it. Good luck," Dino called to Claudine as she walked away. Claudine saw him look at his mobile phone and begin tapping away at it as she left. Despite his claims that he knew everyone who was anyone in the workforce and he could get her a good job with just a phone call, Claudine wondered if maybe Dino didn't know everyone in his 'networking' world of business.

In the conference room, Susan gave Claudine a typing test and asked her to show her aptitude on some bookkeeping and accounting computer programs. She made several notes on a clipboard and eventually looked smartly up at Claudine.

"Right then, very good, Claudine," she said. "You have great typing skills, dead accurate, but your computer skills are a bit too basic for what we need right now. We will keep your resume on file, though, and we will call you if something comes up." She shook Claudine's hand as she walked her back to where Dino was.

"Well, how did it go, luv?" asked Dino, even though Claudine's face plainly said it all.

"Oh, not as cold and impersonal as most, but nothing really promising," said Claudine.

Dino didn't comment any further on the job situation. Instead, he announced he was ready for some lunch. Claudine wondered why he even bothered to come with her on her job interview.

"Listen, luv, now that the job interview is over, you'll feel loads better after you get a hot meal in you and relax," he said as they got back on the road. "I've called ahead to an Italian restaurant of mine to make sure they have the red carpet rolled out for us. That should wipe the frown off your face."

"Oh, I just feel like I shouldn't be counting on you for buying me cleaning supplies and food, or expecting you to make calls for me job interviews. I should be doin' me own buying and makin' me own way, like," said Claudine. She was mostly annoyed that Dino hadn't helped her with the job interview as he promised. But she also remembered Aaron's last email, telling her to not depend on anyone but herself, first and foremost. She knew she was lacking in office skills not because of Dino, but because of her own doing.

"I don't mind buying you things, you know. I want to help you. I can clearly see by your bare cupboards you need plenty of help. Yes indeed, plenty of help, and it's not going to fall out of the sky for you neither. You can feel free to ask me for anything, you know. Anything, and I'd do it for you. I don't think you're a lazy girl, just very disorganized and untidy. You need to establish some sort of order, luv. You need some proper management…"

Claudine tuned Dino out as he rambled on. Before he began lecturing her, she was almost tempted to ask him for a loan for the Syncopation, but she disliked him too much at the moment for calling her untidy. She silently waffled back and forth in her mind. She appreciated that he spent a bon on nice things that day for her home. But she was reluctant to owe him for a favour as big as borrowing a few thousand pounds for her Syncopation business. It could become complicated with everyone else, from Isabella and Mary's friendship to Toasty and Dempsey doing business with Dino. Claudine decided to not even go there.

When they pulled up to the restaurant, Claudine was surprised to see there really was a red carpet rolled out for them. Inside, the warm atmosphere and wafting smells of garlic and baking bread embraced Claudine—like a kind, Italian grandmother. Just as when they were shopping for things for her house, Dino also made sure Claudine had everything *he* wanted her to have, ordering her spaghetti Napolitano and some really nice Italian red wine without asking what she wanted; he ordered a sirloin steak and a jacket potato for himself.

"Trust me with what I order for you. You might think you know good Italian, but I'm really the expert here. I not just saying that because I've been around the world. No, it's because I own the restaurant and I know what's good here and what's goooood here," said Dino, as if he was reading Claudine's mind. Even though Claudine had no choice in the matter, the food was absolutely delicious and the wine he picked paired perfectly with her meal. Dino drank beer, but he asked Claudine if he could pour her another glass of wine.

"Thank you Dino, for planning this all. It's delicious."

"Are you enjoying it, luv?" asked Dino, without looking up from his own food. He was stuffing it in his mouth with authority.

"I am enjoying it. Thank you, yes. And if you don't mind, I'd like to propose a toast," said Claudine. The wine was making her very relaxed and a bit brazen. She was far from a toastmaster; in fact, she hardly ever made toasts to anyone outside of her own family.

Claudine was about to say, "Cheers and thank you, Dino, for a lovely day." But Dino didn't give her the chance.

"That's a thought, Claudine, but if you don't mind, I'll make the toast. Let us raise our glasses and toast to you, Claudine Bellamy, a bloody fine lady!" He clinked his beer mug with Claudine's wine glass, sipped his beer, and smiled for a moment at her before carrying on again with his meal.

Claudine took a little sip of her wine and chuckled to herself, thinking of how Drew would have been amused at her being described as "a bloody fine lady." She could see Dino was trying hard, although he didn't seem to have heard a word she said throughout their meal. She tried not to talk too much about her beloved Drew, but it was Dino who kept bringing up Claudine's previous love life. It was Dino who kept bringing up Aaron's name.

"Claudine, I know who this Aaron bloke is," he said as he sliced off a sliver of steak. "I trained with him and your lad Dempsey. He's not a gentleman and he's not the right man for you. Right, here you are, struggling, fighting for your life for years now. He comes along and you open up your world to him, then he bloody well takes off on you." Dino pounded his fist down on the table and stared sternly at Claudine from under his bushy eyebrows. "I'm making this my business because I'm trying to point out the dead, plain obvious to you, luv. I'm trying to talk some sense into that pretty head of yours. Quit thinking with your heart, because your heart's broken; it's not working proper right now, sunshine. When I get it working proper again, you'll see things differently.

"I also know how men think. Men think with their willies," Dino said, raising one eyebrow. "I've been with plenty of women. I've had way too many young ones who don't know what they want, right up to pretentious middle-aged bitches like me ex-wife. I knew I was done with all that after Trixie, the little half-Polish, half-Greek nymphomaniac – she was a bloody nightmare!" Dino laughed and took a big gulp of his beer. "I gave her the name Tiny Tricks, you know, because she was small. But inside, she was nasty as a big slutty monster. She was the worst self-serving, cheating one of them all, always lying and mean-spirited! They all were, for that matter. Then, when I met you back at my studio for the first time, I knew I finally met the right girl for me. You're a decent, beautiful woman and kind, too. You don't dress like other women, talk like other women or act like other women. You're very special and real. You're that one–in–a–million, Claudine."

Claudine felt taken aback. "But you hardly know me, Dino, and I'm not so sure we are that compatible," she said slowly. "I love animals and you don't for starters. You're dead organized and I'm very disorganized, as you've pointed out to me quite directly today. Untidy, was one of the key words you used to describe me. And then there's Drew…" Claudine shook her head to keep herself from getting too emotional. "I'll never be over Drew, which I'm not sure if you could accept, and I am still not over Aaron either. I don't want to be encouragin' anythin' with you right now, Dino. It wouldn't be fair to either of us."

"Okay, I can understand your never-ending love for Drew," said Dino. "He was a great man; he was your husband, the father to your children, Toasty's partner, and so on. But he's passed on. We both know he's not coming back. But this Aaron bloke, well, he remains in the way because he's still alive and you're hanging on to that hope that he might come back. But truth be told, with this Aaron, what did he ever do that makes him so hard to get over? Really, what makes him so great that you keep putting your life on hold for him? You are wasting your valuable time on something that's not here anymore."

"Well, we were just really connected," said Claudine defensively. "We were goin' to be married. Maybe we would be married by now if he had stayed in England. We were a really good fit. We had plenty of things in common, like me animals, for starters. He might have appreciated this new job prospect that might be a reality for me one day; it involves exercisin' and people. He always understood me."

"Well, you can't build a strong relationship on the fact that you both like exercising and animals," said Dino. "That's like saying you should be with someone because you both breathe air and know how to drive a car. It's too broad, sunshine. But if you'd just give me a chance, I guarantee you will forget all about that bloke. When was the last time you heard from him, anyway? Has he sent you any money? Has he rung you up or texted you or emailed you to see if your alive or starving or dead or pigging fantastic? Has he even called to ask you about your animals or how your exercising is going, since those are the only two pigging things you have in common with him?"

Claudine hung her head. Here, at least, Dino had a point. Claudine suspected that Toasty might have filled him in these unfortunate facts.

"I didn't want to mention this yesterday, with your whole family hanging round," said Dino, "But some of my friends in the film industry said they saw Aaron in Los Angeles with some girls."

"What?" asked Claudine. Her ears were suddenly ringing.

"That's right. I don't know for sure and I don't gossip as a rule, but there it is. And let me tell you something," Dino continued; even he, with his poor 'people- reading' skills, could see that he had hit a nerve with Claudine. "It's not always about being there for the bad times, which I don't see this Aaron bloke pigging doing. And another woman might be involved too; we can't rule that out. But besides the ugly stuff, it's about having someone there with you to enjoy your good moments too. It gets dead lonely for me when I have something I want to enjoy, like a nice meal on my birthday, or some good news, and I've got no one to be there to enjoy it with me. And when I have something nice I want to do for someone, I've only got Mary, really. Giving her nice things is not the same as wanting to run out and buy a dozen roses for me bird because I know she would love it."

Claudine pondered Dino's words as he continued to ramble on in this vein. She looked at him and seriously thought about what he had just said. He was arrogant and he rubbed Claudine the wrong way plenty of times, but other times, he was surprisingly insightful. She didn't want to lead him on. She didn't want to brush him off either because he seemed to want to help her. She just wanted things to stay where they were being friends, yet he was talking about how she was the girl for him. She felt nothing like that towards him.

Dino had changed gears and was now saying something about organization and health. "I can help you with getting rid of all that rubbish cluttering up your life and your home; all that mess isn't good for your quality of life," he said. "Not to mention it makes your home look a right mess. Take pride in your home, luv. Tell you what; why don't we start training together at the gym, like you and Drew used to do? What do you think of that?" He leaned over the table and flexed his bicep in front of her face. "Not bad for fifty-seven bloody years old. Feel it, go on. Not so far off what your Drew had with his biceps, aye? Don't be scared of it love, it's only my arm; go on, give it a good squeeze."

"Are you bloody kiddin' me?" thought Claudine as she unenthusiastically squeezed his bicep. She was offended by his remarks about her home and his attempt to compare himself to Drew, although she was also somewhat amused at that.

When they finally got back to the cottage, it was nearly five o'clock and Claudine was already wanting to go to sleep.

Dino again insisted that Claudine wait as he walked around and opened her car door for her "because we're both old school," he reminded. Then he opened up the boot of his BMW to retrieve Claudine's new things. Cicero crowed loudly at their arrival.

"Bloody hell, what's the matter with him? Daft bird," Dino muttered as he gathered bags of food and cleaning supplies from the boot of his sedan.

Claudine grabbed a few packages too. She walked ahead and opened the front door. Dino was efficiently nudging behind her to keep her moving, his arms stacked high with boxes and parcels. She was just turning the front light on when Buffy raced up the stairs to her safe hiding spot underneath Claudine's bed.

"Crickey! Was that a rat or a cat?" Dino asked as bustled through the front room into the kitchen. He dumped the load of goods onto the kitchen table. Claudine straight away thought about how Buffy never ran when Aaron walked into the house. She remembered how the little cat used to sit on Aaron's stomach and he would say, "Look, darlin', at how special Buffy's face is."

"It's hot as blazes in here. Did you leave that fire on all day?" Dino continued as he took off his classic full-length camel hair coat. "No wonder you can't pay your gas bill, it must be bloody sky high." He got down on his knees and took the liberty of turning the gas fire way down.

"I didn't have a chance to turn it off this mornin' because we left in such a rush," she replied, following Dino into the kitchen to help put the new things away.

Dino was helpful in how he organized all the things he bought for Claudine, but he was also rather nosy and began to take more inventory of what she could get rid of. A lot of his criticism didn't seem very constructive. Claudine just wanted Dino go home so she could relax.

"Thanks so much for gettin' me all these things and putting it all away for me. I really appreciate it Dino. Now, I hate to sound like feeble, but I'm fading now. I'm dead tired," said Claudine, stretching, her arms up over her head.

"Say, do you have any Port Sherry? Or better yet, love, if you have Johnny Walker Blue Label, on ice? That would be smashing. It makes me randy," said Dino with a bold laugh, making himself comfortable on the chesterfield. Annoyed that he was oblivious to her indicating she was worn out, she was couldn't believe he seriously thought she would have expensive whiskey on hand when she could barely afford her daily bread. Offended more than anything however, was Claudine at his remark about wanting to feel *randy*. *Of all the nerve*, she thought hotly to herself.

"No, I don't have either of 'em," she said, sitting down stiffly on the end of the chesterfield. She could smell his body odour now that his coat was off. "No sherry, no whisky. Sorry, ran out o' 'em both just this mornin'."

"Well, I'll have to get you all topped up in your alcohol cabinet for nights when we stay in and watch wrestling. Your Dempsey said that you like to do that."

"Anyhow," said Claudine, "it really has been a great day, but I have to go out and feed the animals and you'll be *wantin'* to get home too." She got up to walk toward the back kitchen, but Dino grabbed her hand.

"I'm sorry if I said things today that seemed dead cheeky. My Mary told me a thousand times not to be arrogant. Sit down, please. I won't bite, you know," Dino said. Claudine did not move. To her dismay Dino did not let go of her hand and after a moment he stood up too.

A wave of body odour hit Claudine as Dino stepped near to her. He once again tried to kiss her. She kept her lips tightly closed and moved her head to the side. Unperturbed, he patted her hair and wrapped his arms around her. "I feel so good when I'm with you. You're so pretty and shy," he whispered in her ear. Claudine stayed still, hoping he would let go soon.

"Dino, I'm sorry, but I'm just not ready for this. And Isabella might be home anytime. She could march right through that door." Claudine was a rigid as a piece of chalk.

Dino patted her hair again, kissing her around her ears. "She'll be with my Mary now working on the documentary. She won't be home for a while," whispered Dino. Then, to Claudine's horror, he confidently began to put his hands up Claudine's cashmere jumper. His lips were back on her closed lips, his tongue trying to force its way into her mouth. Claudine felt herself being pulled and before she knew what was happening she was lying on top of Dino on the chesterfield, with one of his hands pressed against the back of her head and the other up her jumper.

Claudine struggled to pull herself away. Trying to get him to let go of the back of her head was the most difficult part. "Dino, please stop it. I am not ready for this. I can't be doin' this right now. If you expect this because we spent a day together and you bought me some nice things, well, it doesn't work like that with me. You're starting to really hurt me feelings and make me dead uncomfortable," said Claudine sternly, fighting her way back to her feet.

Dino sat up, looking dazed. "I'm sorry! I'm sorry! I get carried away with you, luv," he said and he really did look sorry. "I can be a gentleman. I thought maybe you were just playing hard to get. I understand now; very sorry. I don't want to scare you off. I probably have now, but, believe me when I tell you I'm in love with you."

Claudine gaped at Dino, who held up a hand. "Before you say anything, Claudine, like how we hardly know each other, let me tell you why I love you. You give me such a good feeling, like I've never known before. It's bloody fantastic! You're a proper girl who's nice to look at, who's unpredictable and dead sexy all in one. You're helpless and independent, strong and shy. I couldn't ask for more qualities in a girl I love. I'm sorry for behaving like an animal."

He took his coat and put it back on. In the doorway, he turned around and held open his arms. "Let's just have a hug goodbye?" Dino said.

"Oh, all right," replied Claudine. As she went to give him a hug, she put her bottom out and awkwardly leaned forward, giving him a stiff embrace that barely allowed them contact other than with their arms. He hugged her as best as he could, despite her position, and slipped dejectedly out the front door.

11

LISTENING TO MUSIC AND WATCHING DVDS

By now, Isabella discovered her mum's secret about dancing about and watching the television. She was delighted for her mum.

"I took Syncopation classes in New York, Mum. They were brilliant. I'm very familiar with the whole thing. I've missed not havin' a class to go to over here, but now, you'll be me instructor," exclaimed Isabella.

"I hope it happens, but I need to save some money up for leasing a space and getting a bit of equipment. It'll take some doin' but I'm gonna get there," Claudine admitted.

"Have you thought about asking Uncle Toasty if you can borrow the money from him?" suggested Isabella.

"No, I can't ask him. He's doin' enough for me with inventin' work for me to do so he can pay me something every week. And I wouldn't think of asking our Dempsey after he paid a fortune to get this house back in my name. I still am going to pay him back, but it's all taking some work, literally, on my end," said Claudine, feeling determined.

"If I had the money, Mum, I'd give it 'ya. But I don't 'ave a lot myeself. Didya think of asking Dino, or would that make things strange with 'im?" asked Isabella.

"Yes, that would make things strange, but the thought crossed me mind. He'd be terribly critical of me idea as well. He can't help himself, he's just got no filter and he blurts things out. For that matter, Toasty just says whatever he feels too. So, don't say anything about this to anyone just yet, luv, alright?" asked Claudine.

"I won't say anything to anyone. But if you still need help in a few months with money, maybe by then I'll have some by then I can give you," her daughter smiled.

So for the next while, Claudine practiced her routines in front of Isabella or on her own. She spent many afternoons with Glenda in Manchester. She took care of paperwork for Toasty. She found time she could devote to painting and really concentrate of the smallest of details in her artwork. She even spent the odd day with Dino, usually going for tea with him. Her days were built around a full schedule she felt her growing competence in Syncopation was helping to grow her confidence in everything else she did.

Claudine looked forward to spending her Mondays in Manchester at the Syncopation studio. When she was inside the studio, she imagined herself running her own. She imagined IWF wrestlers coming to her classes at the same time as the women and how it would be on the news that she her studio was the latest way for IWF fighters to stay fit. She imagined Glenda calling her and congratulating her on a job well done. She needed to get her studio started soon because Glenda announced she would be leaving for London eventually to begin training people down there. When that day came, Glenda wouldn't be a car ride away anymore.

The Manchester Syncopation Studio was in a beautiful old building right in the heart of town, with well-travelled-on hardwood flooring and tall mirrored walls and big wooden beams and pillars. It was a modern building but had been a dance studio for years before Syncopation leased it. Glenda had decided to keep the smooth wooden ballet bars up for use in some of her classes. There was a storage room for mats, weights, and other fitness equipment in the corner. One full wall was made of windows facing the street and passing women often peered curiously at the classes or even came in to join. When the crowds weren't too thick, Claudine liked to look across the street at the old cinema house where her parents sometimes took her, Toasty, and Drew as children.

At noon, though, Claudine was feeling a little nervous. Glenda was teaching the first class herself at 12:30 p.m. Patsy, another instructor-in-training, was student-teaching the classes at 2:00 and 3:00 p.m. today. Soon she would be certified and be taking over the Manchester lease to start her own studio. Claudine could tell that Patsy was ready to start teaching full classes of her own. It was inspiring to see a fellow-student ready to leave the nest, but it made Claudine panicky. If she didn't get going on her own franchise, she feared she would get left behind.

Claudine was student-teaching a few routines for her very first time between 4:30 to 5:30 p.m. The class consisted of sixteen songs in sixty minutes, including routines for legs, abdominals, shoulders, biceps, triceps, stretching, and a final routine to get the class back on their feet; Claudine was responsible for three high-intensity routines right in the middle of the workout, plus an arm routine and one stretching routine to finish the class.

"Would we be able to keep the blinds shut, while I'm goin' over things with you?" Claudine asked.

"Of course, sweetie. We'll open them up when the classes start and see how many people we can get in here off the street," Glenda said. Claudine gulped at the thought.

"Now don't you worry, it'll be fine," said Glenda with a laugh. "Ye've been training at these routines for three months now. Ya know all of them by heart, ya just have to get used to teaching them. You got plenty of time before you go on, so just relax, kiddo."

Glenda looked stylish as usual in a shiny shocking blue and fluorescent green Lycra tank top that accented her fiery red hair. Her fitted black leggings and trendy neon-colored trainers completed the look. Claudine wore black leggings too, and a a sleeveless black top. She had fished it out of a discount bin at a nearby fitness store a few days earlier. She wanted to look professional on her first day of teaching.

Glenda showed Claudine how to use her headset and the stereo remote control, then suggested they have an abbreviated walk-through of the first routine.

"Well, I guess I have to just do this and get it over with. It's not going to go away," Claudine said, trying to be fearless, although she was terrified. Glenda smiled and started the music. "Relax girl. The class hasn't even started yet. You're gonna be fab!"

At 12:30 p.m. Glenda opened the blinds and unlocked the doors. Claudine took advantage of all of Glenda's classes every Monday, using the opportunity to review the moves and observe an experienced teacher. Glenda was such a natural and so confident while she was up on stage. Today, Patsy was oozing confidence too and her class flew by without a hitch. Claudine, on the other hand, was a nervous wreck by the time she was supposed to go up.

It was quarter past four. A few women who had heard about the class from Glenda a few days earlier were already arriving. Claudine used the toilet twice, just out of sheer nervousness and when she returned there was less than five minutes till class began. She put her headset on again and stood at Glenda's side on the stage.

Claudine's anxious eyes lit up when Isabella walked in. Spotting her mum immediately, Isabella waved and promptly changed her sandals her black trainers, choosing a spot to stand at the back of the room even though there was plenty of space. The room was rather empty, with only a handful of women gently warming up, waiting to see what was in store for them.

"See that girl who's in the back corner, with the dark hair, well that's me daughter Isabella," Claudine told Glenda. "I invited her to come today. She's the only one in me whole family who knows I'm doin' this. I'll introduce you later, after we get this out of the way. Oh, I hope that didn't sound awful! I just meant, get it under me belt."

"No need to explain. I understand, Claudine. Don't worry, ye've been ready for this for weeks," said Glenda, who was starting the music for the first routine. She turned on her microphone and started the class.

"Okay, everyone, I'm Glenda and this is my instructor-in-training, Claudine. We want to welcome y'all to Syncopation. Give me a thumbs up if y'all can hear me. And y'all give me a thumbs up if the music needs to be louder, okay?" Glenda was full of energy. The five women in the class tentatively nodded yes.

"We've got sixty minutes of choreographed routines to get our hearts healthy and have a good ol' time," Glenda continued. "Our first routine is a warm- up. Just follow what we do and listen to our cues and let's all have fun."

The first routine was set to a five-minute song by The Black Eyed Peas. Glenda adjusted her headset and began to rock her shoulders up and down in time to the music. Claudine mimicked her moves exactly, staring straight ahead at her small audience. When she made eye contact with Isabella, she was met with a most encouraging look that reflected concentration as well as enjoyment.

As Claudine got warmed up, she barely needed to watch Glenda at all. She really did know the routines by heart.

"Can y'all still hear me okay? Give me a big wa-whoooo if y'all can," Glenda called loudly out to the class. "Wa-whoo!" said the class, with some reservation.

"All right! I'm gonna let my partner here, Miss Claudine, give y'all yer cues for the next few songs," announced Glenda. Instantly, all eyes were on Claudine.

"Right then, we're gettin' our heart rates up slightly more, so the intensity is goin' up now. Remember in Syncopation we have more fun and less stress," Claudine heard herself saying. "So, step right foot forward first, two, three, right arm out, and jazz hands and back." Facing her students, she smiled, spreading her fingers apart. She had to remember to do everything opposite as she was the mirror image of what her students were seeing, but so far it seemed to be going well.

"Good, now repeat that with the left side, left foot back, two, three, and left hand out; good! Then repeat, right foot forward, two, three, jazz hand right, and add some height if you want… now, grapevine to the right side, hands up and down, left foot back and behind, right foot tap. Now to the other side, grapevine left, hands up and down, right foot back and behind, left foot tap. Hands up and down, good! That's it, just like your wavin' your hands through water, feel the resistance, good! Let's do that again, right side first."

Claudine bounded through the next three higher-intensity routines with clarity and energy. The women seemed to be following her cues well and Glenda was adding a lot of enthusiastic "wa-hoos" and "ya got it, girls!" from her own headset. Everyone seemed to be really having fun, smiling and skipping along to the music.

"Super job, ladies! Thank y'all so very much for coming," said Glenda at the end of the class. Claudine stood on the stage, unable to stop a huge, goofy grin from spreading across her face.

"We'll be back here again, same time on Wednesday and Thursday. Miss Claudine is getting her Syncopation certification in the next month. She'll be starting her own classes in Chester hopefully in July, if any of you or yer friends are interested in coming to her classes. I'll put it on the website if y'all want to check that out. Come talk to me if ya have any questions. Now let's give ourselves all a big round of applause for great work and thanks to Miss Claudine for doing an awesome job!"

Isabella, standing in the back, cheered loudly and whistled shrilly like she was at a rock concert. The other women looked about, but Isabella just boasted proudly, "That's me mum!"

Glenda left the stage and to talk to some of the students as Isabella rushed to her mum's side and gave her a big hug.

"You did great; how was it?" they said simultaneously to each other.

"I was nervous. I really was. I hope it wasn't too obvious," Claudine said.

"No, Mum, I couldn't tell. You were brilliant! I could see your teacher was dead impressed too. I loved it. You're a natural up there, you look like a proper dancer. Dad would have been so proud of you."

Claudine carefully took her headset off and gave her daughter a hug. "You always know what to say to me."

"Well it's true. I can't wait until the cat's out of the bag and I can brag about how brilliant you are to everyone, but I promise I won't say a word until you're ready, Mum. Now let me take you out for a meal to celebrate. Do you need a hand putting anythin' away?"

Glenda, who had circled back around, was now smiling and waiting for an introduction.

"Oh, yes," said Claudine. "Glenda, this is me daughter, Isabella. Isabella, this is me mentor, Glenda. And Glenda, me daughter took Syncopation classes when she was in America, in New York, where she was acting in a live theatre production on Broadway."

"Well, my goodness. Two stage performers. And yer both so pretty too!" said Glenda. "I could tell ya had some kind of dancing background, Isabella, just by watching you in the class. Wouldja ever want to become an instructor like yer mom? My own daughter back home is an instructor. We'd be right honoured to have a Broadway star as a Syncopator Instructor."

"Oh, I prefer just being a student. I'm too nervous to go up on stage like me mum just did," Isabella said. The three women laughed.

Claudine's times on stage that night made her feel drastically better about herself. Finally, she had accomplished something entirely outside of the wrestling world she was so familiar with. Up until now, working in wrestling was the only paying job she really felt fulfillment in. She couldn't wait to teach more classes and keep working towards opening her own studio.

"Go on ahead, Claudine. I've got this," said Glenda, looking around the studio. "There's not a lot to do, with it only being a small class. You go out with yer daughter and celebrate a job well done."

"No, I should help you put things away and lock up. Would you like to join us afterwards?" Claudine offered.

"Honey, I'm really about ready to just lock up now," insisted Glenda. "I would love to join y'all, but I need to get back and make some calls to my family before it gets too late. Go out and have a great time, but let me give ya a hug before I say goodnight. Congratulations on an amazing first day." She gave Claudine a hug and starting shutting out the lights.

As it turned out, it was just as well that Glenda couldn't join them for dinner because Isabella had something very serious to discuss with her mum. "I don't like to even bring Aaron's name up, but I want to let you know that Dino hired a private investigator to see what he's been up to these days," she told Claudine as they sat in a little Middle Eastern restaurant a few doors down. "He's been pokin' his nose about hopin' to find some kind of rubbish on Aaron. I guess he wants to make it easier for you to forget him."

Claudine's mind was already boggled enough by the fact that Dino had hired a private investigator, as he had told her he had a friend in the film industry who told him Aaron was in Los Angeles. As Isabella continued, Claudine became even more shocked. "And I guess he did – find something, I mean," said Isabella quietly. "Apparently Aaron is trainin' that American actor, Lucky Boyd. Mary showed me the photographs of them doing some trainin' on a beach near Los Angeles. I did some research too and found out that Lucky is making some big boxin' movie – that must be where Aaron comes in. So, now you know who the film star is. Not that it will make you feel any better, knowin' about young Lucky Boyd's reputation for bein' ravin' wild."

"You're right, that doesn't make me feel better," said Claudine. "I am imaginin' all sorts of things now that I know it's Lucky Boyd he's with. Probably Aaron has been up to all sorts of explicit things. Yah, it makes me feel rather sad, actually." Claudine took a big sip of water and tried to not let the news ruin her euphoric mood.

"I'm sure Dino's hopin' all this makes his chances with you better, but I think nothin' he says about Aaron, even if it's dead bad and true, will matter if you're not ready to move on, unless you are, that is. I know it's hard, but are you…ready…to move on?" Isabella asked slowly.

"Oh, I don't know," said Claudine. She felt like a cauliflower ear that keeps getting hit, filling up with fluid, getting drained, becoming harder, and then repeat.

Isabella put her hand on Claudine's arm and looked at her sympathetically. "Let me tell you what Mary told me that day you first met her and her dad," she said. "Mary told me that right when he first met you at the studio; her dad got it in his head that he's goin' to marry you. She didn't think much of it, because he's gone all gaga over tons of women; this young Spanish singer and then for some 'French wench,' as she called her, and then some young American girl and then some Polish girl, and her list went on. Anyway, she said he's made loads of dead bad choices. All those girls were just usin' him, you know?"

"He said somethin' about that to me once when he took me out for one of our first meals," said Claudine. "And then he said I was one-in-a-million."

Isabella smiled. "Well, he's right about that," she said. "Mary said he just got accustomed to bein' with bad girls and in bad relationships, but then he met you. Now you're all he talks about. He really believes that you are the one, which is kind of sweet, Mum. I don't think he helped you get that job because he thinks that if you get really desperate and have no money, you will turn to him and, I guess just marry him, and make his dreams come true, to put it mildly."

"Oh, I don't see that happenin' too soon, but it is a bit amusin', except the part about him not helpin' me get a job," said Claudine, laughing a little despite herself. "I guess I have to simply find summat without his help." She smiled, even though the idea Aaron cavorting with Lucky Boyd was still at the edge of her thoughts.

"And let me tell you this, Mum, I hope you'll find it funny. According to Mary, her dad also said that Dad, himself, and Aaron have the same physical features you like, so the physical attraction is already there between you and him. He said it's just the mental connection that he needs to secure with you."

"Well they all had cauliflower ears, though your dad barely had his for long and they are all big lads," Claudine replied, "but I don't see that Dino's got very much in common with any of 'em. Aaron and Drew have way more in common, and Dino is hairy and he has bad body odour."

"Oh come on! Don't let Aaron be in with Dad, while you leave Dino out," said Isabella. "I know I never actually met Aaron, but from what everybody says, Dino's got more to offer than Aaron. His business sense is helpful to everyone and he likes to be in the mix. That Russian trip he's plannin' for the IWF could be pretty lucrative. He seems a better man than Aaron from where I'm standin', but maybe you know him differently."

"If Dino came along a little later, or wasn't so bloody pushy with me, or didn't interrupt me or finish me sentences with summat nowhere near what I was thinking, I might be more receptive to him, and he really does smell bad," said Claudine indignantly. "He makes a lot of windy speeches about his greatness and he physically pushes himself on me. He's like Pepé Le Pew. A skunk! Literally too. But he is determined, I will give him that," she said as Isabella giggled. "He's just ignorant about what he thinks I like and then he'll even argue with me about it. He'll insist I like the colour red after I just told him how me favourite colour is blue. But maybe he's right, maybe me favourite colour is red, not blue. What do I bloody know?"

"Well, that does sound a bit annoyin'. It's funny, but I think Uncle Toasty is miffed that you turned your nose up at Dino, but would he want a female version of Dino bothering him? Wait, I take that back. He likes all the girls, so he'd probably love it," laughed Isabella.

"I'd bet he would," said Claudine, although picturing Dino as a woman was both difficult and amusing. "Maybe I'm a fool to be so disapprovin' of all this flattery. Maybe I shouldn't be so indifferent to Dino's attention, but I just don't want it right now and I feel dead terrible for not puttin' him over. But when I do, he's just too much."

The food came and interrupted the conversation. As they munched on their kebabs, their chit-chat turned towards Syncopation.

"I know your dad would have loved this concept," said Claudine between mouthfuls, "because it's an hour of choreographed aerobic and anaerobic exercises. I know about twenty songs all taught to me on a DVD, right now, to get me started. I'm scheduled to take the exam on the mechanics of the body at the beginnin' of July. I also have to pass a performance audition, but I already know all the routines and I'm not too nervous 'cuz Glenda will the only one judgin'. After that, I'm basically ready to instruct on me own."

"Wow, this is all happenin' so fast! Glenda said you'd be offering classes in Chester… do you already have a location?"

"Well, I have to have one to open me own franchise," Claudine admitted. "The company will finance me for the mats, the weights, the sound system, and rubber tubes, because there are choreographed routines for all that too. I just need to find a building to rent for me studio, do some eye-catchin' advertisin', get the students to sign up and I'm in! If I can get twenty students and teach those twenty people five times per week, just to get started, I'd be makin' at least enough to keep me going."

"That sounds do-able Mum," said Isabella. "I love Syncopation classes. Mary and I can be your first two students and we'll get plenty of girls signed up to take your classes, too. You'll get more than twenty students a week in no time."

"I am so glad you'll come to me classes. I think I'll be happier in the long run gettin' by with this career, even if I make less quid right now while I'm gettin' started, than by workin' at a dreadful dead-end job, where I'm not happy at all. And I can keep doin' odd jobs for Toasty too," Claudine said.

A few days later, on the last Sunday of the month, there was a big party at Bonham farm. There were two reasons to celebrate: Leilani's birthday and the impending IWF Russian tour that had been gradually come together for Toasty with Dino's help. Toasty excitedly called the tour "the biggest thing to happen to IWF since CrazyBest." Dino and his team had organized the entire thing, including meetings with Russian television and radio stations to try and get IWF on Russian TV.

This party was to be a fabulous running buffet. Dempsey was making his famous Spaghetti Bolognese, Toasty was baking Italian bread from scratch and Dino was bringing Greek Domades with rice and grilled eggplant drizzled with balsamic vinegar syrup along with a generous supply of his favourite Chianti. Mary and Isabella brought a diablo torte and a big tub of pistachio ice cream for desserts from one of Dino's restaurants. There was a glass dish full of different colours and sizes of fat, meaty olives. Claudine contributed a lovely Greek salad, made from an old family recipe. She didn't have anything big enough to mix this giant salad in, so she divided it up into two big brown paper bags from the market. Folding up each bad, she vigorously shook up each one before emptying each into a separate container, but then she was unable to find proper lids. As she forced ill-fitting lids onto the two bowls, she imagined Dino lecturing her about her lack of organization. He had bought her plastic storage containers with fitted lids, but she had since misplaced them. It seemed that at the Bonhams and the Bellamys, there seldom was a proper lid to go with serving bowls or storage containers and matching socks were never an easy find either.

Dino was the first person to greet Claudine at the party. He was sporting a gold chain as thick as a finger, which hung around his thick neck and hung down onto his furry chest. He had a light pink golf shirt on and faded blue denim shorts, which were cut just above his knee. Claudine could see he had pretty good sized calves and good definition in his quads, from what she could tell from his long shorts; he looked like he had been training more, probably with Toasty. His cauliflower ear was more noticeable due to his recent short buzz cut. As he opened Claudine's door for her, Claudine fleetingly thought that perhaps he had gone with this to particular hair cut to resemble Drew or Aaron. Dino helped her in the door, making sure he gave her a big forceful kiss right on her lips. Claudine looked about hoping someone saw Dino's boldness, but no one except Jersey the Siamese cat was there to appreciate her angst.

Despite the assertive beginning to Claudine's evening, the party was a lot of fun. The home-cooked feast was delicious and comforting and there was plenty of it to go around.

Claudine noticed Mary and Sui-ee were acting pretty cozy, Dino was not giving the pair of them a wide berth. He seemed to be ever-watchful and grumbling under his breath when Mary fussed over Sui-ee. She'd fluff his hair or give him a taste of something and Dino would scowl quietly.

"I think Sui-ee wants to marry Mary, but it's only been a few months for them," Dempsey explained out of the corner of his mouth during dinner. Claudine had managed to seat herself in between her two children. Across from them were Toasty and Dino. Dino was looking crushed, eyeing her from the other side of the table. "Dino would have a fit if they sprang that news on him at the party, because he is rather controllin', you know how he is, right? Dino doesn't think much of Sui-ee because he is barefoot all the time and catches fish with a spear. Meanwhile, Dino stuffs his feet into alligator skin shoes from Italy and goes yachtin' about for fish that he never catches." Both Claudine and Isabella were laughing so hard at this that they had to be careful not to choke on their food.

At one point, after the cake was gone and the coffees had been passed around, Claudine disappeared into the library to sit in the old root beer-brown mohair wingback chair. It made her think about how, in this very room, Drew gave her his first love note.

Someone opened the door, startling Claudine out of her happy memories. It was Toasty, dressed up in a beautiful custom baby blue Batiste silk shirt that brought out his eyes. He always wore unusual clothing. No one had the body, the guts or the personality to pull off clothes like that, except for Toasty.

"Claude, I thought you might be in here," he said, pulling up a chair and sitting next to her. "I appreciate you bringin' up the salad, it was lovely."

"No problem, thanks for hostin'," said Claudine. She could tell something was bugging Toasty.

"Hey, Claudine, I need to ask you a few things," he said. "I heard the other day that Dempsey paid off the mortgage on your cottage just a while back. Dino heard from his Mary that it was to the tune of £25,000. Is that true?"

Claudine sighed and looked up at the ceiling. She had known that she would have to tell Toasty about what had happened to her inheritance eventually, but that didn't make it any easier. "Toasty, you'd best shut the door," she said. "I don't want anyone walkin' in on this conversation."

With a confused look on his face, Toasty did as he was asked and came back to sit by Claudine. Drawing a deep breath, Claudine steeled herself. "I'm ashamed to say it is true, Toasty," she said finally. "I was waitin' for the mortgage term to come to an end, so I wouldn't have to pay any penalties for an early pay-out. I only had a few months left, so I just left the inheritance money in the bank. Meantime, Aaron proposed to me. Just before he left, he told me about this promisin' investment in Germany… he said that if I was willin' to invest the money I had, along with his money already in this fund, it would pay us about two thousand pounds a month and we would get the initial investment back in six months, returns on our investment."

Toasty's hands were already balled into fists, but Claudine kept talking, tears forming in her eyes. "I thought with all the extra money comin' in from this investment, that I could go to university and get me degree in something, maybe become a teacher and try to find a suitable job. But then I started gettin' discouraging statements from the investment company and within three months the entire thing went belly- up. I lost it all, Toasty. And I guess Aaron did too. So just after that, Aaron wrote me and said that I needed to find ways to count on meself first and not keep expectin' others to save me, that I deserved better than him, that he needed his freedom and things were complicated. He finished it off with wishin' me the best of luck," sobbed Claudine, her face in her hands.

"Son of a bitch! Motherfucker! If I ever see that robbin' bastard again I will kill him!" Claudine heard her brother saying. "He knew you'd have nothin' if this didn't work and he still took your money. He never ever should have asked you for it. Yah, well, one day, I'll see him and I will stretch the shite out of him, I promise you. He's done with this family. It's a small world, you know."

"Well, Toasty, Aaron didn't even know I had the money until after he asked me to marry him and I then I mentioned it to 'im. I wish I hadn't now, but in his defense, de didn't demand it from me. I have to take some of the blame," defended Claudine.

"That's bloody bullshit, Claudine. He knew you loved him and he took advantage of that. He's a right bastard and you've got to realize that. It's ruinin' yer life, Claude," Toasty said in a serious voice. He felt like he needed to be easy on her right now, as he knew she was still fragile. He felt still felt guilty about how he treated her after Drew and their father died. Her younger brother very much wanted to protect her now.

Toasty was rubbing her shoulder now, gently, but Claudine could feel adrenaline coursing through him. "I want to tell your Dempsey and Isabella about this, but I can't tell them the whole story because it'll show them what an areshole I was for withholdin' your share of Dad's money that whole time."

Claudine got out of the chair and threw herself on Toasty, who caught her like she was no more than a rag doll. "I am a fool. I am such a fool," she sobbed into his chest. "What a failure I am to have had me son pay me mortgage off with his life savings. I deserve to be exposed, Toasty. I don't deserve any special considerations for being so stupid. That cottage is all I have left, you know. It is so much a part of me and Drew, it's an extension of the family, and to have nearly lost it because I trusted someone who obviously didn't want to be a part of the family just shows what a fool I am. I'm ashamed and embarrassed. I betrayed me family by puttin' Aaron above everythin' else. I truly never dreamed he would have taken me for such a rough ride. I can't believe I meant so little to him. You should see the email where he told me good luck, after the money was lost. It was so obvious he couldn't care less. I'm so ashamed of meself. I don't deserve to be a part of this family. I'm a disgrace to mum and dad, and Drew, me children, to you…" She sobbed uncontrollably.

"Don't talk that way, Claudine. C'mon now," said Toasty, hugging her. "You're too hard on yourself. But I don't think there is any point in openin' up this whole mess to Demps and Isabella. We'll still just keep it between us." He pulled a folded throw-blanket off the chair and tried to wipe Claudine's face with it. Gratefully, she unfolded it and, started dabbing at her sopping-wet, red face.

"You've got the cottage paid off and it's yours for good. One day, things will be really rolling smooth for you. You'll look back on all this and it will make the good things seem even more brilliant. Who knows what can happen with this trip to Russia, right? It could be really good for the promotion and maybe, if you can tolerate Dino, you can do more work for us here at the IWF. Anyway, Claude, I feel for you and I am sorry that you got done by that bastard. What comes around goes around, just remember that, right? He'll get his, I promise you. And I won't say anything to anyone." He gave Claudine one last squeeze and left her to collect herself.

12

Why Can't You Just Behave Yourself?

"Hi, Glenda. Thanks for drivin' all the way out here," said Claudine as she approached her friend. It was a hot July day and Glenda looked fabulous as usual in a lavender-coloured summer dress and flats.

"No problem," said Glenda, smiling grandly. "We have a few things to do this morning, but first and foremost, there's this." Glenda drew a manila envelope out of her large tote and handed it to Claudine. Although Claudine thought she knew what was inside, she couldn't suppress a sigh of relief when she saw the certificate.

"You passed your written and practical exams with flying colours!" Glenda exclaimed as Claudine grinned. "Congratulations! You are now Syncopation's newest fitness instructor." She gave Claudine a big hug, which Claudine happily reciprocated, holding the manila envelope out to the side so it wouldn't get crushed.

"Now," said Glenda, "I want to show ya something." She turned to the building behind her and Claudine looked up at it for the first time. It was handsome, made of brick, with wide windows and a big "for rent" sign in the front. There was a mature man in a polo T-shirt and navy blue walking shorts standing in front of the door, looking at the women expectantly.

"Claudine, this is Louis Johnson, the landlord," said Glenda, striding over to him. Louis held out a hand, smiling broadly.

"Pleased to meet you, miss," he said.

Louis showed Claudine and Glenda around the building. It was in a superb location and was in an ideal place to hold classes; Claudine could see why Glenda had wanted to act fast. The studio was big enough to hold a conservative figure of about fifty students. It had hardwood floors, two exits, two lavatories, a small kitchen, heat, an equipment room, and loads of floor-to-ceiling mirrors. The ceilings were arched, which made for excellent sound, and the windows opened with a lever and a big ceiling fan had recently been installed. That, combined with the open windows provided plenty of ventilation for exercise classes.

"Now, I can hold the place for you, but I've got someone else interested in it as well," said the landlord at the end of the tour. "I'm chargin' £1,200 a month for it and I need that plus the £500 deposit for starters."

"Oh," said Claudine, her smile vanishing. She had no idea where she would get that kind of money. Louis saw her expression and furrowed his brow. "Tell you what, though," he said to Claudine. "If you'll let me wife and her sister come to your classes for free, I'll knock £200 off each month's rent. Me wife's been tryin' to lose weight, you see."

"Thank you so much, that's very generous of you," said Claudine, smiling gratefully. "Would you mind terribly if I took the evenin' to think about it? I need to take stock of me finances."

"Not a problem," said Louis kindly. "Here's my card. Just make sure to call me in the mornin'. Otherwise, I might have to give it to another."

"Let's go get a coffee," said Glenda after they had thanked Louis and said their goodbyes. "I want to go over some numbers with you."

Claudine was getting more and more worried as she and Glenda headed to the coffee joint on the corner. They found a nice seat outside of the coffee shop, at a table shielded from the sun by a big umbrella.

"Listen, I know ya probably realize this, but that place is as good as it gets. I saw it listed online and called straight away for ya," said Glenda excitedly, coffee in hand. "We can getcha started right away, but ya need £300 for liability insurance and £200 for your franchise fee, plus £1,500 for your first month's rent and deposit. Basically, it'll be £2000 minimum to get this going. If you had the money right now, we could have you up and running by the end of the week."

"I know it's perfect," moaned Claudine. "But I have no idea how I'm goin' to scrape together that much money in a day. That's £2000 total and the bank takes weeks to process loans."

"I know, but if we don't move on this right away, I think you will lose this studio location and it's ideal," said Glenda, chewing on her wooden stir stick. "It's got everything plus parking.... I know it's a lot of money to put down. We kind of knew this was coming, but I didn't know it was going to happen so quickly." She tapped her fingernails against her chin, thinking. "When I started my first franchise, my sister lent me a little bit of cash for the deposit, now that I think about it. I paid her back within the first week. Is there anyone in your family who would help you out? As long as you advertise properly, you'll earn the money back real quick, so it won't be anything long-term."

"Maybe," Claudine admitted. IWF had been doing amazingly lately and she knew that Toasty and Dempsey both had money in the bank. But Toasty was leaving for Russia in the morning and she knew he had a lot on his mind. "Let me talk to me family and do some research on other options. I'll let you know tomorrow. I'll just have to figure somethin' out. I won't lose this space. It will change me life, to get this going." Claudine sighed and took a sip of her coffee."

Glenda clasped Claudine's hands. "This will be the beginning of a new chapter for ya, I just know it. If I can somehow put together any money for ya, I will hun. I want to see you get a break. I don't know if I can get anything together before tomorrow, but I'll try," Glenda said. "I gotta get goin' though. We'll call each other in the morning, deal?" Claudine nodded her head and finished her coffee as she watched Glenda walk away.

On the short drive home, Claudine pondered the issue of funds. She knew that it was unlikely, but she figured she would at least look up some local banks and see if anyone offered same-day loans, if that was even an option with her poor credit history. As soon as she got home, she jumped on the computer. It was a huge shock for her when she saw an email from Aaron in her inbox.

Hi Claudine,

I hope you're checking your email because it's real important you go to your dad's house on the last Friday of this month. It's coming up, so I hope you get this message in time. Go there to your dad's house before 9 a.m. and wait all day there if you have to for this lawyer. He's gonna deliver something to you from me. I can't do it myself. I'm working still and it's complicated, but I wish I could be there to see your face because I think this will make you happy. There'll also be a letter from me to explain a lot about things I can't risk telling you in an email. My email isn't secure or private anymore.

Aaron

Claudine sat there staring at the screen for a long time. She wanted to believe that Aaron still had some inkling of feelings for her. Otherwise, why would he wish he could see her? She habitually hit the 'reply' button and was about to type out a quote from Oscar Wilde: "If you are not too long, I will wait here for you all of my life." She didn't have a chance to ponder this idea though, because the telephone rang louder than it ever seemed to ring before. It was Glenda.

"Hey, I just wanted to mention that if ya need anyone in yer family to talk to me about Syncopation, I'd be glad to."

"Ta, Glenda. I've not made any calls yet, still planning how to go about asking me family."

They talked for a while about how fantastic it would be for Claudine to get this opportunity signed, sealed and delivered. By the time Claudine got back to the computer, she realized it would be better not to write anything back to Aaron at all.

Late in the afternoon, Claudine was working on her painting of Buffy, trying not to think about Aaron and focus on how, if at all, she should talk to Toasty or Dempsey about a loan. Claudine stared at a photo of Buffy that she had propped up next to the canvas; the little kitten was only about six weeks old in the photo. Buffy seemed to know something to do with her was going on and was taking a long nap on the chesterfield. She usually napped upstairs in the bedroom.

"I hate to ask Dempsey for more money after what he did for me with the cottage," Claudine told Buffy as she worked on her painting and thought out loud. "Toasty's been buggin' me to do something that makes me happy and brings in money I think he'll see that this is a good opportunity for me. I guess I'd better ask Toasty. But then, he's leavin' tomorrow and I'm sure he's busy. I should at least call him right?" Claudine said to Buffy, who stretched out her tiny claws in response.

She dialed out Toasty's number and let the phone ring. It was rang and rang but no one picked up. She tried his cell phone but it said his mail box was full. "That's nothing new," she impatiently said to herself.

Claudine returned to her painting of Buffy. It was nearly finished. She was methodically painting the little individual hairs in Buffy's bushy tail, trying to figure out what to do about the rent money, when she heard an abrupt rapping at the front door. Buffy was off like a shot. "Oh rats," muttered Claudine as she stuck her brush into a can of water and went to get the door. She was surprised to see Dino standing there holding several large paper bags.

"Hi, Dino," she said, opening the door. "Can I help you with somethin'?"

"Well, seeing as tonight's my last night in town I thought I'd stop in and say hello," he said, walking right in as if he had been invited in. "I brought you some things too, to tide you over while I'm gone."

"Oh my, thank you," said Claudine as Dino pulled jars of caviar, wedges of fancy cheese, gourmet crackers, a box of Belgian chocolates, bottles of red and white wines, and tall blue box of Johnny Walker Blue Label whiskey out of a large paper bag. "This is extremely nice of you. You didn't need to do all this, but thank you."

"I told you I'd fill out your liquor cabinet for you, didn't I?" Dino said jovially as he pulled boxes containing wine goblets and short liquor glasses from another large bag. He busied himself with washing the new glassware while Claudine set out the crackers and cheese. *What was he doing here?* she wondered. She didn't mind seeing him, but she knew from experience that it wasn't always pleasant being alone with him behind closed doors.

When she turned around, she saw Dino downing a half full glass of Johnny Walker Blue Label Whiskey, in one big gulp. Catching her eye, he wiped his mouth with the back of his hand and grinned, pouring himself another big splash. "Don't like to drink too much and then drive, luv; waited 'til I finished driving and landed here before I had any more to drink and now I'm having more to drink," he said, as if he had just done something exceedingly clever. "Just a stiff shot of my old friend 'Johnny', to get me where I need to be. Now, you will have to let me stay a while, seeing that I've had a bit too much drink in me, eh? I'd just like to stay a bit, maybe have some of these treats and watch the telly with you, luv. I won't bloody bite you. I've told you that before. Mary says I need to chill, so will you let me chill with you?"

Claudine thought he sounded weird saying "chill" at his age and she was bothered by the calculated lengths he had gone to make sure he could stay. Nevertheless, she grabbed the tray of cheese, crackers, caviar and chocolates and walked him into the living room. She put the telly on and sat down on the chesterfield.

"Sunshine, I need to get this off my chest," said Dino as Claudine sat down. "Clear the air, so to speak, and get rid of the clutter that's messing up my mind. Claudine, if you think your hero is Aaron, then I need to tell you, he's a waste of your time. Your Toasty's totally finished with him for some reason that he won't tell me, but I can tell you with complete certainty that he's not welcome back here."

"All I'm asking, sweetness, is for you to give me a chance," he continued, draining his second glass of whiskey and pouring himself a third. "I've got money, cars, houses all over the world, restaurants, race horses, yachts, connections, power, and so on and so forth. Not to be blowing my own horn, but I think, if your Drew hadn't been around and I met you back then, I would have been the one to sweep you off your feet.

"I feel it's my turn now," he said, banging his barrel chest with one of his fists. He seemed to feel an entitlement to Claudine. "I've been patient with waiting and haven't I always been there for you since our first day out? And I will continue to be there, not just to catch you, but to keep you, so you and I can be together for the long haul. I've earned some kind of chance with you, don't you think? I think so. We get along so smashing and your family loves me. I don't know what's holding you back, luv. We have this fabulous chemistry too; I could cut it with a knife, sometimes, it's that pigging strong!"

Claudine helped herself to some cheese and crackers, saying nothing and deliberately avoiding Dino's gaze. He was presumptuous and misreading their supposed "chemistry," but Claudine believed Dino was a good man at heart. He just didn't seem to know better. She imagined this was how Buffy thought of Sally; Buffy could co-exist with the sweet bull terrier, but Buffy didn't want Sally jumping on the bed with her when she was trying to sleep.

"Whoa! What's that?" asked Dino, who had noticed the painting in the corner of the room.

"Oh," she said, bashfully. "It's of Buffy, me little cat. It's almost done."

"That's very good, Claudine," said Dino, standing up for a closer look, his once-again empty glass of whiskey in one hand. "I didn't know you were still making art. I have one of your drawings on my wall at the studio in Manchester. You should do more of this." Dino seemed surprisingly sharp for the amount of whiskey he recently consumed.

He turned and looked at Claudine as though something had just occurred to him. She could see from his unfocused gaze that the whiskey was starting to take effect. "Can I have this when it's done? I'll pay you for it. What's it worth? I have to have that cat. What's it going to cost me?"

"Oh, I'm not sure," said Claudine. "Buffy, well, she's priceless, but me painting? I don't know. Drew sometimes sold me artwork, but I personally have never made a sale, so I couldn't even tell you what I'd charge, to be truthful." She looked at her nearly finished piece, feeling rather proud.

"Well," replied Dino, "I think it's worth a thousand pounds. Tell you what – I will give you £2000 if you give me the original. Have we got a deal?" He walked to the cheese and crackers and helped himself. "I want somethin' that no one else has. I want that one."

"Oh, I can't take that kind of money from you. You've already been so generous." gasped Claudine.

"Nonsense, luv. Can I pour you a glass of wine?" He asked. "I notice your liquor cabinet is still empty. Le' me 'elp ya put these bottles in there. That's why I bought these for ya." He held up the bottle of white wine and pointed to the red wine sitting on her kitchen counter.

"Ta, Dino. I appreciate that, but nothin' for me right now. We can put the wine in the cabinet though and I'll 'ave it another day. Maybe when you get back, eh?" Claudine replied, and noticed he was starting to wobble a bit as he stood holding the unopened bottle of white wine. She felt bad for him, because he seemed to have a different idea of how their evening was going to be.

"Not much fun, are ya? Can we watch tele?" he asked and almost sat down, but he did an about face and looked at her painting of Buffy again. "Would you take a couple thousand quid for it if I was a stranger buying it at an art show?" he asked.

"What, the painting of Buffy? Well, probably I would, if I was sellin' it like that. It's just that I've already accepted plenty o' things from you, so to take £2000 from you for me paintin' of Buffy isn't right, don't ya see? Well, umm, how about if I give you one o' the lithographs when I get round to having that done? Would that work? That would be a gift from me to you then, for your kindness and generosity."

"No, no, luv I insist! And I want the original," said Dino and he promptly whipped out his wallet and began counting out £50 notes until he reached £2000. "That paintin' is absolutely extraordinary," he slurred. "I insist, an' I know what'll get you to accept the money. Take the money, or gimme a proper romantic kiss tonight, before I leave for Russia."

"Oh, Dino, you've had too much too fast to drink. You're being boastful now. I can't take yer money, but thank you," said Claudine, feeling pity combined with rising impatience for her uninvited guest.

"If you can't see fit to kiss me, then you take the money instead. I'm gunna make it £3000 if ya don't decide soon, luvy," he negotiated with the triumphant air of a lawyer about to win his case. "If ya 'ave trouble accepting 2000 quid, 3000 isn't gunna be any easier. Eh? Eh? Pick one or th'other, m' dear, the kiss or the quid. How's that for bargainin', sunshine?" said Dino slickly. He spoke in a loud sloppy way now and he counted out several more £50 notes from his roll of money and threw it down on the table with the first £2000.

Claudine didn't know what to do. Dino stared her down and got closer, reiterating his offer clearly and slowly. "Take the £3000 or we 'ave a proper kiss. That's where I kiss you an' you kiss me back at the same time. That's how kissin' works. That's how it bloody works, right, luv? An' you've not kissed me back proper yet."

"Well, it's not yet finished, the painting of Buffy," said Claudine, feverishly looking for a way out. "You might not like the finished product, but when it's done, I'll let you know what my answer is, alright? Maybe I'll give it to ya then, okay? You've had way too much to drink, Dino. You don't know what yer sayin'. Now wait here, I'm goin' to put the kettle on an' see how the animals are."

"Listen, Claudine, jus' sit down an' relax, piggin' hell! Why don' ya come over 'ere an' feed me?" said Dino playfully. "The bloody spoiled animals'll be fine, 'ave a glass of wine, aye? I made a point o' bringin' you wine, cuz I read somewhere that it helps you relax."

"Where did you read that?" asked Claudine suspiciously.

"Wait, no, I didn't read it, uhmm, I meant… I 'eard you liked it from when your Toasty, back when I 'ad me first dinner at the house," said Dino quickly.

"I'm okay. I'll just sit," said Claudine, easing herself back down to the chesterfield. She started to flip through the television channels, trying to ignore t Dino slowly leaning in closer to her.

"On second thought, I'm goin' to fetch a glass of water. Would ya like one?" Claudine asked, standing up again. Dino didn't answer. Instead he stood up too and knocked the cheese tray off the table. The expensive caviar blended into the colourful pattern on the Oriental rug. The cheese and crackers looked like part of the design. "Sorry, luv. I'll clean that up later." He whispered in a slur as he approached the other side of the big sofa to block her way to the kitchen. Claudine rolled her eyes and smirked. He was daft, like a big, silly puppy. She was slightly amused until he grabbed her arm and boldly pressed his lips against hers. He forced his sticky tongue in her mouth. Claudine froze and stiffened up, recoiling at the strong taste of alcohol and smell of his body odour. She wasn't amused now.

Dino put his strong arms around Claudine like he was about to give her a belly-to-belly suplex. Staggering, he backed her into a corner in her front room, kissing her as he pinned her against the wall.

"Stop it, Dino! I don't know what's gotten into you," protested Claudine.

"Toasty didn't tell me…I saw it in your book, Claudine, that you were scared to have sex," he murmured in her ear. "I understand, luv. I know that's yer secret problem w'th us. Don't worry, I'll be gentle w' you. I love you."

His hold on her was getting tighter, despite his words. Claudine could feel his hands moving up the back of her shirt. Thinking fast, she let herself go limp for a moment and he released his grip. Suddenly she yanked herself out of his arms. It almost worked, but he still had too much of a hold on her. Snatching her legs out from under her, she fell into the soft chesterfield. Dino pulled her down to the floor where she was trapped between the coffee table and the chesterfield and Dino straddling her. He used his body weight to hold her down.

"Dino! Stop it!" urged Claudine.

"Tell me that ya can't do it 'cuz yer scared," he whispered, forcefully kissing her neck. "Tell me yer scared. Tell me not to hurt ya. C'mon, say it, Claudine." Still straddling her with his thick legs, he clumsily tried to get her clothes off. He struggled to pull up her shirt, breathing hard as he leaned his chest heavily on top of hers.

"C'mon, Claudine! I won't hurt ya if ya tell me not to. Say, 'don't hurt me."

Claudine froze and said nothing. Dino forcefully kissed and groped her all around her neck, across her chest and towards her pelvis. She could smell the caviar and hear the crackers being crushed into her hair as she rolled her head back and forth to avoid Dino's kisses.

Finally, Claudine snapped. With a terrific effort, she partially twisted out from under him and leg pressed him off her with all her strength. She got enough leverage to break free.

"Get off me, Dino! I'm still in love with Aaron. Can't you see that?" she screamed as she scrambled away from him. Then she put both fingers in her mouth and whistled. Sally came bounding down; she was getting harder of hearing these days, but she never failed to hear Claudine's loud whistle. Usually so tame, she now put herself between Claudine and Dino and bared her teeth at him.

"Bloody hell, Claudine! Bloody hell! Why do ya 'ave t' bring *his* name up?" said Dino, using the chesterfield to help himself stand up. He moved cautiously away from Sally. "I don't understand. Ya play games with my head, Claudine. I thought y' were warmin' up to me, an' then ya go ice cold on me. If you'd just go t' bed with me, you'd feel different about us. Can't you forget that about that jack-off and give me a chance? I luv ya so much. And you'd love me too, if you'd only try."

Claudine wasn't sure if she was going to cry or punch a hole in her wall. "Why do you always think you know what I want, Dino?" she yelled, furious tears falling from her eyes. "If I were givin' you false hopes, well I'm sorry, but I don't think I was. Why can't you just behave yourself? I'm not sure what got into you tonight, but you need to go right now. Leave me alone. Don't call me or come 'round here anymore."

It was far too late for a normal rooster to crow, but Cicero broke out into a couple of very rusty cackles as a drunk and dejected Dino walked out of the house. He wanted to turn around and try to smooth things out with Claudine but he knew he blew it. "Sleep in your car, since you're obviously too drunk to drive. But in the mornin' I want you gone. I don't want you botherin' me anymore," shouted Claudine, with tears rolling down her cheeks. She slammed the door and hastily locked it while Sally stood by protectively.

In the sitting room, squashed cheese, crushed crackers, smashed caviar, and money littered the floor. Drew's picture on the wall seemed to oversee it all, his beautiful hazel eyes shining.

"I miss you. You were always so good to me," Claudine said out loud as she looked at the picture. Then she went to her upstairs bathroom, took a sleeping tablet and got ready for bed.

As she lay there, still trembling with anger, she hugged Sally gratefully. Sally jumped into the bed, then bounded across to the big comfy chair, where she circled around a few times before curling up in a ball and closed her eyes. Buffy joined Claudine on the bed once Sally was in the chair. Buffy's tail was up and promptly sat on top of Claudine's head. Mr. Wonderful laboriously jumped up on the bed to make the group complete. As they all fell asleep, a confused Claudine wondered if she had done the right thing by turning away Dino's overwhelming advances yet again. She had only had two relationships, both of them serious, and never had she been treated like this. She recalled Noah, the brewery owner's son who attacked her in his car when she was a teen. *Did boys behave like Noah and Dino or did they behave like Drew and Aaron, except that Aaron abandoned her.* She didn't know what was appropriate for a man to treat a woman. She wondered if Dino was a good thing she was throwing away. Or was she getting desperate, thinking that his forcing himself on her was perhaps acceptable? *Was she at fault for allowing Dino to buy her all those gifts? Was Dino capable of changing? What was Aaron's email about? Would he ever come back?* She didn't know what to think anymore. Her sleeping tablet took affect and Claudine finally fell asleep.

When she woke up the next morning, Claudine groggily went downstairs for some coffee. Sunlight streamed through the windows, promising a beautiful day. She put the kettle on and wandered into the living room. On the floor, the colourful £100 notes glowed in the morning sun.

Claudine suddenly felt very awake as she stared at the notes. She collected them all and counted them. There were thirty-two £100 notes. She had £3200 in her hands. She looked at her painting of Buffy and bit her lip in thought. She dialed Glenda's cell phone number.

"Hello," answered Glenda.

"Hello, Glenda. I hope I'm not waking you am I?" asked Claudine.

"No, yer fine girl. What's up?" asked Glenda.

"I just want to tell you I got the money!" declared Claudine.

"Oh my word! That's absolutely fantastic! Did you get it from yer brother?"

"No, my cat Buffy got it for me and that's the truth," said Claudine, matter-of-factly.

"What? Well, okay. Umm, I guess you should call Louis the landlord and let him know, before it gets scooped up. I'm real happy for ya, sweetie. And you got one great cat!" said Glenda before she and Claudine hung up with each other. She'd find out the details another time. But at the moment she wanted Claudine to get the lease signed, sealed and delivered.

Claudine hastily went to her purse and pulled out Louis' business card. She hurried to the telephone and dialed his number.

"Hello, Louis Johnson here."

"Hello, Louis, this is Claudine Bellamy. We met yesterday."

"Oh, Claudine! Good morning," said Louis, sounding genuinely pleased to hear from her. "How can I help you?"

"Well, is your buildin' still available?"

***

Claudine went to the bank and deposited her £50 notes. She delivered a cheque to her new landlord and signed the rental agreement. Louis looked pleased for her and gladly presented her with the keys to her new studio.

"I'll ring ya when I 'ave questions, Louis. I'm rushin' about today, just getting' things in order, so I apologize if I seem rude. I really need to get some things done." Said Claudine anxiously.

"You're alreet, luv! I can tell ya the buildin' is in good knick an' I don't think there's much else we need to tend to right now. Jus' ring me when ya need somethin'. Good luck, luv. I'll send me wife an' her sister and anyone else I can think of yer way. T'ra!" said Louis.

"T'ra!" said Claudine.

A few hours later, Claudine was hurrying around the Bellamy cottage. She grabbed a hammer and nails, some wire, and a ruler, putting them all into a big cloth sack. Into another cloth sack went a single wine glass. She looked in her cupboards for a bottle of wine. There were several there, all from Dino. She hesitated; she wanted something that was not associated with him.

"Well, this won't do. It has to be unadulterated," she said to herself with a smirk. "I suppose I can just nip in and get meself a little bottle of bubbly on me way. Now, I mustn't dilly-dally," Claudine chirped to herself.

Claudine searched under her bed and behind her wardrobe and cabinets. Her artwork began to emerge from different hiding places. Carefully she made a pile of her work on the middle of her bed and sifted through it. After much consideration of all her artwork, Claudine selected four framed pieces that happened to already be in attractive frames. One was a drawing of Drew; she had painted it from a black-and-white photo that was given to Drew by a wrestling fan and she loved the expression on his face in it. The other drawing was of Isabella holding Mr. Wonderful as a kitten. There was also a painting of Dempsey after he lost his first baby tooth and the fourth one was of her dad's house.

As she stood up, a framed collage she had made for her mother caught her eye. It was of different photographs of the family, right up to around the time of the Sardinia fiasco. Her family's beautiful, soulful eyes stared back at her from the collage, as if they were all still alive.

Claudine grabbed the collage and added it to her stack of artwork. She carefully loaded everything into the boot of her Cortina, but the boot would not even come close to shutting. "Ah, a square peg in a round hole is right up me alley," she said as she looked at her awkwardly packed boot. Looking about, she spotted a scruffy old bungee cord sticking out of the grass.

"Ah-huh!" she said as she picked it up and stretched it apart with both hands. "Yup, this will work!" Claudine declared.

She fastened the boot closed and jumped in her car. Her next item of business was getting some bubbles to celebrate with, so she popped into Bernie's News and Booze and purchased a 75cl bottle of dry pinot rose Prosecco. She met the landlord and signed the paperwork, giving him the cheque. It felt wonderful to turn the key to her own studio. She put on the lights and propped open the door with a brick so she could bring her precious commodities inside. The empty walls looked like blank canvases to her and she immediately began to visually space out where her artwork would go.

Claudine tapped the walls, looking for supporting beams. She hung her painting of Drew on the biggest wall, then found spots for Isabella, Dempsey, and the farmhouse. The collage went last. Then all that was left was to unscrew her little bottle of rosé and pour it into the wine glass. A tear of pride rolled down Claudine's cheek as she looked around her studio and made a toast to herself.

Soon, the artwork wasn't the only thing in the studio. A fitness stage, two feet high, twelve feet wide, and ten feet deep, took its place at the front of the room. Technicians came in and hooked up stereo speakers. They also installed a small CD sound system with a USB port in the front, next to the stage, and wired it to a cordless headset with a remote control. Mary was very helpful in donating twenty sets of five, eight, and ten-pound dumbbells to the Syncopation studio on behalf of one of the weight rooms at Thronos Productions in Manchester. It was all in place within two weeks and soon, Claudine had enough interested students to begin teaching classes.

13

What It Looks Like It Ain't How It Looks

The trip to Russia was carefully planned, with no room for error or failure; Dino's micro-management skills and Toasty's determination really shone. Their first meeting was at the privately owned NTV regarding advertising their potential live shows they would bring to Russia.

Their next meeting was at the National Legislature of the Russian Federation. Toasty and Dino hoped to persuade the Federation to allow Imperial Wrestling to promote their live shows, which would then be advertised on NTV.

Actually getting their television show from England on Russian television would come later, if they established a strong trusting relationships; first they would prove themselves by running live shows in Moscow. Dino and Toasty thoroughly explained how watching wrestling was not something that was challenged by a Russian/English language barrier because wrestling was so universally understood and that one day the shows in Britain, with Russian wrestlers could be of interest to Russian television audiences.

Dino arranged for Toasty to be photographed by the *Moscow Times Newspaper* with members of the All Russian Athletic Federation. It was invaluable exposure for Imperial Wrestling. If Toasty could at least begin a relationship with the Russian people it could open the doors to something if not now, then later on down the road. Toasty was intrepid at testing these uncharted waters. He saw this as the beginning of making his wrestling promotion a worldwide conglomeration.

In ensuring things were never misunderstood, Dino hired a translator named Vlad who accompanied them at all times, as did Yuri, their driver. Dino scheduled a dinner with some famous retired wrestlers as well. Meeting the tough veterans of the sport was a priority for Toasty; it wasn't every day he had the chance to meet Russian wrestling champions in Russia. If they had time, he and Dino planned to do some sight-seeing and take in some amateur hockey games.

About halfway through the tour, Dino and Toasty made their way to a gymnasium with a wrestling ring in St. Petersburg. They took a beautiful train ride to St. Petersburg with their driver, Yuri, and translator, Vlad, accompanying them. They hired a car and drove through the brilliant buildings and parks in the Bath Block. They bought international phone card chips for their mobile phones. They went shopping, tasted Russian vodkas, and saw an amateur hockey game which they had never seen before live. They marveled at Peter the Great's Summer Palace. They stayed at a hotel near the Peterhof State Museum and enjoyed spicy borscht, caviar blini. They felt like kings.

While they were sightseeing, Vlad found a wrestling gym where Toasty wanted to train and also recruit talent to eventually bring back to England for Imperial Wrestling. Vlad called the gym owner ahead of time to see if Toasty could train at 6:00 a.m. The Russian gymnasium owner was happy to oblige, saying there would be someone there in the morning to let them in.

After a wonderful night's rest, Dino called Vlad and Yuri on his mobile phone to drive them to the gym. They would all eat breakfast after Toasty and Dino trained and then visit the Faberge Museum. With Yuri giving directions to Vlad, they arrive at the gym. The parking lot was empty except for one other car.

"Let's go do weights first," suggested Dino. "I heard a load of amateur and pro wrestlers come by around 8:00 a.m. so if we lift weights first, we can roll around with them in the ring afterwards, *capiche* ?"

"*Capiche*… I was thinking, are the rings here the same size as ours in England?" wondered Toasty.

"Have you had to use different size rings before?" asked Dino, surprised.

"Some rings I worked in over in France and Italy were a couple o' feet smaller in diameter, so the wrestlers had to change their footin'," Toasty explained. "If the rings are different, the lads'll just have to improvise, but it's important to spot these things now so the wrestlers can prepare, if they come to us or we come here."

"See that man?" said Vlad suddenly, pointing out a man and a woman having a cigarette outside on the gymnasium's front steps. "He is American actor, Lucky Boyd. He is in St. Petersburg making a film. You know him?"

Dino and Toasty looked at each other and nodded as if to be impressed. It was out of the ordinary to see someone like Lucky Boyd at a gymnasium at 6:00 a.m. in Russia, but what piqued their curiosity most was where, Aaron, his trainer was.

Yuri the driver came round to opened the car door. The men stepped out of the car and stretched. Vlad walked with Toasty and Dino towards the gym doors. It was already bright outside on this early morning in July. Lucky, easily recognizable from movie posters, could pass as a boxer; his chiseled, muscular frame was clearly visible from under his t-shirt. The only thing that suggested he wasn't a seasoned boxer was his incredibly handsome baby face, which made him look like he was about to star in an ad for gym clothes. There were no cauliflower ears or a crooked nose on his premises.

But Toasty wasn't looking at Lucky. He was looking at the short, dark-haired woman next to him. She was dressed ready for the gym in a bright pink velour training suit and white trainers. Her face was pretty, but her eyes were blank. There was no expression or warmth in them at all. "I swear I've seen that girl somewhere before," Toasty said quietly to Dino as they approached the building. "I can't place her exactly, but I know I know her."

Dino, congenial businessman that he was, wasted no time in chatting up Lucky. "Hallo, Lucky Boyd? I'm Dino Tsillas of Thronos Productions, Manchester, England. This is my business partner, Toasty Bonham, who's also the uncle to CrazyBest Champion Dempsey Bellamy. I read somewhere you are a fan of our Dempsey's?"

"Oh, I sure am a fan of his. Nice to meet you both," said Lucky, shaking their hands. He had an easy-going California accent. "Yea, that Dempsey's the coolest fighter out there. I love his style. Wow, this is amazing to meet you, Toasty, and you too, Dino."

Lucky looked at Toasty like he couldn't believe his eyes. "Man, I love your fighting style too, Toasty, you're iconic. Can we get a picture together in the ring, if that's cool? I'm getting ready to train in there. My trainer Aaron is inside getting set up, but his wife, Velvet here, well she and I needed our cigarette first. Bad habit, I know, my bad. And your bad too, Velvet." said Lucky as he turned to Velvet.

Velvet was squatting on the ground, searching about in a gym bag for something. Toasty's eyes zeroed in on her lower back. Below the fringe of her lacy orange G-string knickers, the word *' holiday'* was tattooed on her lower backside, clearly visible for everyone to see. She glanced up at them and nodded in disinterest, continuing to root around in the bag.

"Velvet, this here, Toasty Bonham, is for a fact one of the greatest shooters ever," Lucky said as Velvet finally straightened up, holding a stick of chewing gum. "Hey, Toasty, is your nephew ever going to go to the States? I would love to see him fight in Vegas – they have some crazy big prizes there and…"

"Oh, sorry, mate, you just reminded me," interjected Toasty. "I should call Dempsey right now. He'd go mad if he knew I was speakin' with you and didn't put him on the phone with you to say hallo. Would you mind? I'll only be a minute gettin' him on me mobile."

"Yah, cool, man! I'd love to talk to him," said Lucky with a grin. Velvet grinned too, snapping her gum flirtatiously at Lucky. Lucky didn't notice.

Dino carried on a casual conversation about the state of professional wrestling with Velvet and Lucky as Toasty walked out of hearing distance. He dialed a number and quietly spoke into the phone.

"Hey, Eddie me man, it's Toasty. I can't talk long, but this is dead important an' I've got no time to explain; I'll tell ya later, but can ya answer a question for me?" asked Toasty, with urgency in his voice.

"Sure, mate. What's the question?" replied the wrestler on the other end.

"Do you still see that girl in Japan, that Romanian one?"

"Aye, the Romanian one, her name's Velvet," said Eddie. "Yah, I'll be hooking up with her next month in Japan. I was with her only a fortnight ago. She's got a couple of girls working with her who aren't too shabby, if you want me to fix you up. Are you heading over to Japan again?" he asked casually.

"Listen, Eddie, I 'ave to go, but that's all I need to know for now. Thanks mate, you're fantastic. I'll call ya later. T'ra." Toasty closed up his mobile phone, put on a disappointed face, and walked back over to the group. He tried not to look at Velvet.

"Oh, I can't get me nephew on the phone just yet. The cook says he's still in bed. But he's gettin' him up an' ready so he can have a chat with you in a bit," said Toasty apologetically. "He isn't a mornin' person, our Dempsey. Say mate, your trainer is Aaron Gabrielle right? Is he inside? He and I go way back. I wouldn't mind saying hallo to him before I start on the weights. Dino and I are goin' to train on the weights and then go do a bit of shootin' and scoutin' in the ring with some local blokes. By then, Dempsey will be up and we can get a decent picture with us all pumped up."

"That's cool," said Lucky. "And yah, my trainer's Aaron. I know he trained your nephew, that's actually why I was interested in him. You know, 'cuz I'm such a crazy Dempsey fan. I don't think there's a fighter out there today walking God's green Earth that could get him to tap, whadya think?"

"Well, he's pretty good – hey, he beat me," said Toasty good-naturedly. "Right, then Lucky, I'll just head inside. I got to take a slash. Nice meeting you, Velvet," said Toasty, his mouth almost watering as he opened the gym door.

"Tell Aaron I'll be right in; I'm still waking up," said Lucky, chuckling. Toasty waved his hand in the air in acknowledgement and hurried inside with a purpose. Dino stayed and stalled Lucky and Velvet outside the building. Toasty knew he could count on Dino's gift of gab to keep Lucky occupied for a few minutes and Velvet wasn't going anywhere without Lucky.

The lights were on inside the building, but it seemed dark and lonely. There was a lone caretaker heading towards the toilets with a scrub brush and spray bottle. Toasty walked about, searching for Aaron, and at last saw the ring through a pair of windowed double doors. He spied what looked like a skipping rope going around. Taking a big breath, he pushed the double doors open and went inside.

Aaron was four years younger than Toasty, but similar in size. Both possessed advanced skills in mixed martial arts, but

Aaron had the advantage of having seen Toasty's wrestling psychology on video and in the ring against his Dempsey. Toasty had never seen Aaron's strategies; he only watched him train guys on the punching bag and work on their conditioning. But Toasty was not at all concerned about who was better. There was no doubt in his mind that he would leave Aaron just short of messing himself.

"Hey, Toasty," Aaron said, somewhat surprised. He walked toward Toasty to shake his hand.

"Don't fuckin' give me that 'hey how are you and the fuckin' handshake' bullshit, you arsehole," spat Toasty. "What the fuck is your excuse for takin' me sister's money and fuckin' off on her like she's wet shit on a brick? I met your little Romanian princess outside, Velvet, is that what she goes by?"

"Hey, fuck man, ya don't understand," said Aaron. "It ain't how it looks. I knew that girl before I ever knew… your sister."

Toasty walked right up to Aaron so they were just a few inches apart. "You're a fuckin' piece-of-shit-coward!" he hissed into Aaron's face. "You can't even say Claudine's name because you haven't got the fuckin' backbone, you spineless bastard! I'm done talkin' with you. Get in the fuckin' ring right fuckin' now or I'll punch your rotten teeth down your throat and skull-drag ya in there. Don't give me too long to think about it, mother-fucker."

"Toasty, ah can't do this," said Aaron. "You've been knocked around an awful lot. Claudine told me what the doctor said. If you got another severe hit to yer head, another concussion, you could go blind or even die."

"Save your fuckin' cowardly horseshit excuses," yelled Toasty, holding the ropes open for Aaron. Toasty still had so much fight and fire left in his belly and seeing Aaron made the fire inside him rage like an inferno. "Are you fuckin' deaf? Get in this ring and let's have a go. What, you can't fight a retired wrestler with bad knees and too many concussions? Bet you thought you'd never get caught. Get in the ring."

It was at this point, as Aaron finally climbed into the ring that Dino, Lucky and Velvet came through the doors to the ring room. To Lucky, it looked like the men were having a pull for old time's sake. Neither Lucky nor Velvet knew Toasty was out for revenge. Lucky headed over to the punching bag, keeping one eye on the ring. Velvet followed him and started doing some half-hearted stretches.

It was on. The two wrestlers walked around, about to lock up. Aaron, well-poised, tried to punch Toasty in the face, but Toasty ducked and deftly swept him off his feet, quickly grounding him to the canvas. Toasty reached in front of Aaron and seized both of his biceps, holding them high in place with his left hand. Aaron's shoulders and arms were trapped and in this awkward position he could do nothing to break free.

Toasty cupped Aaron's face snuggly with his hand and dug his raspy chin into Aaron's eye socket. He pushed down on him, folding him in half like a hairpin. Dino and Lucky recognized the classic "thread-through" hold. Aaron did too, rather acutely, since he was the one presently suffering the suffocating effects of it. He tried to tap out, but his hands were nowhere close to being in a position that they could even touch the mat. He fought to breathe through his covered mouth. His eye watered profusely and his nose began to run from all the tears. Aaron's face got slippery and Toasty's hand slid off it, only to go right back onto to cupping Aaron's mouth. Toasty was toying with him like a cat with a mouse.

"Boy, that Toasty is putting on a regular ol' shoot-fighting clinic in there," said Lucky as he punched and kicked the bag, trying not to look overly concerned by Aaron's extended shrieks. "What the hell is he doing? Some of his stuff blows my freakin' mind. I've never seen moves like this, not live, not ever. Wow, I wish I had a film crew here to capture this. I should make a movie about this guy."

Oblivious to the praise, Toasty was calculating. Each time Aaron screamed, Toasty was showing him that he could finish him off for good. Toasty knew from watching his father how the lads would panic and squirm, making themselves frustrated and more tired. After some of the more torturous sessions, they would actually get to the point of messing themselves, purging all human waste from their body before taking their last breath. Billy would let them go before they reached that point. Toasty knew the art of Billy's tactics and was deeply aware of what he was doing now. He was not intending to kill Aaron, just let him repeatedly believe he was going to die. Fueled by anger, he went well beyond the mark of proving his point.

Lucky's partial interest was now that of a fully tuned-in member of the audience. He walked away from kicking the bag altogether and approached the ring, leaning on the ring apron and watching keenly. Even Velvet took a break from her light stretching and lack-lustre kicking on the huge canvas bag to stand with Lucky.

Lucky watched on, completely fascinated as he heard Aaron shrieking and screaming for durations as long as ten solid seconds; then his yelling faded out. Lucky watched on as his trainer struggled and then would just give up; then he would struggle again and then give up. Whenever this happened, Toasty was giving Aaron a little life to let him try to pry his way free, but each time, he was lured into the master's web even more. It was like a spider with a fly caught in its sticky web. Dino, Lucky and Velvet had a ringside view of it all.

"Hey, uh, maybe Toasty should let Aaron go, whad'ya think?" said Lucky to Dino after about ten minutes of this. "Looks like my guy's about to expire."

"I agree, I think your lad's done for the day, and it's not even seven a.m." Dino snidely said to Lucky.

"Ya think?" asked Lucky, who was actually nodding his baby face in agreement. Next to him, Velvet was blowing bubbles with her pink chewing gum. She dramatically cowered into Lucky's chest whenever Aaron screamed.

"Uh, maybe you better ask Toasty to go easy on Aaron now," urged Lucky as Aaron began screaming at the top of his lungs yet again. By now his voice was hoarse and his screams were becoming less piercing. Aaron had very little fight left in him now.

"I've never seen him without *some* kind of defense! Hey Aaron, c'mon, Dude, don't be so lame! Fight with a little effort, c'mon, your nose is bleeding all over the canvas and you've got stupid-crazy mat burn all over you," shouted Lucky.

"Oy-yoy-yoy! Concentrate Aaron," Velvet yelled, clapping her hands together a few times and looking confused. Neither she nor Lucky had ever seen Aaron so completely helpless.

Finally, Toasty completely released Aaron and stood up.

"It's not what it looks like, Toasty," was all Aaron could mumble. The whites of his eyes were bloodshot, making his copper irises appear brilliant gold, like something from a science fiction movie. Blood dripped from his nose and sticky pink phlegm crusted in the corners of his mouth.

Before Toasty left the bloodied canvas, he kneeled back down to where Aaron was lying in a crumpled heap. It appeared as though he was checking to see if Aaron was okay.

"By the way, smokin' cigs and chewin' gum lead to prostitution," he said in a quiet, cold voice. "Your dirty wife just serviced me mate in Japan only a fortnight ago. Oh yeah, and she'll be servicin' him again next month. Me mate is Dr. Eddie bloody *Holiday*. Why do you think your skank's got the word 'holiday' tattooed on her bloody ass? And you broke me sister's heart and stole all her money for that dirty slag?"

Toasty stood up and walked out of the ring.

"Aye, mate," he said loudly to Lucky, "I've just stretched the shit out of your trainer Aaron 'cuz he fuckin' did a number on me sister from promisin' to marry her to taking her inheritance money so she'd lose her house. This has nothin' to do with you, Lucky, but not sure it's proper to get a photo with you now. Seems kind of tight, ya know what I mean?" He walked out of the gym without another word.

Dino followed, taking one last look at everyone. There was Velvet, unknowingly displaying her tramp stamp to her tortured and wincing husband as she riffled through his training bag looking for something to clean him up with. Velvet shuffled back to him with a towel and water. She slouched down and put them next to him, stepping away quickly like she didn't want to be near him. Leaning on the bottom ropes, Aaron swished some water around in his mouth and spat it out, a mass of blood and phlegm, right at her feet.

"Ewww, gross," she exclaimed, jumping back.

Dino shook his head in disgust, wondering what Claudine ever saw in Aaron.

14

She Who Laughs Last

It was the last Friday of the month and Claudine was overwhelmed with anxiety as she drove to the farm to meet Aaron's solicitor. To make things even more stressful, she would also be seeing Dino for the first time since he got fresh with her. Tonight was their welcome home party for the Russian tour.

It seemed odd for Claudine to be heading up to the house so early in the morning. The 8:00 a.m. BBC news was about to start, so she turned up her car radio. The news was mostly grim today, but the last bit of local news really shouted out to Claudine.

"And the entertainment company Rocket Productions, headed up by Toni and Ernie Orr, filed for bankruptcy yesterday before the Queen's Court. Rocket Productions is responsible for the television reality series such as 'Diva Dentists,' 'Diva Doctors,' and 'Pimp My House.' Gross misrepresentation of the dental and medical professions led to international and local broadcasting corporations, as well as the National Physicians Association, in filing suit against Rocket. A court-ordered inquest exposed these programs for blatantly casting actors instead of authentic professionals on their reality television programs. Toni Orr also co-authored the controversial autobiography *The Blank Canvas* with Claudine Bellamy, the wife of late wrestling superstar Drew Bellamy. Rocket Productions' risky expansion into the American film industry lead to massive lawsuits against them for fraud from the American footballer…"

What a terrifically fabulous way to start my day, Claudine thought with immense satisfaction. The horizon this morning appeared rather bright through her windscreen, even though it was raining. Thinking about her new career and the splendid morning news, Claudine wondered if this was 'the first day of the rest of her life.' The popular expression hadn't ever significantly inspired her before, but today it seemed appropriate.

Claudine pulled up to her father's house and saw no unfamiliar cars; the lawyer hadn't yet arrived. In the kitchen the dogs Jeep and Betty greeted her with wagging tails.

"Well, Betty, I imagine your daddy's still asleep after his big Russia trip. You miss him when he's gone, don't ya? I miss Buffy when I go away, even for a few hours," Claudine said to the black Rottweiler, whose back end wiggled back and forth in agreement.

How slowly the minutes passed by as she waited. She was bursting with anxiety about what Aaron could possibly want her to see after all this time. *What was in the letter he wrote?* That was what she was most curious about.

Claudine would tell Toasty and Dempsey the news about Rocket Productions in person when they woke up, but as she was texting Isabella about the bankruptcy, she saw Betty run to the front door. A silver sedan was pulling up. Anxiety grew by the second in Claudine's chest as she watched a man get out of the car with an attaché case. He walked up the front steps to the door where Claudine greeted him.

"Good morning, I'm Claudine Bellamy. I believe I am expecting you, if you're the solicitor who Aaron sent," said Claudine as welcomed the man into her father's home. The man looked vacantly at her.

"Do you have photo identification? I need to see some government proof you are who you say you are," replied the man. He spoke a Russian accent. Claudine went through her purse and pulled out her driver's permit with her photo on it.

"See, it is me. I am who I say I am. Are you the solicitor Aaron sent?" she asked again.

"Yes," said the solicitor, looking at the ID card and handing it back to Claudine. "Aaron Gabrielle hired me to deliver this to you. I will need you to sign a document to verify that you received this attaché case." Claudine signed it and waited for her next instruction.

"The code to open the case is 830," said the solicitor. "Dial that into the combination lock."

Claudine did as she was told. The thin briefcase unlocked with a click, but she did not yet open it.

"It is none of my business what you see or say now that you have what Aaron wants you to have," said the man. "You may open the briefcase now. I have done all that is asked of me. I will let you discover whatever is so important to you and him. Good day." The man abruptly turned and walked away.

Claudine shut the door behind him and returned to the table. She slowly opened up the case. When she saw what was inside, she nearly collapsed.

Inside the briefcase lay a thick, grey, paper envelope. It was large and old, folded in half, and about the size of a paperback book. Faded blue letters spelled out "Drew Bellamy UGA" across the front.

The envelope crinkled in her trembling hands as she opened it. Inside was a stack of American one-hundred dollar bills.

Claudine put the envelope back into the briefcase. Careful not to close it, she carried it to the library and sat down. Physically she sat very still, but her mind was rush of emotions. Before she counted the bills, she wanted to know how this all came about and what else Aaron had to tell her.

Opening the briefcase back up, Claudine reached for the other envelope in the case. It was white and puffy, with her name printed across its front. When she reached inside, a big pile of paper currencies from different countries spilled out along with his letter. She saw euros, American dollars, francs, roubles, and yen, along with some currencies she didn't recognize.

Shoving the cash to the side, she opened the letter. It was four pages long and handwritten in jagged, backhand writing. She carefully read the words over and over.

Hi Claudine,

Let me get to the point first and explain the rest after, if you even care to read it. I found Drew's money. It's in the envelope. I don't know how much is there, not my place to count it, but you go right ahead, darling. I hope it's a fortune still and I hope you are doing great.

Now, let me start this long story, from the beginning:

I managed to find your family's IWF address over the internet and I figured it was a safe place to have you go to for all this. First off, I hope you're doing better than before. I need you to know you aren't to blame for the way things fell apart and I'm real sorry for what I'm about to tell you. I told you many times how special you were and you still are to me. I remember you saying animals are much better than people. You got that right. Most people are full of shit. I got lots of things to fix in my life so I don't remain one of those people who is full of shit.

I left for Germany telling you I'd see you soon. I'm not sure you believe me now, but I thought it was the truth. Then I lost my clients soon after I got there because of injuries and stuff, but I got a contract to train Lucky Boyd, the actor. He's taken me around the world and I've seen some pretty wild stuff. I'm no angel, but I'll leave it at that.

I told you once about a girl I was in love with in Japan. Her name is Velvet. What I didn't tell you was I was married to Velvet. I'm sorry I didn't tell you. I didn't think it was relevant at the time.

Anyway, our marriage ended because she picked a life as a prostitute over being married to me. That was in Tokyo. And then one day, she just shows up at the gym in St. Petersburg where I'm training Lucky because he's making a movie here. Velvet tells me that we're still married. She said she never signed off on the divorce papers. She tells me she wants to change her life and not be a prostitute anymore and asks if there's a chance for me and her to work things out. I tell her NO WAY, because a) she's a prostitute, and b) because she and I were done a long time ago, and c) because I am in love with a girl in England (YOU)!

It was after I met her in St. Petersburg that I wrote you the email, telling you that we needed to go our separate ways. Still being married, and to a prostitute, and losing all our money, well, I figured I should just set you free, sort this fucking divorce out, and then try to get your money back. If I could do all that, I might stand half a chance of starting again with you. My head was a real mess when I sent you the email, but once it was sent, I couldn't take it back. The next day I regretted sending it to you and I wanted to tell you everything, but I read your email reply to me and I saw how much I hurt you. I figured I better just fuck off. I didn't want to stay married to Velvet after I broke up with you, but when she said the name Hagra, I decided to keep her around long enough to find out more. I went back to LA twice with Lucky, but basically St. Petersburg has been home to me for months now. The movie keeps getting delayed due to weather and directors changing. Stuff I can't control, unless I quit, but I can't because I signed a contract with the movie studio.

I don't want to torment you with all this drama, or torture you with boring details but I think you should know the whole story, for the sake of closure. I know how you don't like uncertainty. So here is the next part. I'm sorry, darling, but I think you need to know it all.

Velvet tells me our divorce papers are at her dead Madame's apartment in downtown St. Petersburg, along with her valuable jewelry and gold ounces and gems and stuff. She says her dead Madame's name is Hagra.

Velvet says she will go back there and get the divorce papers and sign off on them for me if I help her get her stuff. I figure, since I need the divorce if I want to ever be with you again, I may as well help her. I feel bad for Velvet too and as much as I want to get my divorce from her, I want to help her get away from prostitution. She seems to really want to turn her life around.

So we meet at the movie set in St. Petersburg. We take the studio car and drive off downtown to get Velvet's stuff (and the divorce papers). She is nervous at her apartment, so I tell her to go have a cigarette on the balcony. I needed to get her out of the way quick so

I could look around in the freezer for Drew's money – I remember you said that that's where Drew's dad hid it.

I went straight to the freezer and searched in there and sure as hell, hidden way at the back underneath a bunch of freezer-burnt shit I find this plastic bag with an envelope in it. I didn't have time to check it out, so I stuffed it down my pants. I don't even know how much is left, but it's amazing, really amazing that it didn't get stolen or spent after all these years. I guess no one who's a drug addict like the pimps and prostitutes working for Hagra really care about freezer-burnt meat, which is what this looked like when I found it. And maybe Hagra figured the money was too hot to spend. I'm just guessing.

Meanwhile, Velvet is back inside grabbing all her stuff and she says she can't find the divorce papers. We're arguing now and as fucking fate would have it, one of her pimp's buddies comes by and tries to cause trouble. I end up punching him in the face and he falls and hits his head. We take off in a hurry. We weren't hard to find, the studio car had advertising all over it.

I immediately dump Velvet and all her stuff off at my trailer and go to Lucky's trailer to find him and hide this package in his trailer, away from Velvet, and get it off to you. He's in the toilet, so I pull the package out of my pants and I'm just on the verge of opening it up to take a look when one of the producers comes looking for me. He's all hysterical. He says the police are on set and need to talk to me. Lucky comes out of the bathroom and I gave him the wrapped-up package and asked him to hang on to it for me. I told him it was a bunch of love letters I needed to read in privacy. He promised he wouldn't look and kind of laughed, but he could tell I was serious about it being private. I knew he wouldn't look.

The police took me right from the studio lot directly to jail for questioning. It turns out the john had a heart attack after I punched him and went into a coma. I stayed in that jail for three months on charges of aggravated assault for punching this asshole in the face. I couldn't email or use the phone, couldn't do anything. Lucky finally got me out but one of the problems that kept me in jail is that, because we were in a foreign country, it took forever. I wouldn't say to the police why I really hit the john, because I didn't want to expose Velvet as being a prostitute, so that made it take even longer. I didn't want her going to jail for being a prostitute because then I figured I'd never get the divorce. I just maintained that this guy was trying to rob us so I hit him in the face. Velvet backed my story up.

In the end, it came out that the guy had high blood pressure and diabetes and was doing way too much coke, plus a million other things wrong with him. They couldn't prove whether I caused him to pass out of if it was all the other stuff. It took a couple months and I was held in jail for the whole time, but Lucky got me a real smart lawyer and the charges were dropped

When I was finally released from jail and got the package back from Lucky, sure enough, it was an old envelope with Drew's name on it. I opened it up and saw a big wad of American hundred dollar bills. It's none of my business to count it, so I didn't. So, for whatever it's worth, here's what's left of the hundred grand Drew always wanted you to have.

I am very very sorry I hurt you. I fucked things up real bad for us darling and I don't blame you for never forgiving me. I should have just leveled with you and told you I had been married. I should have leveled with you when Velvet resurfaced, but I didn't. She seems to be turning her life around though. This divorce is just a fucking long process and it still isn't final. She says she needs to go back to Japan and finalize something on it and that should be soon. I'm not really sure what's taking so long, but I'll let you know when it's final, for whatever it's worth.

I hope things are great for you again and you're happy. You probably moved on to better things already, you sure deserve them. I hope God brings us together again, with the past behind us both, but I understand if you already walked away. But Claudine, just know that when I open my hand, I still see you as one of my five fingers. I always will see you that way.

I wish you the best, you deserve it and I will always be very, very sorry that I hurt you.

Aaron

PS: Here is some other cash that goes with this letter. It's all in different currencies that I saved from all the countries I worked in. I don't know what you will get for this at your bank, but I think is close to £3,000. I'm sending it to you now to help repay you for that terrible investment.

Claudine had to put the letter down so she wouldn't soak it with tears. When Aaron held open his hand to show her his fingers at the airport, she had believed she really was one of them. Now, she believed he was writing these things not for her closure, but for his own closure. He didn't sign it "with love" and that seemed to speak louder than anything else. Her feelings for him, however, still ran deep, but what she had to do now was just keep going forward. The whole situation reminded her of when a wrestler takes a pile-driver so severe that he sees stars and his footing is unsure. He still has to carry on and finish the match just the same. Maybe she would see Aaron again one day, maybe not. She had to tell herself with certainty that it was over; otherwise she would fall into another depression and get nowhere, or even worse, go backwards.

She went into the living room with her packet of money, too exhausted to count it presently. Laying herself down on the chesterfield, she closed her eyes and fell asleep.

Claudine was still asleep when Dempsey lightly dragged a piece of paper across her lips to wake her up. It was an old trick her dad used to do to wake her and Toasty up for school. Half asleep, she bit her tickled lips with her teeth.

"How long have you been asleep?" he asked.

"I've been here since about eight this morning," she said, sitting up and blinking her eyes. "Did you hear about Toni?" she asked.

"Yeah, I heard the great news," said Dempsey.

"Is Isabella here yet?" Claudine asked.

"Yeah, Mum, it's already twelve. Why are you napping here?" asked Dempsey.

"If you can go get our Isabella and Toasty and meet me in the living room right away, I will tell you all about it," said Claudine.

When they all gathered around, Claudine showed them the cash. She gave them an abbreviated explanation about what Aaron wrote to her and asked them if they could help her count the money. She decided to keep the letter private; one day, she would tell everyone about Aaron's complicated life. Toasty listened quietly; he had a secret too, but he also wasn't ready to tell everyone about his little visit with Aaron in Russia.

As it turned out, there was $69,900 American dollars left in the envelope. They seemed to be the original bills, although no one was sure. It was a miracle that Hagra hadn't used it all, although the rationale of a heavy drug user was difficult to comprehend. Dempsey, like Aaron, suggested that Hagra might have been nervous that the bills were marked. Everyone was amazed that Aaron somehow found it and they were surprised that he chose to do the right thing in sending it to Claudine.

"Well, Dempsey, I guess I can pay you back for the cottage now," said Claudine with a smile.

"And then some," said Isabella joyfully.

"And on the day that Rocket Productions went down, too," laughed Dempsey. "This couldn't be more perfect!" Everyone was happy, including the dogs. They rolled on their backs and ran circles around Dempsey's legs.

All of this was just the beginning of an evening of celebration. It was a full house that night for the welcome home party: Toasty, Dempsey, Isabella, Mary, Dino, Sui-ee, Leilani, and a few newer wrestlers from Samoa and Japan were all there.

After an hour or so, Claudine stepped into the library, wanting to read Aaron's letter again. Instead, she felt a tap on her shoulder.

"Umm, hi, Claudine," said Dino tentatively. "May I have a word?"

"Well, you always go overboard, so 'a word' must mean some be some windy sermon about our untapped love," Claudine said.

"I'm not at all interested in your rubbish. You behaved like such an ass, Dino."

Dino stood there for a moment, staring at his feet. He was wearing a two-tone tan and white velour tracksuit that made him look like a giant teddy bear, but he didn't look cute or cuddly to Claudine. "Please hear me out, Claudine."

"No. It's against me better judgment, summat you don't have any of. I'm only toleratin' you right now because of the circumstances. I don't want to spoil this great party by causin' a scene with you and you're takin' advantage of that situation. You are brilliant at takin' advantage of situations."

"Well, if I have to take advantage of this situation to tell you that I am cursed with stupidity and that I am sorry, then I will," said Dino.

"Too late, Dino. I want nothin' to do with you," said Claudine. "Don't stand there and look offended. You've been a cad and a creep. Why don't you go off in some corner and lick your wounds in some unnatural way?" Claudine was mad, but she wasn't as mad as she let on. She had been blessed with so much today that she felt like she should be less mean, but she needed to get Dino to behave himself for good.

Dino, to her surprise, smiled a little. "You are unpredictable, Claudine. Only you could have thought of that. I am incredibly stupid and I'm sorry, but I'm not so stupid to know you are one of a kind. Now I will go find somewhere to 'lick me wounds in some unnatural way,' as you put it. If I can do that to your satisfaction, can we at least give it another go – be friends again, for starters?" He held out his hand.

Claudine stood there for a moment and looked at Dino's embarrassed face. She didn't hate Dino, she realized. She subtly glared at him for another moment longer before shaking his hand and smiling, slightly.

"Thank you for hearing me out," he said, relieved. "I'll leave you be now."

"Oh, wait," said Claudine, remembering something. She went to the corner of the library and picked up flat cardboard package loosely tied with yellow ribbon around it.

"Here's your paintin'," she said, handing it to him. "I don't owe you anythin' now."

Dino pulled the yellow ribbon and unwrapped the pretty paper, stopping to stare at the finished painting of Buffy. There was a moment when Dino looked like he was about to cry as he looked at the painting. He held it up and cocked his head back and forth, studying the different angles.

"Well, luv, I do appreciate this. Thank you. I'll have it framed and put up at the studio straight away."

Claudine left the library and ran right into Dempsey, who handed her a lovely glass of chilled white wine. "C'mon, Mum," he said, steering her into the kitchen. "I was just about to start a toast. Where's Dino?"

In the kitchen, Dempsey hit his glass with a spoon for silence. "First off, our Isabella's got big news to tell everyone. C'monnnnn, Toasty, Mary, everyone get your glasses of wine and let's hear our Isabella's news."

Everyone raised their glasses and Isabella lifted her head dramatically. "Okay, I have the stage, no pun intended," she said as the guests laughed. "I literally do, though, thanks to Mary and her father, Dino, who have opened up business relations with Goldsmith Pictures in Hollywood. I'm now under contract with them to make five films. The first one begins after we officially finish the documentary on me dad, so let's have a toast to me father."

"Yes, let's drink to me father and cheers to me sister, Isabella, her brilliant movie career and her brilliant documentary," added Dempsey. Everyone cheered and clinked glasses.

Toasty cleared his throat. "I want to make a toasty toast to Dino and Mary," he said, "for makin' this first-class documentary with me niece Isabella and helpin' the IWF get noticed over in Russia."

The Samoans began making toasts and the glasses of champagne and wine were refilled often and generously. It was like a festival of toasting and everyone was grinning ear to ear.

Claudine started to think about making a toast herself. She was ready to share her good news about Syncopation; there was no reason to keep it a secret anymore. Before she could, though, she heard Isabella taking care of it for her. "But wait, me mum's on stage now, too," she boasted, lifting her newly filled glass.

"Let us all toast me mum and her success in getting her new Syncopation classes started down Chester. She's a fitness teacher now. I know Dempsey and I would never have made it without her and I know our dad would be so proud of Mum, eh Demps?"

"Yes, he would. Thank you, Mum, and thank you Isabella for that nice toast," said Dempsey. Claudine could tell from his demeanour Isabella had already spilled the beans to him, but since the franchise was already up and running, Claudine didn't mind. "We are proud of you Mum and congratulations! You've got the eye o' the tiger 'cuz you're a survivor. Can wrestlers take your classes?"

The sounds of laughter, applause and clinking glasses filled the room once again. Dempsey turned the lights on and off several times and all the dogs started barking and running about. The scene was only complete when the Betty, the young Rottweiler and Jeep the old Bull Mastiff, instinctively jumped up only on Dino, who spilled red wine all over his two-tone tan tracksuit. After that, a satisfied Dempsey finally stopped the light show, but the delightful cheering frenzy still carried on.

In the midst of all this, Claudine stepped back and took a deep breath. In the next room, a small fire glowed in the beautiful brown tortoise glazed-brick fireplace, lighting up the pictures and trophies on the mantel. Raising her glass once more, Claudine made a private toast as she looked at all of the faces there. Her family's soulful eyes stared back at her. Taking a step closer, she looked at her mum, her father, and Drew, Dempsey, Isabella, and Toasty. Here they were hugging animals, sitting naked and tiny in bathtubs, wrestling in the ring. One picture showed them all together; it was taken just before the tour to Sardinia, at a Sunday tea when everything was magical and fun. Claudine held her glass up to that framed picture.

"This would never have been possible if it weren't for all o' you and everyone who is still here today," she said quietly. "Thank you, God. Mum, Dad, Drew, I know you are watchin' us all right and smilin.' And we're all smilin,' too. Here's to all of us." She took a sip of her wine to complete her toast.

When she turned around and saw the group still clapping and laughing, she hurried across the room to join their silliness. Opening her arms, she gave her brother and children a big hug. "I wish this moment could just freeze and we could come back to it whenever we wanted," she cried. "We finally did it! We did it! " Claudine began to laugh and soon everyone in the room was laughing with her. She wondered if this was what was meant by the old saying, 'she who laughs last laughs best,' and not because she was the last one to get the joke.

EPILOGUE

Claudine looked out of the window of her limousine, staring at the spectacle before her. The most majestic theatre in Manchester was awash in media and fans lined up three people deep along the street. There was a queue of at least a dozen limousines leading up to the entrance, waiting to be received by the throng.

"Hey, Mrs. Bellamy, we're fourth car in line, so it won't be long now," said Byron from the limo's driver's seat. "When we get there, wait for the valet to open your door. By the way, you look like a film star."

"Oh, do you think so?" Claudine was wearing a sleeveless chiffon dress, high cut in front, with a plunging backline to show off her muscular back and arms. The pale blue colour of it made her eyes stand out like pieces of the summer sky. She looked stunning.

"You do! Just take a deep breath and relax and enjoy your night."

"Okay, I'll try," she said. "Let me just take a moment to collect me thoughts." She sat still and poised, thinking about how she got to this moment. Her first year at Syncopation had ended with a profit and she had gained a lovely following of women who depended on her nearly every day to motivate them. Now, she was a big part of many of these women's lives. One student asked Claudine to be her child's godmother; another often asks Claudine for advice on her cats. They all leaned on Claudine, and as they did, Claudine leaned right back on them. Claudine remembered Glenda telling her this was a perk of being a dedicated Syncopation instructor; another benefit was looking and feeling better than she had in years. She didn't look worn out or sad anymore.

Claudine's paintings had become quite a hit too. One of Claudine's students turned out to be an art gallery owner. She began exhibiting Claudine's work in her gallery and had managed to sell several pieces.

The limousine moved forward and stopped with a slight jerk, bringing Claudine back to the present. She heard her driver put the big, sleek vehicle into park. The valet opened her car door to a flash of cameras and crazy cheering. People were shouting her name as she gracefully stepped out of her limousine and walked down the red carpet. This was actually the second time she had walked down a red carpet; the first time, Dino had the red carpet rolled out on their first date to one of his restaurants. This was quite different than that.

"Hey, Claudine! Hey, over here! We love you and we love Drew!" chanted the crowd enthusiastically. Claudine looked over in the direction of the cheers and saw some of her Syncopation students waving excitedly at her.

"Hallo! Thanks for coming," she called, happily waving back to them. She glanced around, then looked way up at the dark sky, hoping her family that had gone too soon was watching this wonderful evening from the heavens above. Looking back down, she paused momentarily as her eyes fell on a familiar face. Her heart seemed to skip a beat and she hesitated for a moment before straying from the straight path she was supposed to take towards the entrance of the theatre's grand hall.

"Aaron, my God!"

"Hi darlin'. Congratulations!" He looked healthy and tan, with long hair in a plait. His square, thick-rimmed tortoise-shell eyeglasses had almost kept her from recognizing him. This look was very different from what she remembered, but it worked on him.

"It's not a good time now, but are we able to talk later?" they both asked of each other simultaneously.

"Sure, I'd like that."

"Mrs. Bellamy, is there a problem?" asked one of the hired guards.

"No, no. But can you please see that me friend gets a ticket and is escorted backstage right away?' she asked anxiously.

"Right, you got it, Mrs. Bellamy," said the guard.

Claudine got back on her red carpet path and went in the front entrance of the theatre, smiling and waving politely. She then hurried into the back of the hall, anxious to meet Aaron before Dino or Toasty threw him out.

"Hey, there you are, Mum," cried Isabella.

"Oh, luv, you look beautiful. I'm so proud of you," said Claudine, wrapping her daughter up in a hug. "I know your dad is watchin' over us beamin' with pride. You're a *dream-come-true daughter*, Isabella."

Dempsey was just approaching the pair with a big bear hug when a photographer called out.

"Can we get a picture of you three?"

"Remember, Bell, that when the food gets here, it's goin' to be good, right?" said Dempsey, posing with the two women.

"I'm pinchin' meself," said Isabella excitedly.

Claudine smiled and nodded her head in agreement. "Listen, I just saw Aaron outside in the queue," she said under her breath as the photographer snapped away. "I had security take him to the back because I want to talk to him. I don't want to make a big production of it, just please let me talk to him and get a number where I can reach him later. I don't want this to become anythin' to take away from this perfect night."

Her children looked at each other in surprise before looking back at their mum.

"Well, how was he?" asked Dempsey.

"He was very complimentary and asked if we could talk," said Claudine. "He's got eyeglasses now and he's wearing his hair in a plait off the side of his head."

"Well, of course he'd be complimentary! I guess talking to him again… well, it's summat you're going to do, regardless," said Isabella, always the diplomat. "But you should make it brief and arrange to talk with him another time, another place. This is your night too, Mum, not just mine."

"I'm dead surprised he's here," admitted Claudine. "But since he is, I will find him and keep him from runnin' into Toasty and Dino."

"I'll keep an eye out for him," said Dempsey. "Hey Mum, Bella, I want you to meet Falon."

Claudine and Isabella turned to the young woman who had just approached. She had huge green eyes shaped like a cat's and her long, wavy brown hair was pinned back on one side with a white flower. She was slender, nearly a foot shorter than Dempsey, who reached out and held her delicate waist.

"Oh, my, what a lovely surprise! Very nice to meet you, Falon. You have a lovely face," said Claudine.

"Thank you, Mrs. Bellamy," said Falon, reddening. "So honoured to be here."

"Dempsey's told me lots of lovely things about you, Falon," said Isabella. "So nice to meet you. I am happy to have you here on this big night for me and me family."

Other people came over to say hello. "We should take our seats in about half an hour, thereabouts," Isabella said before greeting them. "Please make sure you and Falon sit with us, Dempsey."

They went their separate ways, pulled in different directions by people wanting to get a picture or a quick word. Finally, Claudine was able to get away and go to the hospitality room. It was full of celebrities and friends enjoying champagne and there was jazz music playing in the background. Claudine smiled and looked around for Aaron.

"Excuse me, Miss Claudine," said a handsome man with a thick French accent, blocking Claudine's progress. He had straight, dark brown hair, cut in a blunt bob just below his jaw line. The short goatee he sported made him look very artsy, a look accentuated by his loose-fitting linen blazer, white t-shirt, and boot-cut dark denims. "I'm Pascal from *Le Tigre Magazine* in Paris. Would you grant me a quick interview?"

"Uhmm, sure, Pascal, oui, just give me *cinq* minutes," said Claudine. Aaron at last appeared at her right side.

"Oui, merci," Pascal replied, smiling.

Claudine and Aaron stared at each other. She was unsure of how to greet him, and he seemed unsure how to greet her too. Finally, she smiled at him and he reached out to her, catching her in a tight embrace. When they broke away, he looked fondly at her.

"Ah see you have a big interview in five minutes, so ah won't keep you," he said. "Ah'd love to get with you later, or tomorrow, to talk more. Ah got so much to tell you and ah wanna hear all about you, darlin'. You're lookin' fantastic, by the way. You really are. How are the kids? An' Buffy, how is our little cat?"

"Oh, why thanks, Aaron," said Claudine. "Everyone is brilliant. Buffy misses you though. How are you? I see you've grown your hair out. It's actually a good look on you, with the glasses and all. Not everyone could get away with that."

"Darlin' ah'm good. Ah saw an actor wearing his hair, braided and pulled over to the side like this. He was on one of the movie sets and I thought I'd like to try it on myself. I've had it for a while. D'ya like it?"

"Yes, it's different; it's nice. So, are you still married?" she asked. She was impressed with herself for getting to the point.

"I've been divorced for about four, no, five months, which I was gonna tell you as soon as it was done, but I wanted to get a few loose ends tied up before coming back."

Claudine was stunned. "Why did you wait so long to tell me and why did you pick tonight of all nights to reappear?" she asked. "You couldn't have picked a busier night. I'm sure you know Toasty is going to be here any minute too."

"Well maybe my judgment's bad, but ah'm here now. Ah'm working on a movie in London, doin' stunt work, starting a couple weeks from now. Ah wasn't sure you'd want to see me, but ah wanted to see you so much so ah took a risk. Ah ain't bothered one way or the other about seeing Toasty. Ah figure we got it all out of our systems a year ago."

He stepped towards her. "No one knows better than ah do the mess ah got myself into," he said softly. "I'd like to start repairing things with everyone, but I ain't gonna do that here tonight. It's not appropriate, but ah ain't scared of what anyone's gonna say to me for being here for five minutes with you."

Claudine said nothing and Aaron looked at her with the serious gaze she remembered so well. "Ah care about what you think, though, so let me explain in short form. After the divorce, ah went back home to Texas to visit my family. Ah wanted to call you then, but ah needed to get my head together. Once ah got here, ah decided to come to the premier and ah couldn't help myself. Ah wasn't callin' your name out, jumpin' up and down, or tryin' to catch your eye. Ah didn't want to cause any problems; ah still don't. Ah'll be in London for about four months. Man, I hate rushing to say all this, but do you think we can start again?"

Aaron's look was pleading. For a moment, Claudine wanted to bring him right back into her life. But as she stood there, dumbstruck, she heard a voice over her shoulder.

"So sorry to interrupt, Ma'am," said a man. She turned and saw a couple that looked as though they had just walked off of the silver screen. She recognized them immediately: it was Dave and Lemon Duffy, the movie star duo that had walked out on The Blank Canvas film.

"We just wanted to say it's an honour to be here tonight," said Dave.

"Why it's an honour to meet you both," said Claudine, quite surprised.

"We'd love to talk more with you about a movie idea about your life, your story, your way, if you're interested," said Lemon. "We did not want to be involved with any production that didn't involve you directly. Here's our contact information."

"You can call us or our agent," said Dave. "Congratulations to your daughter." The pair of them drifted away as suddenly as they had appeared.

"Wow, wasn't that a shocker," said Claudine, turning back to Aaron. "I'd like to hear them out; I'll get Isabella involved with that for sure. But anyway, Aaron, I wish we had more time to talk and perhaps we can another day. There's too many distractions here. But I must say a few things right now."

"Okay, Claudine, shoot. I wanna hear it all, good and bad," said Aaron. His demeanor was sincere.

Claudine fixed Aaron with a penetrating stare. "Do you realize how long and hard I prayed to hear you say those things you just said to me? Do you realize how long and hard I cried over what you did to me? Do you realize how hard I had to work to get me life together after you left? Maybe if you hadn't come here tonight, I would have imagined I'd jump at the chance to be a part of your life again. But you weren't there for me when I needed you. Not even an email. Nothin'."

Aaron hung his head in shame as Claudine continued. "Maybe a year ago, it would 'ave mattered that you still want me now. But you 'ad so many other priorities an' I don't know that I was one of them.

You helped Velvet the prostitute get her shit together, then ya went home to Texas an' weighed out your life for five months before decidin' to come here. I'm not sure if you're so shallow that you came back because you think I'm not a loser anymore, or if you came back because you really want to see me really shine."

She was more sad than angry, but her eyes stayed perfectly dry during all of this. Aaron's face was bewildered as he looked up. "Ah am sorry, Claudine, ah really am," he said. "And, yes, ah'm a shallow person for lots of reasons, but wantin' to see you 'shine' ain't one of them. Ah'm real proud of you. Ah wanna show you how much ah love you. Ah wan'cha back. You might think that's never gonna happen, but never say never." He looked so handsome to Claudine, despite how much he had let her down.

"Right. Aaron, I won't say never, but it's probably never going to happen," she amended. "I've managed to not get emotional and break down like I might have done once upon a time. If you really want to do something proactive, write me a letter, how about that? Now, I really need to go and I think you need to go too." She walked away, leaving him standing there for a moment before heading out the back door and into the night.

For the first time since she had known Aaron, Claudine just wanted to be far away from him. She felt a bit rattled but quite amazed that she had stood up for herself. As she searched for a distraction, she saw the French reporter who wanted to talk with her. Smiling, she started walking towards him when she was cut off by a very robust torso in a suit.

"Where is that piece of shit? I'm gonna annihilate him, but I want to have a word with you, Lady Jane!" Dino was clearly agitated; his face was tense and red with anger and his eyes darted furiously all around in hopes of spotting Aaron. "I'm disappointed in you for having him back here. How could you do that to me? You owe me an explanation. I've been patient with you and your pigging animals and your pigging disorganization."

"Dino, calm down. Aaron is gone," Claudine said calmly. "If he was still here, were you goin' to break some chairs over his head on Isabella's big night? You probably would, by the looks of it. You're gettin' upset over nothin'. And I don't owe you the kind of explanation you think I do."

"How did that shithead even get back here?" Dino demanded.

"I invited Aaron back here. I didn't do that to spite you though, Dino. And he's already gone anyway. I wanted to talk to him; I needed to."

"Well, you should have asked me for permission first and I don't want you talking to that bastard again. Do you understand?"

"Dino, I have a past with Aaron," Claudine said with exasperation. "There are still things between him and me that need to be addressed. But that's between *him and me*. And I don't need your approval, I can think for meself."

"I don't bloody think so." mumbled Dino.

"Dino, you've helped me family a lot and I'm grateful to you for that. But your business endeavours with me family don't have anything to do with your supposed relationship with me. You and I are not courting. We are friends. Obviously we aren't ever going to fit together. You still think I'm a dreadful slob, you don't understand the unconditional friendship I have with me animals and I don't know if you even appreciate that this past year I've really started a career for meself. I don't have to answer to you about how I live me life."

Dino opened his mouth to say something, but Claudine kept talking right over him. "I am not interested in startin' up again with Aaron, but I am still not interested in bein' more than friends with you. I didn't invite Aaron back here to hurt your feelings. I just needed to say a final goodbye to him; I needed to tell him that in person. Please, let's not ruin our friendship over this. We have a great night ahead of us and the movie is going to start soon. Now, if you'll excuse me," she said and politely pushed past him to the waiting reporter.

Pascal was looking at his mobile phone, standing off from where Dino and Claudine were talking. His rather pointy-toed black boots made him seem even leaner and taller than he already was as he stood against the wall.

"Sorry to keep you waiting," Claudine said. Pascal didn't indicate he had heard any of Claudine's conversations. Instead, he smiled and shook Claudine's hand.

"Oh you have a good handshake," she said.

"Thank you, you as well." he replied back. "Now, let me ask you a few questions."

In the front of the room, Toasty was walking through the crowd of celebrities and guests in the back stage area, saying hello and nodding his head in acknowledgement. He had a lovely woman on his arm; she was tall and blonde, with the figure of a gymnast and the face of a film star.

"Are you all right?" he asked his guest.

"Well, I'm overwhelmed but I'm dead excited," she said with a smile. "Thank you, Toasty, for thinkin' o' me after all these years."

"Oh, I see Mary over there. She's Isabella's best friend," said Toasty, pointing Mary out. "She's married to Sui-ee, who's one of me main wrestlers now. Mary's father, Dino, is me business partner. Let me introduce you to her, she'll know where everyone is."

Mary looked preoccupied and slightly frantic when Toasty approached her. "Isabella is behind the curtain with Dempsey and Sui-ee, but they're going need to get to their seats soon. She's going to say a few words after the curtain goes up. But listen… Toasty, you need to find my dad and talk to him. Even stop him."

"What's up?" asked Toasty.

"Well, he's going to go after Aaron, who showed up out of nowhere to wish Claudine luck. Isabella's worried that you're the one who'll go after Aaron, but Dempsey said you and Aaron settled your differences and it's me dad we have worry about, because he's still thinking he's first in line for your Claudine. And I just want this night to go smoothly for everyone," she said, on the verge of tears.

"So that bastard actually had the balls to show up again?" said Toasty with a smirk. "Well, don't worry, Mary, I'll find 'em. They must be all right or we'd hear the fightin'. Oh, by the way, Mary, I'd like to meet a dear long-time family friend, Claire."

The lights in the hospitality room went on and off a few times, indicating the audience needed to take their seats.

"Claudine, 'ere is my business card," said Pascal, wrapping up the interview. "I would love to talk with you more, especially about what you 'ave done in the past year. Please call me."

"Thank you—." She stopped abruptly as Toasty covered her eyes from behind.

"Sorry to interrupt here, but I've got a big surprise for me sister. Say, you're that French magazine writer, Pascal. You used to box, didn't you? Glad you made it," Toasty said, keeping his hands firmly across his sister's eyes.

"Thank you. I am very 'appy to be here. Claudine, Toasty, I will give your family some privacy," offered Pascal.

"Well, you're stayin' for the show, right?" said Toasty, still keeping his hands covering Claudine's eyes.

"Yes, of course. I will take my seat and perhaps we can reacquaint after?" Pascal suggested. He stepped away, but as he neared the doorway, he paused to watch the expression on Claudine's face as the mystery guest was revealed to her.

"This suspense is killing me, Toasty! Let me see!" she said.

"Claudine, I brought us a big surprise all the way from America," and he dropped his hands down.

"Oh my God! Claire!" Claudine exclaimed and gave her old friend a huge hug. Tears came to their eyes.

"So, Claudine, I hate to ruin the moment here, but where's Aaron and where's Dino?"

"Oh Claire, you look so beautiful," Claudine said, still hanging on to her friend. "Thank you for bein' here tonight. Toasty, I didn't even know you kept in touch with Claire. And Aaron is gone for good and that's all fine. Dino is off in some corner licking his wounds in some unnatural way." Claire burst out laughing.

"Claudine, I'm so proud o' you. Toasty told me all about what you've done for yourself this past year. I can't wait to meet your children after the show. I wanted to tell you that I was comin', but Toasty wanted it to be a surprise. He flew me out here, we've been keepin' in touch through the internet," Claire excitedly explained as she moved in closer to Toasty. He looked back at her affectionately.

The lights in the hospitality room went on and off again as the crowd filed out to the auditorium and took their seats. Claudine worked her way through the masses of people and took her seat next to Dempsey. She saw Claire and Toasty sitting in the row ahead, along with Dino, Mary and Sui-ee. There was a friendly tap on her shoulder. She turned around and saw it was Pascal.

"It's going to be a good show. I can just feel it," he said, placing his hand briefly on her shoulder.

"I can hardly wait for it to start," she said, smiling proudly. .

The lights dimmed and Isabella came out onto the stage. The spotlight shone on her as she held a cordless microphone to her mouth.

"Thank you all so much for bein' here," she said, her voice amplified in the large auditorium. "It's been quite somethin', gettin' this true story about me dad, Drew Bellamy, produced. I want to thank Dino and Mary Tsillas of Thronos Movie Productions, who really made sure I got to do this and do it the right way. It's the real deal, this film, and I couldn't have made it without Dino, Mary, me mum Claudine, me brother Dempsey, and me Uncle Toasty, who are all out there in the audience somewhere. I want to thank all the people who shared their stories with us, as you'll see soon in this film, and so many behind the scenes who brought it to fruition. I also want to thank me family who is up there," she said, and she waved her arms upward toward the ceiling as if she was reaching for heaven. "Me dad, me grandparents Billy and Louisa Bonham, and me dad's family who all helped to get me to this moment right now. Please enjoy the show and thank you again for comin' tonight."

The audience applauded loudly as Isabella left the stage. A heavy auburn coloured velvet curtain lifted, the lights dimmed and the movie began to play on the big white screen. "Regrette Rien" by Emile Lardeux played as the opening credits of the film began to roll.

Claudine sat gripping the sides of her seat, impatient for the movie to start. Seeing her daughter setting the story straight about Drew, which *The Blank Canvas* should have done, gave her tremendous satisfaction. She was so proud of Isabella and she was pleased to see her son and brother with companionship on this monumental evening. How wonderful it was to see Claire again and with her brother, Toasty, too.

Pascal tapped her on her shoulder again, offering her some of his popcorn. Suddenly, she felt giddy. Claudine's ecstatic smile said all that her words could not. Her cauliflower heart felt a little softer tonight.

The End (The Beginning)